BLOOD CRYSTAL

Blood Crystal

By Jannifer Hoffman

Have fun reading

Jannif Hoffm

Resplendence Publishing, LLC
http://www.resplendencepublishing.com

Resplendence Publishing, LLC
P.O. Box 992
Edgewater, Florida, 32132

Blood Crystal
Copyright © 2010, Jannifer Hoffman
Edited by Tiffany Mason
Cover art by Rika Singh
Print format ISBN: 978-1-60735-142-9

Electronic release: January 2010
Print release: May 2010

DEDICATION

To my special flowers in the master's bouquet

Henry and Maggie Quaschnick (my parents)
Patrick Quaschnick (my brother)
George Goettle (my nephew)

Very special thanks to those who helped along the way

First and foremost Alan Woehrle
His knowledge of airplanes and helicopters far exceeded my needs

Tony Hoffman who knows more about guns than anyone else I know

Cherie Hoffman RN and medical adviser
If she doesn't know it, she looks it up

Royette Merkel long time friend
who knows all about Indian marriages

Lyle Christie master of the "King's English"

Arnold Lovato for the use of his last name

My readers Bonnie Barrett & Mary Bender

My wonderful editor Tiffany Mason

Table of Contents

PROLOGUE

On a tranquil August evening on the Island of San Delta, eight councilmen, called together by their concerned president, Bama Kendu, mulled around a campfire.

Located in the Indian Ocean seventy miles off the coast of India, San Delta consisted of only seventy square miles. Their only natural resource came from a spring-fed river flowing from the mountains. In spite of the pristine beaches and balmy climate, they had no facilities to bring paying tourists. Their sole income came from selling vegetables and handmade trinkets to the tourists on the mainland or the neighboring Maldives.

As things stood now, the young people couldn't wait to spread their wings and leave. Each year the population diminished while the average age increased. Their little country was dying a slow death.

This was why Bama Kendu had requested a council. For years they'd turned away the large hotel chains offering to take over the soul of the island.

Maybe it was time.

As they discussed the folly of turning their welfare over to strangers, one man suddenly pointed to the sky. A giant red fireball hurtled toward them. They stared in awe as the molten mass hit the earth with quaking force not more than a hundred yards from where they sat.

They rushed toward the site to find a black smoldering

meteorite, the size of a truck motor, imbedded in the ground. At the top, it emitted a brilliant red glow that faded as it cooled, leaving an iridescent crystal that looked to be the size of a hen's egg. They observed it for some time, talking in hushed tones as though it might hear them.

When the lava rock had cooled to the touch, one of the men produced a tool to pry the crystal object out of the porous stone. Once freed, the man handed it to Bama Kendu.

Bama turned it over in his hands, wondering at the curious apparatus. Still warm, its smooth surface, clear in some spots, opalescent in others, had the distinct size and shape of a toddler's heart. It fit comfortably in his hand. As he wrapped his fingers around it, the color darkened with the rhythm of a pulsating heart, getting brighter and warmer with each beat. At once, Bama screamed and dropped it to the ground where it immediately ceased pulsating and faded back to its original color. He stared at his scorched palm. It burned as though he'd gripped a live coal.

This was a thing such as he'd never seen before. Even if it was an evil thing, surely there were people who would pay a high price to own such a treasure. Perhaps this was the miracle his people had prayed for. Perhaps this Blood Crystal, as he called it, had the power to bring life to their dying country.

Chapter One

If Stephen Douglas had realized he'd be driving down the back streets of a seedy Los Angeles neighborhood, he wouldn't have rented a red Cadillac convertible. Instinct told him he should put the top up, but it was easier to see the house numbers in the fading September light with it down.

He pulled out the post-it note he'd written the directions on and reread the address. Damn, he had to be close. For the third time, he made a right-hand turn to circle the two block area when a medley of rapid-fire cracks split the air. They were followed by a cacophony of men shouting and more shots now recognizable as gunfire.

Shit.

He pushed the lever to fold the top over him. It was halfway closed when a body literally flew into the back seat. He hit the brakes at the same time a husky voice yelled, "Keep moving. Stop the car and you're dead."

For emphasis, a hard object jammed his ribcage between the bucket seats with enough force to make him wince. He had no reason to believe it wasn't a gun. The top closed into place and he moved his foot back to the accelerator.

"What do you want?" Stephen asked the hunkering figure behind him.

"Just drive a few blocks and I'll get out. Stop now and

we're both dead."

That's when Stephen realized the voice came from a female. What the hell. She was no less threatening than a man, however, not with the weapon biting a dent in his side.

"Make a right turn at the light. Don't speed and don't make any noticeable moves. Drive normal."

"It's tough to drive normally with a gun puncturing my ribs," Stephen said.

A sound that might have been laughter came from the back seat. "Better than bullets, which we'll both get if we're caught."

Stephen made the right turn and continued straight for another two blocks. He pulled to the side as two police cars, sirens wailing, passed him from the front. At the same time, he heard more gunshots, muffled by distance now.

"How far do you want me to drive?"

"A couple of miles. Make a left at the next light."

"Since I'm obviously cooperating, would you mind getting the stick out of my ribs?"

He couldn't believe it when she actually chuckled. She pulled the weapon back just enough to let him know it was still there.

"Who's after you," he asked. "Good guys or bad guys?"

This time she full-out laughed. "You're certainly curious for a man with a gun on him."

Stephen glanced in the rearview mirror, hoping to get a glimpse of her, but she was plastered to the floorboards. "In situations like this, I like to know who I'm dealing with."

"You're an idiot," she said. "What the hell were you doing driving a forty-thousand-dollar car around this neighborhood with the top down?"

"Maybe I was looking for a hooker."

She made a noise of derision. "And here I thought you were a priest coming to save me from the fires of hell."

He'd already driven the two miles she asked him to.

"Don't you have a car or something where I can drop you?"

"Only if you have a death wish."

"Then it is the bad guys after you?"

"I wouldn't bet my life on that if I were you," she said.

"Exactly what would you do if you were me?"

That made her pause. He made another turn, a left this time.

"That should be far enough," she said. "You can stop and I'll get out now."

He couldn't let her go without knowing who she was. "What will you do then?"

"Why do you care?"

"Maybe my life is in the crapper and I need something to care about. Do you need any money?"

"You're shittin' me, right?"

This time it was Stephen's turn to pause. He took a moment to consider what he was getting himself into. He had a thousand dollars in cash on him. Driving a Cadillac convertible, she might have anticipated he had money on him, but all she asked for was a ride out of the danger zone. She couldn't go back to her car, so she'd be stranded. He wasn't sure why he should care, or trust her, for that matter.

The voice behind him interrupted his thoughts. "I'm not a hooker, if that's what you really were looking for. You do seem squirrelly enough to come to a neighborhood like this, in a rich boy's car, looking for a two-bit tramp to get your rocks off. If you are, watch yourself, because if I was a cop, I could arrest you."

"And what if I was the cop?"

She made another snorting sound. "Cops don't drive Cadillac's—unless they're crooked."

"Know a lot of cops, do you?" He made another turn, wending away from the place he'd picked her up. When she didn't answer, he prodded her. "What's your name?"

"Why?"

"So if they mention names on the evening news, I'll know which one is you."

She swore, using words he'd only heard in back-alley

barrooms.

"Does that mean you'll be on the ten o-clock news?" he asked.

"Life's a bitch and then you die," she muttered, pulling the gun out of his ribcage.

Stephen smiled to himself. "So...who will they say you are?"

"Dani," was all she said.

Hot damn and bingo. Danielle Lovato. How lucky could a man get?

Stifling a grin, he pushed his hand back between the bucket seats. "Hello, you can call me Stephen."

Danielle slapped his hand. "Four million people in this city, and I abduct a lunatic. You think you're my guardian angel or what?"

"Sounds like you're in need of one," he said.

"Stop the car and I'll get out."

"I want to help you. Why are you fighting me?"

"Because I'm getting bad vibes. Are you part of Deluca's gang?"

"I have no idea who Deluca is. I'm not even from LA. Besides, you have the gun."

Danielle considered that. She did have the gun. "Why do you want to help me?"

"Do I need a reason?"

"In my world, nobody does anything for nothing. What's your game, *Stephen?*"

"All I'm offering you is a place to get cleaned up and distance from whatever trouble you're in."

Danielle hesitated, trying to decide if he was for real. "And what do you get out of it?" she asked.

"The feeling that maybe I did someone a good deed."

She snorted. "Oh, yeah, I believe that all right." She pushed herself up on the seat, staying far enough to the side so he couldn't see her in the rearview mirror. She looked around, trying to determine if they were being followed. She saw no cars closer than a block.

"Well, you must. You took the gun off of me."

"It's pointed straight at your back, so unless your fancy seats are lined with metal, consider it still on you. What were you doing in that part of town anyway?"

"A personal favor for a friend."

Danielle swore. "Halleluiah, St. Stephen. You are so full of crap."

He had a deep husky laugh. It actually made her smile. It had been a long time since she smiled.

"So… St. Stephen. Where are we headed?"

"My place."

"Bad idea. If we're being followed, you'd be up to your neck in more trouble than you want."

"We're not. I've been watching."

This guy was starting to worry her. She reached for the door handle, intending to bolt at the next light. She heard the door lock slide in place and knew he must have anticipated her move.

She leaned over to glare at him in the mirror. "What was that for?"

Pale gray verging on blue eyes stared back at her. She could tell by the crinkling around them that he was grinning.

"We're only a couple of blocks from my motel," he said. "You can run then if you want to. At least there's a bus stop out front."

"Motel? You're in a motel."

"I told you I'm from out of town. I'm here on— business."

"Where are you from? The loony bin?"

"Minnesota."

She rolled her eyes. "Well that should explain it. Except your car has a California license plate."

"It's rented."

"Just don't tell me you're a psychiatrist."

That husky laugh again. "I'm not. I'm a lawyer."

He drove to a Holiday Inn and pulled up in front of room number one-twenty.

"Is this your room?" she asked.

"No, I'm on the upper floor right above it."

"Don't park here," she said. "Go around to the back."

"Why?"

"Just do it! This damn car sticks out like a full blooming rose in a potato patch, and if anyone saw me get in it, they could be on top of us before you turn the lock on your door. I see no reason to make it easy for them."

"Who are these people?"

"It's a long story."

He pulled around to the back as instructed, thinking it might be a good idea after all, and found a spot by the dumpsters where the lights didn't reach. He was taking a chance on it getting stolen, but hell, it was insured.

When they got out, he waited for her to bolt, but she stuck by him. He saw no sign of the gun, but she pulled a knapsack out of the backseat and slung it over her shoulder. The first thing he noticed was her height. She was only about three inches shorter than he was, and he was over six feet. He wondered how she'd manage to scrunch up on the floorboards of such a small car even as slim as she was. She wore a frayed Lakers jacket and baggy cargo jeans with multiple pockets. A dark blue cadet cap covered her blacker than midnight pixie hair.

As she followed him up the back stairs, her eyes kept flitting back and forth as though she expected the boogieman to leap out at them. He kept glancing back, prepared to stop her if she decided to run.

At the room, when he stepped back to let her enter first, she hesitated.

"Just remember," she said, "I still have my gun and I know how to use it."

"I never doubted that for a minute." He went in ahead of her and she followed, though he was certain it was reluctantly.

Her gaze quickly scanned the expansive room. "I need to use the bathroom," she said, walking past him down the short hall, mumbling something about being able to afford a suite with a sitting room.

Stephen flicked the TV on and moved to the far corner of the room to yank out his cell phone.

Danielle looked in the mirror and groaned. A shower would have felt good, but she didn't have time for that. She had to get out of town fast. This place seemed to be safe for the moment, but she wasn't ready to trust the dope in the next room. She noticed his shaving kit unopened on the vanity. Everything was clean, no towels used, even the stupid little vee still decorated the toilet paper roll. In the bedroom, she'd seen an unopened suitcase on the bed. Somehow it didn't feel right.

She heard the TV and figured he really was trying to see if the raid was being televised.

Quickly taking care of business, she wasted no time stepping back out into the sitting area—just in time to catch him hanging up his phone. In a heartbeat, she jerked her 9mm Beretta out of the knapsack and trained it on him.

"Who the hell were you calling?" she asked.

He held out his hands, palms up in a peace-offering gesture. "Don't worry. It's okay."

"Who were you talking to?" she repeated, her voice going up an octave.

She edged toward the door keeping the gun zeroed in on his chest.

"Don't go," he said quickly. "You're safe. I was talking to your father. He'll be here to pick you up in fifteen minutes."

An angry flash of color exploded like skyrockets in Dani's brain. She forced her shaking fingers not to squeeze down on the trigger and rid herself of this menace.

"My father's been dead for over a year, you numbskull, and if we're not out of here in five minutes, we'll both be history—unless you're one of them, and even if you are, you'll most likely still be dead."

She knew by the widening of his eyes that he believed

her.

"Let's go," he said, running past her. Sirens screamed in the distance.

Dani still didn't know if she could trust him, but right now, he seemed like her best bet. If the idiot crossed her again, she could always shoot him in the foot.

She followed him out the door and down the back steps. By the time they reached his car, red lights flashed in front of the motel.

He leaped into the driver's seat, swung the passenger door open with one hand, starting the engine with the other. She hopped in and the car moved before she'd pulled the door shut. With no lights, he drove forward into the alley.

She noticed with some surprise that he had the foresight not to race the engine and draw attention to them. A couple of other observations came to mind. He had a distinct limp, a powerful body, and at least a three-day beard covering what appeared to be a better than average looking face. Coffee brown hair hung over his ears a bit shaggily like he hadn't had it cut in a couple of months. One lock fell over his forehead, giving him a rakish look.

Stealing repeated glances at the rear view mirror, he stuck to the alleys the length of two blocks before turning out on the street. It seemed there was more to this peculiar stranger than met the eye. At the moment, however, he seemed to be working on her side. She stuck her gun in her knapsack but kept it on the floor, pressed against her leg. As far as she could tell, they weren't being followed.

About two miles from the motel, Stephen pulled into a dimly lit Walgreen's parking lot. He shut the car off and turned to Dani.

"We need to talk, Ms. Lovato."

Chapter Two

"You damned right we do," she all but yelled, dark brandy colored eyes flashing. "For starters, who the hell hired you and what did they hire you to do?"

Stephen clenched his teeth. He absentmindedly shoved the lock of hair on his forehead back and glared at her. "When I said we need to talk, I was looking for answers from you. After all, you were the one who jumped in my car. Why are the police after you? What have you done?"

"I have a news flash for you, buddy—they're after you too."

"Yeah, because of you."

"Somehow, I'm not picturing you as an innocent victim here. You were the one who called them and blabbed where we were. Who were you talking to on the phone?"

Stephen took a steadying breath. Yelling at each other didn't seem to be getting them anywhere. "A man I believed was your father."

"Obviously the rat was not my father. So who was it?"

"Hell if I know. He...approached me...with a proposition—"

"What kind of proposition?" She glared daggers at him when he didn't answer. "Just exactly where did he approach you?"

She was asking questions he wasn't ready to answer.

"I'll tell you when you tell me why they're after you."

She stared at him for several beats. "You've given me zero reason to trust you," she said finally.

"I got you out of that mess back there—isn't that enough reason?"

"You got me out then put me right back in with that phone call you made. Describe the man who hired you."

Stephen shrugged. That seemed like a safe enough question. It was a starting point at least. "He looked to be about fifty-five, give or take a couple of years, short, about five foot nine. Overweight by about sixty pounds, balding across the top of his head. He had dark gray eyes, close together and kind of beady looking. And he wore a fucking badge."

Dani swore before he even finished the description. "I don't suppose you got his name?"

"At the time, I thought I did. He told me his name was Peter Lovato."

"More like Lieutenant Brick Mays," she muttered.

"I take it you know him," Stephen said.

"Oh yeah. He's the LAPD prick I'm supposed to report to."

Stephen stared at her a moment, trying to understand. "So why are we running from him?"

"You heard the gunshots back there?

Stephen nodded. "Yeah?"

"That was Lieutenant Mays and his cohorts murdering my partner."

Stephen swore under his breath. "So what are they after?"

Dani gave him a long brittle stare. "We have to get out of here and ditch this outrageous car. Trust me, they won't give up. Did you give the plate number when you registered at the motel?"

Stephen made a sound of contempt. "They won't have to ask. Mays' credit card paid for it—he said it was a company card. That's why I rented the Caddie."

Dani gave him a string of obscenities that pretty much

described him as a blooming idiot. The worst of it was, he agreed with her.

"I know where we can get a car," he said.

"You can't rent one, they can trace it. We'll have to steal one."

"Won't be necessary. How far are we from Malibu Beach?"

"Five, maybe six miles. Why?"

"I can get a car there. Just get me in the area and I can find it."

Dani gave him a doubtful look but directed him north out of the parking lot and onto Highway 101. A half hour got them to Malibu, and it took another forty-five minutes cruising up and down the beach front to find the house. All this time, Stephen refused to answer her questions.

The sprawling home facing the Pacific Ocean looked about as formidable as a fortress. Stephen cut the lights on the Cadillac and coasted up the driveway.

"Whose house is this?" Dani asked. "If it belongs to a relative, it's the first place they'll look. Plus they'll be dragged into it."

"No relative," he finally said. "My ex-wife."

Dani made an indelicate sound through her nose. "And she's going to say *here honey, you can have my car*?"

"She's in Hawaii. It was my car before I—before we divorced. I always stashed a spare key on a magnet inside the rear fender wall. I doubt she even knew about it. If it's not there, I can hot-wire it. Give me a minute and wait here like a good little girl." He quietly opened his door and stepped out.

"Well as long as you put it that way," Dani mumbled opening her door and getting out too. There were no other houses even visible through the heavy Elm and Chaparral coverage.

"I asked you to wait in the car," Stephen snapped irritably.

"No you didn't ask. You told me."

Stephen swore and walked to the side of the house, ignoring her. She was beside him in an instant. "Be careful," he groused. "There's a steep rock wall up ahead. Don't go falling over it."

"Are you asking or telling?"

He made a hissing sound. "You're starting to get on my nerves."

"Maybe I can help."

Stephen stared up at a two-foot square window at least eight feet high. "Fine, cup your hands and boost me up."

"Why don't you let me go in?"

"Because I've been in there before and I know what I'm looking for. Besides, I have to break the window. Do you want to help or argue?"

She shrugged and removed her jacket. "Here," she said. "Wrap this around your arm so you don't cut yourself."

He gave her a skeptical glare but did as she suggested. With a boost from her, he was able to pull himself up to the window ledge. Using his elbow, he slammed it into the window. When glass shattered, he listened before positioning the jacket over the jagged edges of the glass. With an agile leap, he disappeared through the small opening before Dani could blink.

Her Lakers jacket vanished inside with him. Seconds later, she heard the garage door open—at the same time, light spilled out of the opening doorway. The light went out almost as fast as it had come on. She hurried around to the front and watched in the semi-darkness as he fished around under the wheel well of an older model Buick Skylark. Making a triumphant sound when he found the key, he wasted no time getting in behind the wheel. The car purred to life after only two turns.

"Can you follow me and we'll dump the Caddie someplace not too close—please," he added quickly.

She saluted, grinning, hopped into the convertible and backed out to give him room. He pulled out of the garage and the door slid shut behind him on well-oiled rollers. She followed closely behind him back to 101 where they left the car in an inconspicuous corner of a Best Western parking lot.

She opened the back door of the Buick and tossed her knapsack on the seat. Keeping an eye on him to make sure he wasn't paying attention, she stuffed a small package into the crease of the back seat. When she jumped into the front beside him, she held out the rental papers. "I thought we might as well take these, no sense giving them any extra info."

"Good idea," he said. "Now, this is your town—where are we headed?"

"How long do you think we have until this car is missed?"

"I'd say close to a week. They're on their honeymoon."

"She remarried?" she quested.

"Yeah," he answered with a distinct edge of irritation. "Where to?"

"East on ten, then northwest on fifteen toward Las Vegas. We need to get out of California before they put up road blocks."

His brows rose a notch. "What in the hell did you do anyway? I think since I'm in this up to my neck I have right to know at least that much."

"I didn't do anything but my job."

"And what, pray tell, was your job?"

Dani took a deep breath and released it slowly through her teeth. "Take a left at the light; it'll get us on Interstate 10. I think we're safe, at least until they find your rental and realize we switched cars." She sat back in the seat and waited until he'd turned onto ten. "I'm an undercover agent and I was on assignment attempting to recover some stolen diamonds."

"You're a cop?"

"Agent."

"And...did you recover them?" he prompted.

"No."

He gave her an impatient glare. "Well gee, I guess that explains it. You went undercover to find some diamonds, which you didn't find, and now we're racing down the interstate in a stolen car with the LAPD on our tails. Yup, that sure clears it up for me."

She gritted her teeth and put her hands over her chest and stared out the window at the oncoming traffic. "Before I tell you any more, I need to know exactly how and why you got involved. And don't say it was when I jumped in your car."

"Like I said, this guy, Mays you called him, approached me with a proposition."

"Follow the signs up ahead to fifteen east. Where and why? You said you were a lawyer."

"I was before—"

She gave him a frowning look. "Before what?"

"That's irrelevant."

She made a disgusted sound. "Well, at least I know you really are a lawyer. You know how to double talk. What was the proposition?"

"I was supposed to find you—his daughter—there was going to be a raid and I was to get you out of harm's way. He gave me an address, but I'm not familiar with LA and I got lost."

"And I'll bet he said not to tell me he was my daddy. Right?"

Stephen shrugged. "Yeah."

"And he probably said to tie me up and haul me out if necessary."

Stephen gave her an odd look. "And now you're going to tell me what's going on that I don't know about."

"First, I'd like to know what he offered you, a lawyer for Pete's sake, to drive into the bowels of hell. Why would you even do it?"

"I was in a bit of a jam and he offered to clean my slate."

"What kind of a jam?"

"Again, that's irrelevant."

Dani let out a weary sigh, pulled her cap off, threw it on the consol between them and ran a frustrated hand through her short hair. "How the hell could he think you were capable of getting me out of there?"

"I've had some…experience."

"And your experience told you to drive in there with a red convertible?"

"All right, that was stupid. I'll give you that much. But I was in a foul mood. My life's been in the toilet for a couple of months and Lieutenant Mays had his mitt on the flusher."

Dani gave him a long look. "I can see that," she said. "You look and smell like you haven't showered or shaved in a week. And you're eyes are bloodshot. My guess is you've been on a two-month boozing binge."

He gave her a piercing glare. His eyes flicked to her hair. "Coming from a woman who resembles a skunk. Why would anyone bleach a white streak down the center of black hair? And how long have *you* been sleeping in those clothes?"

"I told you I was working undercover," she snapped.

"As an agent. To me that say's government."

This idiot was no dummy. It was time to change the subject. "I'm hungry," she said.

"So am I. And we need to fill gas anyway," he grumbled. "You have any money on you?"

"I don't know. I'd have to check the backpack. You were offering me money back there. Don't you have any? And don't even think about using a credit card. They can trace that in a minute."

"You actually think I don't know that?"

"Yeah, actually I did. So how much money do you have on you?"

"Your *daddy* gave me a thousand dollars to deliver you. I was supposed to get another five hundred after the job was done—at the price of gas, that won't go very far. And why don't you know what's in your backpack?"

She stared out the windshield a moment before

answering. "It's not mine. I grabbed it when they put a bullet through my partner's head. I'll take a look when we stop."

Thinking of Roger made her heart ache and reminded her of the dulling pain in her left hand. As Stephen pulled off the road into a Shell station in Barstow, she absentmindedly blew into her palm to ease the burning.

CHAPTER THREE

Stephen noticed her tending to her hand, but this wasn't the time to bring it up. Later, when they were back on the road. Right now they needed gas and food. He pulled up to the first pump, then opened his wallet and handed her a hundred dollar bill.

"Here, run over to the Subway next door and get me a foot-long meatball sandwich, get whatever you like for yourself. I'll get coffee inside when I pay for the gas. You can check your backpack later. You want coffee?"

"Yes, please, decaf, one cream, two sugars."

When she reached for the door handle, he stopped her. "For God's sake put on your cap and tuck that white stuff underneath it; a clerk would remember that stripe in a heartbeat."

She sent him a hostile glare but jammed the cap on her head, pulling it down to cover her *stripe*. "Where's my jacket?" she asked through the window where he was opening the gas cap.

Stephen shrugged. "I guess in the confusion I left it back at the house. Don't worry, we can get you another one. It's not that cold out here."

"Don't worry?" she hissed quietly, walking up to him. "My badge is sewn into the lining. It'll take the LAPD forty-five seconds to put two and two together."

Stephen swore, but before he could comment, she

whirled around, mumbling to herself, and marched toward
the Subway. He cursed himself for his own stupidity, and
aimed a few choice words at her while he was at it. If they
got out of this without killing each other, it would be a
small miracle. How the hell were they going to get out
anyway? He hoped she had a plan. After all, it was her
mess.

Inside the station, he stopped to take a leak, got two
large cups of coffee, and went to the counter to pay. Other
than a couple of teenagers trying to buy cigarettes, he was
the only customer. While he waited, he glanced at the
soundless television playing above the clerks head. A
newsflash covered the screen. He nearly choked when a
two-way mug shot of himself, taken when he'd been
arrested, filled half the screen. Beside him, a frowning shot
of Dani Lovato appeared, fortunately without her skunk
stripe. Next came a photo of the likeness of his Cadillac
convertible. He didn't need sound to know they were being
hunted. His stomach sank to his toes when ARMED AND
DANGEROUS – DO NOT APPROACH slid across the
screen followed by a phone number to call.

When they got back on the road, he was going to
shake some answers out of Ms. Lovato one way or another.

The clerk had finally convinced the kids they wouldn't
be getting any smokes, so they took their time choosing
candy bars and chewing gum. On the TV screen, a video of
the raid appeared. In slow motion, it showed Dani shooting
toward the camera, then it switched to Dani prying the
backpack out of her dead partner's fingers. The picture was
blurred to the point where, if he hadn't known it was Dani,
he wouldn't have recognized her.

He'd have liked to blame Dani for the mess he was in,
but in truth, he'd gotten himself into it when he drove his
SUV into a storefront window after he'd had not enough
sleep and too much to drink.

Their only chance at getting across the border into
Nevada was if no silent alarm alerted the police at Nadine's
house when they took the car. Right now, the authorities

were still looking for the convertible.

Dani was waiting for him in the car. She didn't say anything while he pulled back out on I-15.

"How far are we from the Nevada border?" he asked when she handed him half of his meatball sandwich.

She answered though a mouthful of her own food. "About a hundred miles."

"Our faces are both plastered on TV."

She nodded. "I know. I was waiting for you outside the Shell station and I saw it through the window."

"We need to get cleaned up and change our appearances. What happened back there in that raid? Did you shoot your partner?"

She gave him a withering look. "Of course not. That's what they want people to believe. A part of that tape was obviously edited out."

"What's in the backpack?"

"I haven't looked yet."

Stephen turned on her angrily. "Don't give me that crap. You were ducking bullets back there, and yet, you took the time to grab it. There's something in it they want. What is it?"

"Where did they get those mug shots of you?"

"You're changing the subject."

"Fine, when we stop, we can look in the backpack together—satisfied?"

"I'm not sure."

She made a sound of distain. "You are one hard man to please."

"So I've been told," he muttered.

"And you're grumpy too."

"Don't push it, woman. I'd be willing to make a bet, cop or not, you'd be parked in jail right now if it weren't for me."

"Well, you'd lose that bet because I wouldn't be in jail; I'd be in the morgue."

Stephen held out his hand. "Give me the rest of my sandwich." When she passed it to him, he took a large bite, chewed, swallowed, and continued to question her. "I sure wish you'd explain what went on back there. If you and your partner were undercover agents, why were the cops shooting at you?"

She stared out the side window and didn't answer.

"What are you hiding?" he persisted.

"First tell me when they got those mug shots of you?"

"When I was arrested two days ago."

"What did you do? Rob a bank."

"Why is it I'm always the one answering questions?"

She contemplated that for a moment. "I've known two men in my life I've trusted: my father and Roger, my partner. Both of them are dead and neither one turned out to be what I thought they were."

"It seems to me," Stephen said, "you have a low capacity to trust."

"Right on, buster. And for all I know, you were set up by those assholes back there to—"

He waited for her to go on, but instead, silence stretched between them.

"To what?" he asked finally.

"If you have nothing to hide, explain about your arrest."

Stephen sighed long and heavy. "It's not that I have anything to hide. It's just that I'm not very proud of what I did."

"Okay, very few people are proud of getting arrested. Tell me about it."

"I got drunk and drove my car into the front of a Red Lobster."

"They didn't have a takeout window?"

He let out with a belly-rolling laugh. It felt good. He hadn't laughed in two months. He looked over and caught her smiling. She was pretty when she smiled.

"It was 2 a.m. and, by the way, closed. I'd only driven about twenty feet when I realized I was too drunk to drive and pulled over a little too far."

She spent all of eight seconds digesting that. "So, you

got divorced two months ago and have been drinking ever since."

"I didn't say that."

"You didn't have to. Was she worth it?"

The answer was *no, she wasn't worth it*. But it wasn't that simple. "It's a long story. And I really don't want to get into it."

"Okay, your relationship with your ex-wife is irrelevant anyway. Tell me what happened after you got arrested and how Prick Mays approached you."

"You don't let up, do you?"

"I can't. Not if I'm going to answer your questions."

Stephen was certain she wouldn't tell him anything until he could get her to trust him. Honesty seemed to be the best way to go about that. "Like I said, he offered me a thousand dollars to find you and another five hundred when I delivered you."

"You don't seem like a man who could be bought that easily. You needed money that bad?"

"The money was just a bonus. He offered to clear my arrest record."

"Oh, he's good at that all right. But, other than the fact that you look like a thug, what made him think you could or would do it?"

"What do you mean I look like a thug?"

"When's the last time you looked in a mirror? If I'd had a good look at your shabby clothes and scruffy face, I wouldn't have gotten in the car with you."

"And then you'd be in the morgue."

It was her turn to laugh. It was a nice musical laugh. A sexual jolt he wasn't prepared for raced to his groin. He hadn't had a woman in his arms for fourteen months—way too long. He glanced at her, assessing her female qualities. She had nice eyes, the color of fine brandy, and long dark lashes, but over all, she was too thin, not a woman he would normally be attracted to. He'd always liked well-rounded women with big breasts. Giving himself a mental shake, he remembered his ex wore a 36D, and where did that get him?

He passed a road sign announcing forty miles to the Nevada border, and decided he needed to play along with Dani Lovato and get her to trust him. *Keep the conversation light*, he told himself.

"What happened to your hand?" he asked.

The wild-eyed expression she turned on him was anything but light and told him volumes of…nothing.

Chapter Four

Stephen reached over and flicked on the radio. Loud rock music filled the car. "Can you dial in an LA station? The TV in the store was on mute, so I didn't get any details. Maybe we can get some helpful info."

Dani fiddled with the dial a few seconds until she tuned in a news report.

...Lovato is likely traveling with an unidentified Caucasian male, six-foot one, dark hair, gray eyes, twenty-nine years old. If you see either one of them or the red convertible with the license number 6REC 271, do not approach. They are armed and dangerous... The announcer rattled off a phone number to call, repeating it twice, then went on to news of an upcoming election.

Dani switched the radio off and turned to Stephen frowning. "I don't get it—why didn't they say your name? Did they say it on television?"

"I don't know, the sound was off. But they flashed yours across the screen. It doesn't make sense, does it?"

Dani eyes narrowed on his face. "Is there something about you they don't want the public to know?"

Stephen shrugged. "I...don't think so."

"What were you going to say, you bastard? You are one of them, aren't you! You're working for Mays. That wasn't just any police number they gave. It was Mays' direct line."

"Don't be ridiculous—" Stephen stopped talking, his eyes on the rear view mirror. He muttered a vile oath. "We're being followed."

Dani spun around to see the car nearly on their bumper. She grabbed her backpack from the back seat and fished out her gun.

"Don't do anything stupid," Stephen said. "Maybe it's just a tailgater."

"On an open interstate at three o'clock in the morning? I don't believe that for a minute and neither do you."

Flashing red lights gave them their answer. Gritting his teeth, Stephen slowed down and eased over to the side.

"Why are you stopping? We're only twenty miles from the Nevada border."

"You expect me to outrun a police car? Put the damn gun away and quit panicking. They're still looking for the Cadillac. Just stay calm and play along with whatever I say. And put your hat on."

Dani wanted to argue with him, or open the door and run, but she didn't have the time or energy to do either one. Besides, what Stephen said made sense. She watched the statuesque officer get out of his car, wielding a flashlight in one hand, discreetly releasing the strap on his weapon with the other.

She took several deep breaths, stuck her hat on her head, and tucked her gun in the backpack where she could reach it quickly if it became necessary. Certainly she didn't plan to shoot an innocent cop, but if she took him off guard, she might be able to disarm him.

Stephen rolled his window down. "Hello, officer, is there a problem?"

The officer, Hendrickson, his badge read, shined the light into the car, covering the front and back seat in one sweep. Dani shielded her eyes from the bright light so he wouldn't get a good look at her.

"Where you all headed?" Hendrickson asked.

Stephen smiled. "We're going to Las Vegas to get

married."

In the guise of shifting in her seat, Dani reached over and pinched him. The side of his leg was firm as steel. He didn't even flinch.

Hendrickson assessed Dani. "You're a long way from home with those Minnesota plates. You here of your own free will?" he asked her.

Dani nodded her head, using her sweetest Texan drawl, "Oh, yes sir. You see, I kinda got pregnant and my daddy would just kill me if he knew, so I said we have to hurry and get on with a ceremony or Daddy's gonna git out his shotgun. He's a Texan, you know."

Stephen turned to her so the officer couldn't see and gave her a hard warning glare. She gave him her prettiest smile. "Ain't that right, honey bunch?"

"Yeah," he said. "And afterwards, we're going back to Minnesota."

"But poopsie honey," she said in her best whiny voice. "You said you'd take me to Texas to see my daddy."

"No pitty-pat, I didn't. We can't let him see you until after the baby's born. I know he's not too bright but he might figure it out."

Henderson cleared his throat. "The reason I stopped you is your plates expired on the thirty-first of August. You have until the tenth of September, but I thought you'd want to know."

"Thank you, sir," Stephen said. "I appreciate that. I didn't know they'd expired."

Officer Henderson smiled. "No problem. You kids have a nice wedding. And good luck."

Stephen waved him off and put the Buick in gear. As soon as he saw the patrol car make a u-turn on the center medium and head back west, he turned on Dani.

"What the hell was that all about?"

"You said to play along with whatever you said." She grinned. "At least we distracted him enough so he didn't ask for your license."

Stephen shook his head. "You're one crazy lady, but

you might be right. I must be slipping, I didn't even think
of checking the tabs. I still don't know why she wanted this
car—she's had it almost two months and hasn't even
bothered getting California plates."

"Why did you get divorced anyway?"

"She was pregnant!"

"You divorced because she was pregnant?"

"It wasn't mine," he ground out. "And I don't want to
talk about it."

Dani gave him a who-cares-anyway look. "Fine"

"What I want to do is find a place to get cleaned up
and get some sleep. I feel like I've been smashed through a
meat grinder."

Dani expelled a deep sigh. "Yeah, I feel that way too.
We need some clean cloths and toiletries. I doubt we'll find
anything open at this hour until we get to Vegas."

                        * * * *

An hour later, they pulled into the far corner of a Wal-
mart parking lot.

"We should go in separately." Dani suggested.

"Yeah. And if we're lucky, this shift hasn't had a
chance to see that newsflash. The clerk at the gas station
was too busy with the kids to pay attention to it, but I know
with this rat's ass beard I have that I'm easily recognizable
from those mug shots."

Dani chuckled. "Gee, quite a pair we make. You
resemble a rat's ass and I can pass for a skunk. I better pick
up some bleach and dye."

"You still have the cash leftover from the Subway.
You need any more?"

Dani shook her head. She hadn't told him about the
six twenties she had stashed in two different pockets. That
was her backup emergency cash. "I should be able to make
it on what I have. I'm thinking we should only get what we
need. We have a long ways to go yet. I'll meet you back
here at the car."

When she reached for the door handle, his hand
snaked out and wrapped around her slim wrist.

"Ms. Lovato, I'm up to my rat's ass in this—if you have some kind of a plan, I think it's time I knew about it. Where are we headed?"

Dani hesitated. Could she trust him? The possibility he was working for either Mays or Deluca and playing along with her until he had what he wanted still existed. But right now she needed him. He had money and a car. She had to give him something. Maybe tonight she could steal the keys and ditch him—that was the sensible thing to do. But what if he was exactly as he appeared? Not likely, but…his warm fingers on her wrist were sending odd sparks shooting up her arm.

"Washington," she said. "I need to get to Washington."

"That's north. Why the hell did we drive east?"

"D.C.—Washington D.C."

In the dim light, Stephen's gaze held hers for a long moment. When he finally released her wrist, he did so by shoving it away from him.

"Woman, when we find a place to clean up, we are going to have a talk."

Chapter Five

Thinking about *having to talk* had Dani experiencing a sense of doom as she raced around the store grabbing two t-shirts, a pair of jeans, toothpaste, toothbrush, deodorant, and a package of combs. She hesitated only a moment to choose hair color remover and an auburn dye that seemed to come close to her natural shade.

Out of the corner of her eyes, she saw Stephen shopping in the same hurried fashion in the men's department. As tall as he was, she could easily spot him over the racks. Even with ripped jeans and a rumpled cotton shirt, likely a reject from Goodwill, the man displayed a physique to kill for.

She was headed for the checkout when she remembered underwear. Whirling her cart around to the ladies lingerie, she snatched a three-pack of bikini panties off a hanging rack when she spotted a short red lace and satin sleep set. She glanced towards the check out and saw Stephen walking up to it, balancing his purchases in his arms. Stupid man hadn't bothered with a cart. Obviously his wife had done all his shopping for him.

Well, what the hell, she thought, she liked red and she needed something to sleep in. She yanked the sleepwear off the rack, tossed it in her cart, and headed for the checkout just as Stephen walked out the door. Damn, but he was quick. Well, he didn't have to choose hair color.

As the clerk rang her up, Dani added breath mints, a handful of chocolate bars, and a couple bottles of water. The clerk gave her a sly look when she scanned the satin thingy, and Dani, fully aware of how bedraggled she looked, felt a flush creep up her neck.

"I'm getting married tomorrow," she said hastily.

The clerk, barely older than a teenager, smiled and scanned Dani from hair to ancient sweatshirt to ragged pants. "Was that your honey who just came through? Man, is he a hunk."

Wishing she'd kept her mouth shut, Dani shook her head. "Oh, no. Barry's out in the car. He's not much of a shopper."

As the clerk continued to chatter, Dani nearly choked when she saw her impulse buy cost her thirty-nine, ninety-nine. Crap, she could have slept in a seven-dollar t-shirt like she usually did. The total bill came to fifteen dollars more than she had left of Stephen's hundred. Deciding it would take too long to have the item removed since it was already in the bag, she begrudgingly dug out one of her twenties.

At the car, Stephen reached over from the driver's seat and swung the door open for her. Stuffing her bag in the back, she hopped in beside him.

* * * *

Stephen pulled a large bill out of his wallet to pay for the room. On the outskirts of Vegas, the rundown motel looked like it hadn't been updated since the sixties. The Sloski Stop Inn looked like the kind of place that rented rooms by the hour—discreet, no questions, and no ID required.

Mr. Sloski, non-too happy about being roused from sleeping in front of the television blaring in the back room, looked at the bill like he'd never seen one before.

Stephen filled out the form using a fake name and plate numbers.

"One night or two," Sloski asked, turning the money over in his hand and holding it up to the light.

"Just one night," Stephen said impatiently. He was bone-weary tired; he just wanted to take a shower and get a few hours of sleep.

"You realize it's four-thirty in the morning?"

Fucking-A, I realize it. His head felt like a ball of mush. "Yeah, I know."

Sloski handed Stephen thirty-two dollars and seventy-five cents. "Check out time is eleven and we have to be firm about that...need to get the rooms cleaned."

You have at least thirty rooms and only four cars in your lot, asshole. "Not a problem. But can I look at two different rooms. My wife's a bit fussy. She always wants to choose her room."

Stephen thought by the blank stare he received that the man might ask him to pay for both rooms.

Frowning, obviously put out by the request, the old man snatched two keys off the battered rack behind him and tossed them on the counter. "Go ahead take a look. But we run a clean place here and the rooms are all the same."

Stephen thanked the man, hurried outside, stopped long enough to ask Dani to *please* stay put a moment, and then ran up the steps. He found 208, luckily at the far end of the building with a set of stairs going down the back side. He opened the door and turned the deadbolt to keep it from closing, then went back to the office.

He handed Sloski the key to 208. "We'll take 106," he said. He waited until the man wrote it down and handed him the receipt.

Sloski disappeared in the back room before Stephen made it out the door.

As he got in the car and drove around to the back, he noticed Dani's eyes were drooping. Apparently, she was as beat as he was.

"What was that all about?" she asked.

"I asked to see two rooms. He thinks we're staying in 106. We'll actually be upstairs in 208."

She gave him a long look. "Nice move, Hot Shot. Where'd you learn that trick?"

Stephen parked the car behind a semitrailer. "What? You think this is the first time I've had to hide from the police," he said, getting out of the car.

She followed and they both started collecting things from the back seat. "You are so full of crap."

He grabbed his Wal-mart bag and her backpack. As they trudged up the back steps to the room, Stephen glanced down at the office, relieved to see the same dim light that had been on when he'd first walked in. Apparently, Sloski had gone back to bed. Stephen hoped it was to sleep rather than watch television.

The room, one queen bed, one sadly stuffed chair, and a wide beat-up dresser, appeared adequate.

"Give me two minutes in the bathroom to brush my teeth and take a wiz," he said, "then you can have it to do whatever." He fully expected her to rant about the one bed, but she just dropped into the chair and nodded. When he came out, she was reading the directions on a bottle of hair color.

"This is going to take a while," she said. "Do you want to shower first?"

"Nah, go ahead. I'll just lay on the bed and get a little rest. Wake me when you're finished." He threw himself on the bed fully clothed then looked up at her as she headed for the bathroom. "Let's not use any lights except in there," Stephen said. "And when we blow this lovely abode, I'd rather not leave anything behind, including your hair color stuff and clothes." He reached under his head, yanked the pillowcases free, and tossed it to her. "Put everything in here. And, by the way, when you wake me, just call my name. I tend to get startled if somebody touches me while I sleep."

Dani started slathering the color remover on her hair, thinking about his last words and getting a strange feeling about her roommate. She suddenly realized she didn't know his last name. Plus, since she was the undercover agent, it should have been her warning him to keep the lights out in the bedroom and take precautions not to leave anything behind. Who was he? A lawyer? She seriously doubted it.

And why would Mays send him in after her—unless he needed a back up if he didn't find what he was looking for in Roger's knapsack. At that point, he'd need someone alive, preferably not a witness to an undercover cop's murder. But Stephen had screwed up by getting lost. He didn't get her out of there in time.

Obviously Mays wasn't working alone. There was more than one person sending gunfire their direction. Now she had no idea who to trust. For all she knew, Mays had joined forces with Deluca.

It had been Roger's idea to call Mays when they nabbed the Crystal from Deluca. She'd have rather called her own supervisor, Bob Reierson, in D.C., but they both knew Reierson couldn't get there to protect them in time. Besides, he'd turned it over to Mays, which is where Roger's loyalties fell. Lot of good it did him.

Dani stared glumly at her drab yellow hair after she'd rinsed the gunk out of it. She applied the Auburn dye, leery of the results, but she didn't have the energy right now to care, especially since she envied Stephen snoozing on the bed.

As soon as the dye had finished its time, she'd shower and pass out on that bed, and she didn't care who was next to her. She had no plans other than sleeping—and she was quite certain he felt the same way.

Heaven forbid if she accidentally touched him and he went psycho on her. What the hell was up with that anyway?

After her shower, she glanced in the mirror, not liking what she saw. Her hair, still wet had a definite green tint to it—well, she thought, rather a Chia Pet than a skunk.

In view of the sleeping conditions, she opted for her jeans and a t-shirt to sleep in. She emptied the pockets of her discarded pants and put everything into her new pockets. Then decided it was time to tell the bear she'd finished with the bathroom. She'd then have the bed to herself. Actually, she was tired enough to sleep standing up.

For a moment, she just stood there watching him sleep. As men went, he was far above average. In fact, there was nothing average about him. She wondered what he looked like naked, then groaned at her thoughts. Sleeplessness was making her hallucinate. Too bad she wasn't ready to trust him.

Standing at a safe distance, she was about to call out his name when she heard a car door slam. She peeked out the window to investigate and saw three men walking toward a lower room. When one turned around to say something to the other, his face caught the light and her heart dropped to her toes.

Deluca!

CHAPTER SIX

Stephen was back in Afghanistan. He'd fallen asleep on the cold hard ground after six gruesome days of trudging through the mountains.

A man grabbed his shoulder, smiling the evil smile of death, holding a matte-black M-17 in Stephen's face.

Acting on instinct bred by fear and adrenaline, Stephen clasped the enemy's arms, and in a tactical reversal move, yanked him forward and rolled over the top of him, bodily pinning him with a forearm pressed to his throat.

The scream was female. Dani, her soft body beneath his, stared back at him, her eyes wide and laced with shock. Reality slammed into his brain.

"Goddammit woman, are you trying to get yourself killed?"

"No. I'm trying to keep us alive. We have to get out here. Deluca's downstairs."

Stephen charged to his feet, pulling her with him. They each grabbed bags, and she put out the bathroom light while Stephen peered out the window. A black sedan that hadn't been there when they checked in was parked in the center of the lot.

Warning Dani to keep quiet and stick close to him wasn't necessary. He wanted desperately to take possession of the gun in her hand, but that was sure to be met with resistance they didn't have time for.

A loud medley of shouting and door slamming came from below.

"Let's go," he said, exiting through the front door.

Hugging the wall, he reached the back stairway with Dani close at his heels. As they rounded the corner at the stairs, he heard shouting and swearing below. Looking back, he caught a glimpse of two men headed in the direction of the office. Thank the Lord Dani had spotted them. It wouldn't take Sloski but four seconds to put two and two together, certainly not with prompting from Deluca. Who in blazes was this Deluca anyway? And what was he after?

Then there was Dani, damn her hide to hell and back. What did she have that everybody in the whole fricking world wanted? She'd said it wasn't diamonds. What then, information? If that was the case, she wasn't in danger of being killed, unless it was to silence her. Either way, Stephen Douglas was expendable, the only idiot involved who didn't have a clue what was going on. He'd tried to remedy that by searching her backpack last night after she'd gone in the bathroom. He'd found nothing worth risking even a dog's life for. Maybe it was time to ask himself why he was even here.

Instinct told him these guys weren't trying to arrest anybody. But then, he didn't think *apprehending a criminal* was part of Mays' goal either.

The semitrailer they'd parked behind had vanished, probably a trucker with a deadline. He hadn't realized it earlier, but the first glow of dawn breached the eastern horizon.

Wasting no time, they charged for the car. Stephen unlocked the doors; he had it started and moving in less time than it took to blink.

Fortunately, he'd scoped out the parameter as well as he could in the dark last night and they were able to exit stage left without being detected. At least he hoped...

Watching the rearview mirror, he allowed himself to breath, struggling between relief and anger.

He looked over to see how Dani was faring and realized she had her shoes in her hand. This was an inconvenient time for his brain to dredge up the memory of her soft body pinned underneath him. She'd smell good too, damn good, like flowers and sunshine. Thinking about it though only made him aware of his own lack of a shower, four-day beard, and deprived sleep.

"What road are we looking for?" he asked. He knew his voice had an edge to it, but he figured he was entitled.

She blew out a breath of air so deep it raised the hair on her forehead. Green hair.

"Five fifteen to Boulder City, then ninety-three to Kingman where we can pick up I-40."

"Then we're still headed for D.C.?"

Her face screwed up in thought for a moment. "Unless I can come up with an alternate plan."

"Does green hair interfere with your ability to think?"

She gave him a scathing look, but her lips had a distinct twitch to them. "Very funny," she snipped.

"I thought so."

When the sign came up directing them to I-515, Stephen turned short of it.

Dani sat up straight in her seat. "Hey, you turned too soon."

He ignored her as he maneuvered the car around a corner and stopped behind a gas station/pawn shop. He switched the engine off and turned to stare at her.

"It's a long way to D.C. The plates on this car are already expired. There's a grace period, but it's an excuse for every highway cop across the country to stop us. Plus, we both need sleep. It's time we came up with an alternate plan."

Dani face took on a set expression. "What do you have in mind?" she asked, a sarcastic edge to her words.

"I have access to a private plane. But it belongs to a friend and I'm not going to get him involved until I know what I'm up against. That said, I can't, or rather won't, go that route unless I know I'm doing the right thing." She stared at him and said nothing. Satisfied she was listening, he continued. "Let's start with the easy stuff. What are you, FBI or CIA?"

"That's classified information."

He gave her a long hard look. "In case you haven't noticed, I'm risking my life here and I have no idea what for. So unless you can give me some straight answers, I'm going to dump you at the nearest bus stop where you can find another sucker to help save your classified ass.

"Foreign Affairs," she said flatly.

"Okay, we'll leave that one for a moment. Who is Deluca?"

"He's the head of an International smuggling operation. They deal in expensive gems and artwork. High profile stuff—things the average Joe Blow jewel thief wouldn't be interested in. Too tough to get rid of."

"And this man is trying to kill you. That tells me you have something he wants." He glanced down at her butt-hugging jeans. "You can't be hiding anything very big, and it's not in your backpack. So what is this small thing you have that a man as powerful as an international jewel thief could possibly want?"

"How do you know it's not in the backpack?" she asked suspiciously.

"I looked last night when you were fertilizing your hair."

"You went through my backpack?"

"And the next thing I'm contemplating is giving you a full personal body search."

She pressed her back against the door, discreetly sliding one hand down her leg toward the gun in her backpack. "Who the hell are you anyway?"

Stephen anticipated her move. He reached passed her and grabbed her backpack, flinging it in the seat behind him without taking his eyes off her. "I'm not your enemy that's for fucking sure. I'm trying to help you, but your mule-headedness is making it awfully difficult. Just exactly how long have you been a foreign affairs operative?"

For a moment he thought she was going to throw a pout.

"About seven months," she said. Then added, "This was my first big assignment."

"Okay, let's assess this. They sent a greenhorn to flesh out a high profile international jewel thief? To get something valuable and small enough to fit in the pocket of those tight jeans. Doesn't that sound a bit odd to you?"

He had to give her credit. She didn't attack him. She sat there staring and thinking instead.

"Maybe." she said finally.

"How well do you know the man who sent you on this job?"

She shrugged. "Not at all, really. He found me." After a few moments of thought, she slammed her back against the seat and folded her arms over her chest. "Apparently, I'm surrounded by asshole males who think women are brainless fools."

"You have one right here who doesn't think that."

Dani made a rude sound. "I have no idea who you are or who you're working for. And here I sit, trusting you with my life. Maybe I am a brainless fool."

"If you were, you'd have already told me what was going on. Whatever you have, or know, you've managed to do a good job keeping it a secret. You're alive while your partner is dead. And you've managed to evade the LAPD and Deluca, whom I'd guess has a wealth of contacts. I'd say those assholes underestimated you."

She gave him a heated glare. "And you're just another one of them buttering me up to get information."

Stephen laughed. "You are one tough cookie. But for the record, I am exactly who I said I was. What I told you about landing in jail and being approached by Mays is the truth. I just don't know how to convince you."

"I don't know either because you could be lying about everything. I don't even know your last name. And I especially don't know why they didn't mention your name on the news flash. That alone is enough to suspect you of hiding something."

Stephen's cell phone rang as he was trying to decide if he should come clean and explain about that.

"You have a damn cell phone on?" she shouted. "They can trace cell phones and get your exact location."

Stephen unbuckled his seatbelt so he could dig in his pocket. "Christ, woman, relax. It has a scrambler. And my last name is Douglas. I wasn't even aware you didn't know it."

"What ordinary citizen has a phone with a scrambler?"

"This one does," he snapped, unable to hide his frustration.

When he finally got the ringing phone out, she reached over and covered it with her hand.

"If you really want me to trust you, let me answer your phone without looking at the caller ID."

Chapter Seven

He shocked her when he grabbed her hand and slapped the phone in it. She quickly flipped it open and glanced at the caller ID. It read *Virg*. She put it to her ear, watching Stephen, half expecting him to try to grab it back.

"Hello," she said into the mouthpiece.

A man's voice came over the line. "Rando?"

Dani frowned. "No, are you sure that's who you're looking for?"

"Apparently not. How about Stephen?"

She glanced again at Stephen "He's right here…behind the wheel…he handed the phone to me. Who should I say is calling?"

Stephen rolled his eyes at her.

The caller made a snorting sound. "Tell him it's Virgil. But exactly who are you? I've never heard a woman answer his phone. Ever. Put the phone on speaker and have him say something so I know he's really there."

Dani sighed and looked at Stephen. "It's Virgil. He wants me to put the phone on speaker."

Stephen reached over cupped his hand under hers, pushed a couple of buttons, then released her hand and relaxed back in his seat. "I'm here, Virg. What's up?"

"You have a woman in your car answering your phone. That's interesting enough in itself."

"Her name is…Ava. She's questioning my integrity;

maybe you can set her straight."

Laughter filled the car. "She's questioning you? Lord, she must be one suspicious woman."

"That's a bit of an understatement," Stephen answered dryly.

"Well...Ava...what do you want to know about my baby brother?"

To Stephen, Dani mouthed, "He's your brother?"

Stephen nodded.

"Can I trust him?" she asked into the phone.

Again the laughter. "Hell no, he'll say anything you wanna hear to get in your pants."

Dani shook her head, stifling a grin. "Really? You mean he's not a big time Hollywood producer?"

"Am I still on speaker phone?"

"Yeah."

"Well then, I guess he is."

"Too bad because that wasn't what I was looking for."

"Ouch. Okay, what do you want to know?"

"If his name came over the news, would people recognize it?"

"They would here in Minnesota."

"Explain please."

"He spent a year in Afghanistan. Just got home two months ago. He's a decorated war hero. The man has a drawer full of medals, including a Purple Heart."

She cast a look at Stephen who stared out the windshield clearly uncomfortable with his brother's praise. "He was wounded?"

Virgil chuckled. "Oh yeah. But just in the thigh. Nothing you have to worry about. No vitals if you know what I mean."

"So you're saying I can trust him?"

"With your life, honey. With your life. I'm not so sure about your virtue though," he added, chuckling again.

Virgil Douglas seemed to be a likable fellow, not nearly as intense as his brother. "Just one more question. Why did you call him Rando?"

"His name is Stephen, Stephen Randall Douglas. Some of us started calling him Rando when he joined the service." Virgil laughed. "He hates it."

"Thanks," she said smiling. "I appreciate your honesty."

"Good, now can I talk to Rando? Family business. Ma's having some issues."

"Of course." Dani said goodbye and handed the phone to Stephen. "I'm going to get some coffee. Want some?"

"You bet, black for me."

Dani had mixed feelings as she strolled around the gas station. She was still a little miffed because Stephen had gone through Roger's backpack. They should have done it together. Granted, they hadn't had the time, but still...she was right there in the bathroom; he could have told her what he was doing. And then there was the greenhorn comment. She hadn't been with Foreign Affairs that long, but she considered herself a good agent. What she hadn't told Stephen was the main reason they selected her. She knew crystals. She doubted Stephen would consider that important enough to assign a high profile job.

At least one thing was cleared up. The media hadn't been given Stephen's name because of his war hero status. If the public had gotten hold of that, they'd have made a big deal of it and hindered the investigation. Certainly no one would have turned him in.

Well, she decided, she'd show him just how good an agent she could be. Instead of going to the gas station, she headed for the pawnshop. If she could find one of those dragon crystals, and he insisted on seeing what she had, she'd show him that. And if he is who he says he is, he wouldn't be any the wiser. If he made any kind of a gripe about it, she'd know he's not telling all.

A little bell clanged over her head. The shaggy haired proprietor looked up long enough to give her a bodily once over. She must have failed whatever test it was because he dismissed her and went back to sipping on his coffee and paging through an antique book. Probably hoping to price one of his countless treasures. She didn't have a clue as to how he'd know what he had in his shop. The place resembled like a cluttered back-alley flea market.

"Do you have any crystals?" she asked.

His bushy eyebrows drew together in a frown. "You mean like jewelry?"

"Anything, crystal. A friend of mine is a collector. Just point me to what you have and I'll take a look."

He nodded his head toward a round glass-covered case in one corner. "If we had anything like that, it'd be in there. Some of this stuff has been around a while."

No shit, she thought, taking care not to rub up against any of the dust covered junk. She wended around a glass-topped counter covered with watches and rings and two large boxes brimming with miscellaneous computer parts.

The round case was filled with dozens of antique glass bowls and ornamental cups. She did see a crystal butterfly and a turtle, both too small and ordinary to be considered valuable in any way. She opened the door and moved things around finding nothing of interest.

"Check the bottom shelf," he called. "I think there's a couple of crystal skulls. Your friend probably wouldn't have one of those.

Dani knelt down and found them. One as large as her fist, the other about the size of a man's fist, both clear. She picked up the smaller one. The real skulls were life size and extremely valuable. These weren't crystal, they were glass and they weren't life-size, but they were reasonably well done smaller replicas. She'd seen them for sale once in an antique shop. But Stephen likely didn't know crystal from cheap glass, and he probably didn't even know about the real skulls. Very few people did. This looked like something she could pull off.

She glanced out the window making sure Stephen had stayed put, then brought the skull to the counter.

"This isn't crystal," she said. "It's glass. But it is interesting. How much?"

He shrugged. "They run about a hundred dollars. "

He was a scammer and full of crap too. "I deal in this kind of thing," she said. "The big one is worth about fifty and this one thirty-five." She knew they were worth only half that much, but she didn't want to insult him.

"I'll let it go for eighty," he said.

She only had sixty left and she needed coffee money. *How about sixty and a red satin nightgown,* she wanted to say. Instead she countered, "I'll give you fifty."

"Cash?"

Dani breathed a sigh of relief. She asked him for something nice to put it in, and he grudgingly produced a dusty red velvet bag from beneath the counter and charged her two dollars for it. She paid him and hurried out to the service station area toward the coffee bar.

When she got to the car, she found Stephen laying with his head back, his eyes closed. The skull didn't fit in her pocket, so she'd asked the clerk for a bag, and the skull was at the bottom under the coffee. When she got a chance, she'd put it in one of the pockets of her dirty cargo pants. That should convince him she'd had it all along. And fortunately, she knew enough about the real skulls to come up with a believable story.

"That coffee smells like heaven," he said. Without opening his eyes to look at her, he held out a hand.

She took both coffees out of the bag and placed one in his waiting hand. She then crumpled the bag with the skull left in it and threw it in the back seat in the vicinity of the dirty clothes pillowcase.

Stephen sat up, pulled the cover off his coffee, took a sip, and shuddered. He looked as ragged as she felt. In spite of the shower and change of clothes she'd had, she was weary, sadly in need of sleep.

He glanced over at her, eyes drooping. "We need to find a place to get some rest, and I really need to get cleaned up and lose this convict look."

"Gee, and I was just getting used to it."

He scratched at the growth of whiskers on his neck and flicked his visor down to look in the mirror, then shot her a leering grin. "You like it, huh?"

She made a half laughing, half hissing sound through the teeth. "Okay, let's find another motel. You stay in the car this time and I'll go in and pay. The manager likely recognized you at the last place."

Stephen put his visor back up and started the car. "But if he called the number they showed on the news flash, he'd have gotten Mays, not Deluca."

Her tired eyes widened. "You're right. I guess I was too busy and too exhausted to think about it."

"What do you think now?" he asked. "Are they working together?"

Dani shook her head. "I find it hard to believe Deluca would hook up with an LAPD officer, even a crooked one, but I suppose anything's possible."

"I guess we better not make any assumptions until we know something concrete. How do we get out of here?"

"Where is your friend's plane?"

He turned icy blue eyes on her. "Before we go that route, you have something to tell me or show me."

"All right, all right, as soon as we get to the motel."

His look was skeptical, but he nodded and put the car in gear. "The plane is in the ski hills this side of Denver," he said, and then added, "Make no mistake, Miss Lovato; if I find out you're lying to me, I'll drop your ass like a hot rock."

His warning, particularly his choice of words, sent a shiver up her spine, but she couldn't let him get to her. She was a government agent, greenhorn or not, and she'd do what she had to do. She knew what the Blood Crystal meant to Bama Kendu and the people of San Delta. He'd explained it when Reierson took her to meet with Kendu at his hotel suite. He needed it to save his country. Five people, three his own friends, and two US agents had been murdered when Deluca's hooligans stole the crystal. Reierson had explained how the whole thing was an embarrassment to the U.S. Government and they'd taken steps to keep both the theft and the existence of the priceless crystal from the media.

"Go back the way we just came and catch I-15 going north," she said, acknowledging his threat with a slight nod. She had to bite her tongue to keep from saying *ditto*, but the truth was…she needed him. She had no money and no transportation. With zero finances, she couldn't even hop a bus.

He interrupted her thoughts as though he'd read her mind. "In case you didn't know it, there's eight hundred dollars in your backpack."

"What?"

"I guess that means you didn't know."

"How could Roger have that much cash on him?" She didn't realize she's said it out loud until Stephen spoke.

"How would I know? He was your partner. You tell me."

For a moment, she stared at him, not wanting to tell him what she was thinking. Somehow, he knew by her expression.

"Don't tell me he was on the take too?" Stephen said as though he already knew what was going through her mind.

She couldn't answer through the constriction blocking her throat. She'd trusted Roger *just like she'd trusted her father*. Finally, she swore and threw her hands in the air in a helpless gesture. "I don't know what to believe anymore."

"So, if Roger was throwing his chips in with someone, was it Mays or Deluca?"

"Mays killed him!"

"Maybe he didn't need Roger anymore."

Dani remembered Roger calling Mays to tell him they had the crystal and to come and get them out. Roger had asked her to leave. Get out while she could before Deluca discovered the crystal was missing. He'd been angry when she'd refused. She'd told him she wasn't going anywhere without the crystal, but he insisted he should keep it in the backpack. *And then he'd relayed that information to Mays.*

"Or me," she said. "But maybe that explains why

Mays hired you to get me out of there."

"He didn't want to deal with the consequences of killing a federal agent," Stephen said.

Dani's head snapped around to glare at him. The man had an uncanny way of hitting on the truth. Was it a guess or did he know something?

Stephen pulled into a small motel on the north side of Las Vegas. He parked on the side out of sight of the front door to wait for Dani to register.

"Don't use our names or put down the real plate numbers," Stephen said, handing her a hundred dollar bill.

"I'm not a complete idiot," she replied, "and I can use the money in the backpack."

"I know you're not an idiot. But you've been trained by people who know the honest thing to do."

"Unlike you," she muttered, getting out of the car.

"You can pay me back later," he called as she slammed the door.

Even with all the mayhem surrounding them, she found it oddly satisfying to spar with Stephen, or *Rando* as his brother called him. She walked into the motel office with a small grin on her face.

Stephen complimented her choice of rooms, second level, on the end, stairs going down the side. As before, they parked the car in the back, nose aimed toward an easy exit. Not that they expected anyone to recognize her, but they'd learned to be cautious.

Dani grabbed the pillowcase, and in the guise of removing the hair color box and other trash to toss in the dumpster, slipped the skull into an empty pocket in her cargo pants. She had a fleeting attack of conscience about deceiving him, but shoved it aside, considering it a necessary part of her mission.

This time Stephen gave her a few moments in the bathroom before going in and closing the door behind him. Dani went straight to the backpack. She removed her gun and dumped the rest of the contents out on the king-sized bed. She found an old but clean t-shirt she'd seen Roger wear, a couple of James Patterson's books, a collection of crossword puzzles, and a brochure from a hotel in San Juan. She paused over the last item only a moment, allowing anger to seep into her core.

She then unzipped all the side pockets and discovered the money Stephen mentioned. Eight one-hundred dollar bills. Twenty-four hours earlier, she'd bought his dinner because he said he was running low on cash. With no qualms about theft, she stuffed the money in her pocket. At least now if she needed to strike out on her own she had the resources to do it.

When she discovered his cell phone, she quickly checked to make sure it was turned off. Next she found, tucked in a hidden lining, his badge, passport, and a one-way airline ticket to San Juan. She didn't have to wonder why he carried his passport on an undercover mission. Maybe he *was* working for Deluca and double crossed Mays? It didn't matter, though. Either way he was a rotten scoundrel, just one more man who'd betrayed her. It wasn't as devastating as finding out what her father had done, but disconcerting no less.

Still fuming, she emptied her pathetically small personal arsenal of things from the Wal-mart bag. She wasn't surprised it all fit easily in the backpack. Pausing over the ridiculous impulsively purchased red nightgown, she rolled it up and stuffed it in a side pocket.

That finished, she emptied the deep pockets in her cargo pants. The velvet covered skull she tucked in with her clothes, and put the few extra cartridges for her Beretta in her jeans pocket. The rest of them were in a zippered pouch in her abandoned Lakers jacket, alongside the built-in holster to carry her gun.

Satisfied she had all her belongings together, she lay down on the bed with the ratty old bag cradled in her arms. She had no thoughts whatsoever of removing any of her clothing, including her shoes. Her last thought, other than wondering how Deluca had found them, was curiosity about why Virgil called his brother Rando. Was it just one brother poking fun at another or some kind of a code name, and was Virgil really his brother?

Stephen stepped out of the bathroom wondering how a man could feel fresh and alive and dead tired at the same time.

Dani was curled up in a ball, hugging one corner of the large bed. The alive half of him got hard looking at her. *Where the hell did that come from?* He no more had sex on his mind than having a tooth pulled. Noticing she was fully dressed prompted him to do the same. He pulled clean jeans and a t-shirt on along with fresh socks, and as an afterthought, slipped his shoes on too. That done, he stuffed his dirty clothes in the pillowcase with hers, then gathered his other things together in the Wal-mart bag, keeping everything on the desk within easy reach. After a cautionary glance out the window, he walked around the bed to check the small bathroom window where he could look down at the car. It was just as he'd left it. No strangers lurking about. He gauged the stairway outside and found it to be a good escape route, slightly below the level of the floor made it inconvenient to break into but easy to slip out. As an afterthought, he opened the window that was just big enough to slip through, removed the screen, then closed and locked it.

It was one o'clock in the afternoon. Broad daylight. Somehow that thought wasn't real comforting. He felt a whole lot safer under the cover of darkness. He'd seen too many of his comrades wasted in their sleep under a blazing hot sun. With that in mind, he pulled the single chair from the desk up to the door and wedged it under the knob; he also double-checked to make sure the deadbolt was set. Heading for the long awaited comfort of the bed, he shook his head, wondering if he was becoming overly paranoid.

Drawing a deep, pensive sigh, he laid down on the bed beside his mysterious companion. He realized it had been less then twenty-four hours since she turned his world upside down. Hell, what was he thinking, his world had been upside down for two months…no, make that fourteen months…the healing pain in his leg served as a constant reminder.

Near darkness surrounded him when he next opened his eyes. His heart pounded with an adrenaline-induced rush. Where it often took people several minutes to become oriented when they woke in a strange place, Stephen was instantly aware. Something had disturbed his sleep. Something wasn't right. Scratches at the door…faint noises that wouldn't have brought an untrained person out of a deep sleep.

CHAPTER EIGHT

He reached over and eased Dani's backpack from her arms. She stirred, turning, stretching. He fished through the bag and quickly found her gun. In the semi-darkness, he familiarized himself with it, then putting a hand over Dani's mouth, softly called her name. Her eyes popped open instantly wide and frantic.

"Ssssh…be quiet. Somebody's at the door."

She nodded her understanding, shook his hand away from her mouth, and reached for her gun only to see it in his hands.

"Give me that," she hissed.

"Save your arguments for later," he said, pulling her off the bed behind him.

"But—"

"Ssssh."

He dragged her with him to stand against the wall beside the door, safely away from any bullets that could come through it. He motioned her to stay put while he checked the peephole. He saw one man standing and waiting, another bent over working on the lock. No one stared back at him through the peephole.

He pulled her out from behind him. "See if you know who it is?"

She put her eye to the hole and stepped back. "Not Deluca, but it's one of his henchmen."

"Bring your stuff," he said, hurrying to the bathroom window over the stairs. He peeked outside, found nobody there, then slid the curtain aside and unlocked the window.

He handed her the car keys. "I'm going to make some noise out front. When I do, open the window and get to the car. Have it running with the passenger door open. If I'm not out in twenty seconds after the shooting starts, leave without me. Wait two minutes at the Walgreen's on the corner, then you're on your own."

He took one second to plant a kiss on her lips and left her staring back at him with wide eyes. This was one time he prayed she'd follow orders.

Back at the front door, the thug had managed to get the deadbolt open. The chair held up as he slammed his shoulder into the door. Stephen fired two shots into the lower half of the door hoping to hit a leg. The smell of gunpowder assailed his nostrils at the same time a howl of pain came from outside. The entire door splintered under the force of rapid gunfire. He gave a good imitation of a John Wayne yowl so they'd think he'd taken a hit.

Dani, already through the window, had disappeared from sight. Smart lady. She might be stubborn as a bulldog, but she knew how to take care of herself when the chips were down. He'd taken a chance giving her orders like a drill sergeant, but there hadn't been time for mollycoddling.

He fired another couple of shots into the door just to let them know he was still a threat, then ran for the bathroom and squeezed through the tiny window. He heard glass breaking behind him and knew they'd given up on the door and gone for the window beside it. Racing for the car, ignoring the pain in his leg and keeping an eye over his shoulder, he felt a rush of relief to hear the engine running.

He dove through the door as Dani rammed her foot on the gas, fishtailing into the alley. Looking back, he spotted one of their assailants leaning out the screenless bathroom window.

Before they turned the corner, two bullets hit the car, likely in the trunk since no glass shattered.

"Don't slow down," he said. "They'll be on our tail quiker'n you can shake a stick at a pole cat."

"My thoughts exactly," she replied, switching on her headlights and taking a right turn on two wheels. Out of nowhere, a dark green sedan tore across the intersection directly in front of them. Dani braked and veered right to avoid broadsiding it as the frantic eyes of the driver peered like a startled deer into their headlights.

Stephen had only seen the driver for a split second, but was certain he knew who it was. The look on Dani's face told him he wasn't mistaken.

"What the heck is he doing here?" Dani all but shouted as soon as she'd regained control of the car. She kept an eye in the rear view mirror, knowing there was little chance the driver could have recognized them. All he'd seen was the glare of their headlights, yet the way their luck had been running, she half expected Brock Mays to make a U-turn to pursue her.

"That was my question," Stephen said. "They *must* be working together."

Dani concentrated on driving, taking two sharp turns, and winding up on the entrance ramp to north I-15. "I still don't see how that's possible. But even if they are, how did they find us? And if they aren't joining forces, how the hell did they *both* find us? There's no way that teenybopper I registered with this morning recognized me. She had text books spread out all over the desk and was far more interested in her notes than looking at my face."

"We've got to be missing something."

Dani took a deep breath, forcing herself to relax and bring the car down to the legal speed limit. The last thing they needed was a patrol car with flashing lights on their bumper. "Maybe Mays is following Deluca?"

"It would make more sense if Deluca was following Mays. Otherwise, how did Deluca find us last night?"

Dani gave a snort of disgust. "None of it makes any sense if you ask me." When Stephen didn't respond, she glanced over at him. The sight of his bare face nearly caused her to drive off the road. "Holy crap," she said. "Who are you? And what have you done with Rando?"

In the darkness, his grin showed a row of even white teeth. He ran a hand over his smooth chin. "Looks that good, aye?"

"I don't remember saying that."

"Didn't have to. I can tell you like it."

She hid a smirk and refused to turn his way again. "Actually, I liked it better when I couldn't see quite so much of your face."

His deep chuckles relaxed her in one way but sent her female senses skyrocketing in another. Was she actually attracted to him?

"I hate that nickname, you know."

"What nickname?"

"Rando. My brother started that when I came home from the service. He has the whole family using it. I haven't found a way to get even with him yet."

"You like to get even, do you?"

She could feel his gaze on her and wondered if she'd unintentionally hit a nerve. Then she remembered something that raised her ire. "I want my Beretta back!"

He reached behind him, pulled the gun out and handed it to her. "Here, I used four bullets. I don't suppose you have any extras?"

"Maybe I do. Maybe I don't," she said, checking the safety before she tucked it under her t-shirt in the waistband of her jeans.

"That means you do." He looked down at her tight jeans. "Where you're keeping them is a mystery though."

"There were two clips in the jacket you left on your ex-wife's garage floor."

He shook his head. "Shit."

After everything he'd done for her, she felt a twinge of guilt. He'd been willing to stay and take the heat while she left with the car. "By the way," she said, "thanks for what you did back there. You likely saved us both from a nasty situation, even if you did steal my gun."

He shrugged. "The way I look at it, we watched each other's backs. Neither one of us would have gotten away if you hadn't had the car running and ready to go."

"You didn't even say please."

He laughed that husky skin-tingling laugh again. "I didn't have time, but if it's any comfort to you, I was surprised you obeyed orders so easily."

"Yeah, well, don't try it again."

Silence hung between them for a few minutes until they passed a service station touting a trucker's café.

Stephen sighed. "I'm freaking hungry enough to eat—"

"—the asshole out of a skunk," she finished for him.

He flashed her a sly grin. "I was going to say McDonalds. I've recently become attracted to skunks."

Dani felt the odd sensation of a flush creep up her neck. Her heart followed suit by doing a peculiar thumping dance in her chest. She shrugged both off as stress and hunger. "Maybe we should stop at the next place with food. I'm starving myself."

For the umpteenth time, Stephen craned his neck to look out the back window. "The nice thing about driving this time of night is you can spot anyone following from several miles off. I think it's safe to stop. Even if they still have our faces on the news, we don't look much like the couple they're looking for."

About ten miles down the road they spotted another truck stop. Dani turned in and parked as usual in a dark corner with the car facing a clear getaway. The small café had a back door that looked more like it was an employee's entrance, but they tried it and found their way past the restrooms where Dani made a stop while Stephen found a place to sit near the back door, facing forward. From his vantage point, he could keep an eye on both the front door and the activity outside. Right now, two cars and a pickup were pulled up to the gas pumps.

Inside, the only other customers were three truckers sitting at the counter heckling the waitress. Behind them in a booth, a young couple mooned over each other like they'd just come from a wedding ceremony in Las Vegas.

The waitress walked up and gave him a smile that might have brightened his day, or night at one time, but right now he was interested in nourishment. A moment after Dani slipped into the booth across from him, he handed her the menu, having decided on the 24-hour-breakfast even if it was only midnight. It seemed he'd lost track of time, mentally and physically.

He perused his companion while she frowned over the menu. Damn if she didn't look good, even with green hair. Those perky little bumps on her chest told him she wasn't wearing a bra. He gritted his teeth and concentrated on the cars outside, fighting the uncomfortable stirring in his groin. Damn, woman. He could imagine her reaction if he told her she should wear a bra, even if her breasts were the size of poached eggs.

The waitress came to take their order, saving him from his wayward thoughts. When she left, it was time to concentrate on something other than Dani's nipples staring him in the eye.

"So, where and what is this thing we're risking our lives to protect?"

She opened her mouth but instead of talking she glanced around the room. "Maybe this isn't a good time."

"It's a very good time. Even if someone could hear you, they'd have no idea what we're talking about."

She gave a deep reluctant sigh. "Have you ever heard of the crystal skulls?"

He steepled his hands in front of him, trying to remember where he'd heard of them. "There was a movie out a while back hyping crystal skulls. I didn't see it, but I would have thought it was fiction."

"They aren't fiction. There are only a few in existents and they've been discovered in different parts of the world. The first one was found in 1924 in Belize, so they're very old. The workmanship is such that we didn't have the skills to make them back then, so it's speculated that they came from another planet."

He watched her face for any sign she was lying. But she held his gaze and spoke with firm authority. "I still don't understand why you of all people were chosen to recover this rare crystal."

She gave him a dour frown. "In spite of being a greenhorn agent as you so eloquently put it, my area of expertise is crystals. I have a lot of contacts and I was supposed to go undercover in the guise of helping Deluca find a buyer."

"So, how much is this crystal worth?"

She hesitated a moment then shrugged. "It depends. Less if it's sold as a stolen item. It would have to go to a private collector wanting it just because he can afford it. He couldn't display it or legally resell it. Like when rare paintings are stolen. Or anything else high profile enough to be recognized."

"How much would a buyer like that pay?"

"It doesn't matter. It's going back to the original owner."

The waitress brought their food and Dani made purring sounds, turning her attention to eating, obviously deeming the conversation over. He had the feeling she didn't want him to know the value of it, which meant she still didn't trust him. Stephen shoved a spoonful of eggs in his mouth, chewed, swallowed, and went back to questioning her between bites.

"Just exactly where is this *skull?*"

She swallowed half a glass of orange juice before answering. "In the backpack."

"What? Is it the size of a pinhead? I went through that backpack."

This time she'd managed to get half a piece of toast in her mouth to take time to chew and swallow. "I put it in there last night along with my other things while you were in the bathroom."

His eyebrows raised a notch. "That was smart," he said. "At least you got your stuff out. Mine stayed in the motel."

She gave him a Cheshire grin. "Not if you tidied up and put it all back in your Wal-mart suitcase like a good little boy."

"You took my bag?"

She nodded. "Yup."

"Wow, I could kiss you for that. Did you get the pillowcase too?"

"Yes. And you already did kiss me. What was up with that anyway?"

He scooped up the last of his hash browns and shoved them in his mouth. This time he was the one stalling. "I wasn't sure if I'd make it out, so…"

"Well, it wasn't much of a kiss anyway," she said, pulling out one of Roger's hundred dollar bills. She got up to pay the tab and left him staring after her.

The clerk rattled the bill between her hands, gave Dani a suspicious look, and swiped her brown pen over it.

"This is no good," she said, raising her voice with each word.

Dani quickly looked back at Stephen and said in a whiny voice, "Honey, this hundred I won in Vegas is bad."

She actually managed tears in her eyes. Damn she was good.

Stephen got up, pulled two twenties out of his wallet, handed them to the waitress, telling her to keep the change. Out of the corner of his eye, he saw her use the marker before a broad grin covered her face.

"It's okay, sweetie," he said to Dani. "Don't cry."

"But…honey…"

He put his hands on either side of her face and pulled it to his mouth, pressing a lusty sucking kiss to her lips. Ignoring her wide-eyed stare, he released the lip-lock, grabbed her hand and tugged her resisting body toward the back door. "We need to go. Nature's calling."

Once through the first door by the restroom, he turned

to her talking rapidly. "A black car just circled the pumps twice then disappeared behind the building."

CHAPTER NINE

"Quick," Dani said. "There's a window in the women's restroom."

They both shoved into the dark restroom at the same time and charged for the window.

She recognized the two men approaching the Buick, one of them, Marty Alonzo, limped heavily, the other, Harry Andrews, she'd seen through the peephole at the motel. She didn't have time to dwell on how they'd found them...again. They both wielded guns in front of them as though they expected a shootout. To the left, the couple from the café headed for their car, their arms around each other, doing heavy petting as they walked.

Both of Deluca's men immediately holstered their guns and leaned against the Buick as though they idly stood there enjoying the evening. Marty lit up a cigarette.

They stood between the Buick and the building, giving them no cover to duck behind.

Dani moved quickly before Stephen could stop her. She burst from the back door holding her gun with both hands at eye level walking forward.

"Freeze!" she yelled.

When both men reached for their guns, Dani hollered again. "Touch those weapons and I'll drop you where you stand. Put your hands in the air."

Marty obeyed but Harry had his hand inside his jacket.

"Bring out a gun, Harry, and I'll shoot to kill. I promise I won't miss."

He paused, put his free hand in the air, and slowly pulled the other out of his coat, fingers spread, and raised it, swearing, "Dammit, Dani, you should know better than to cross Deluca. We don't want to hurt you."

"You mean like you didn't want to hurt me back at the motel?"

"Well, hell, Dani, you fired first. We just need that fucking crystal."

She walked up to within six feet of them. "You're not in much of a position to bargain now are you? Get their guns," she ordered Stephen who'd come up beside her. "And be careful. If either one of you makes a move the other is dead...understand?"

"Who the fuck is he?" Marty asked when Stephen reached around him and pulled out his gun.

"The man who fired first, asshole. I get extremely crabby when my sleep is disturbed."

While Stephen relieved Harry of his Smith and Wesson, the man started swearing at Dani.

"Dammit, you crazy son-of-a-bitch woman. You can do what you want to us, but you know he won't give up until he has that crystal or until you're dead...or both. He told us to offer you ten percent of the profits. That's four hundred grand, Dani. You're nuts not to take him up on it."

She gave an angry snort. "And I suppose he'll pay me with counterfeit bills like he did Roger. Is that how he pays you?"

"Deluca doesn't pass counterfeits, he doesn't have to," Marty supplied.

While they talked, Stephen patted them down, looking for more weapons. He came up with two cell phones, a small Tom Cat Beretta, and a ten-inch Bowie knife.

Stephen sauntered over to the black sedan where he bent down and shoved the blade into first one front tire and then the other. "That's for the holes in the trunk of my car," he said. Both men let loose with a volley of curse words as the air hissed from the tires.

"Pick up that little box they kicked under our car," Dani said to Stephen.

Stephen shoved Harry aside, pushing him into his partner who howled when his towel-bandaged leg got bumped.

Bending down to retrieve the box, Stephen stood up shaking his head. "Well I'll be dammed. A tracking device. They have a bug planted on our car. Where is it?" he snarled at Harry.

"How the fuck should I know. Ask Deluca. Who the hell are you anyway?"

Stephen reached in his waistband and pulled out Harry's pistol. He aimed it at Marty's good knee. "Give me a reason to pull the trigger," he said in a voice so low and deadly, Dani got shivers up her spine.

"It's in Roger's phone," Marty blurted out.

"You wouldn't be lying to me now would you?"

"Fuck no. It ain't no good without the transceiver anyway."

"I think we're done here," Stephen said. "Shoot 'em so we can go."

Harry started swearing franticly. "Don't listen to him, Dani. It won't do any good to shoot us. You know Deluca. He'll just send somebody else. You think he's gonna to let you walk off with a four million dollar crystal"

"See that field behind you?" Dani asked. "Start walking and don't turn around until we're gone."

"I can't walk," Marty whined.

"We might as well shoot you then," Stephen said matter-of-factly. "That's what they do to horses."

Marty threw his arm around Harry and both men hobbled amid a medley of colorful words that would have made a pirate cringe.

"Where's Roger's phone?" Stephen asked quickly.

"In the backpack."

"Get it, hurry."

She went to the back seat, brought the phone out, and

handed it to Stephen. He took it to the sedan and came back without it. "Gimme the keys and let's get out of here before they find a weapon I missed or somebody calls the cops."

He stopped between two tarped semitrailers and heaved Harry's phone on top of one and Marty's on the other. "That ought to throw a wrench in their search," he said, getting back in the car.

Dani laid her head back on the seat and concentrated on breathing evenly and deeply. She'd tried to give the aura of being a tough cop back there, but most of that came from watching movies. Truth was, although she was a crack-shot, top in her class, she'd never actually shot a real person. The closest she came was shooting at Mays after he'd gunned down Roger.

That brought another thought to mind. If Deluca didn't pay off Roger, who did—Mays? He'd certainly have access to confiscated counterfeit bills.

She glanced at Stephen. Apparently, he was winding down too, satisfied with the silence between them.

That thought lasted all of ten more seconds.

"When in the hell were you going to clue me in on this four million dollar figure? No wonder you avoided that question. Evidently, you still don't trust me. Just what on God's green earth does a guy have to do to get that elusive commodity from you? Somebody in your past must have done a major number on you."

Right on, buster. "I do trust you," she lied.

"Like fucking hell you do. I want to see that crystal. Now."

She sighed heavily from the depths of her being. She wanted to trust him. She really did. But...reaching in the back seat, she dug through her bag and pulled out the red velvet sack. This was the moment of reckoning. She'd laid the groundwork. If he accepted the skull, she'd know he wasn't aware of the real Blood Crystal.

She opened the little bag and slipped out the skull. The setting couldn't have been more perfect with the red and green lights glowing in the dashboard. As she held it upright in her open palm for him to see, it picked up the colors shimmering eerily in the dark car. The hollow eye sockets glowed ghostly red and the mouth emitted an evil toothy smile.

Dani stared at the interesting play of luminosity. She knew it was simple glass, and yet it appeared prismatic, haunting.

Stephen interrupted her musings. "Jesus," he whispered, drawing his brows into a deep frown. "Anybody who'd put out four million bucks for that God forsaken thing needs to get a life. So what's it worth in the underground market?"

She wanted to lie to him, but showing him the fake skull somehow maxed out her energy to lie. But after all, she reasoned, if the skull were a genuine artifact, it would be priceless, easily into the millions.

"That is the underground price," she admitted, gently easing the *priceless* fifty-dollar glass skull back into its bag. They were coming up on St. George, Utah and she wanted to get it out of sight before they got into the city lights.

He took his eyes from the road to watch her. "You weren't tempted to take the ten percent Deluca offered?" he asked. "Just to get him off your back if nothing else?"

She took a deep, steady breath and slowly shook her head. She wanted him to understand the value of her mission…their mission. "The owner of the crystal is from a poor island off the coast of India. The Smithsonian had made him an offer that would have revived his little country and take them out of poverty. He's a kind, caring man and genuinely concerned about his people. If I don't get the crystal back to him, he'll have to go home with no hope to offer his countrymen."

"Do you know how long we stay on I-15?" Stephen asked.

"About a hundred miles or so. We turn east on I-70, and that takes us straight to Grand Junction and then Denver. We should probably gas-up when we get to 70. There's a long dry spell after that."

"You've traveled this road before?"

"Just once." She didn't want to get into why she'd left LA and moved to D.C. He might ask about her father and that's the last subject she wanted to get into…now or ever. Fortunately, it was curiosity that pulled him back to their original conversation.

"So…how did Deluca get his hands on it?"

"Bama, the president of San Delta, sent it with three of his guards along with two U.S. agents. All five where murdered. Speculation is that one of the agents contacted Deluca. If so, he lost his life for that betrayal. Deluca doesn't like to leave loose ends. Plus, he has a peculiar sense of honor. He figures if a man betrays once, he'll do it again."

"By and large, that's true," Stephen said a touch of bitterness in his voice. "It makes me wonder why a man would marry a woman who cheated on her husband. Why would he think she wouldn't do it again?"

"Or vice-versa," Dani replied. *And what about the children who get destroyed in the process?*

Stephen agreed and for some time, silence hung in the air. Suddenly Dani remembered something. "What did you do with Roger's phone?"

Stephen chuckled. "I planted it between the cushions of those assholes' car." He reached between the seats and pulled out the transponder. "Now we can keep track of where *they* are."

Dani laughed. "Oh my God. You are too clever. Where did you learn that little trick?"

He bobbed his eyebrows at her. "I'm the youngest of two, make that three, brothers. I needed tricks to survive."

Dani could only imagine what it was like to grow up in a big family. "So you're the youngest?" she asked.

"I have a younger sister. How about you?"

There it was. Why did everything come right back to her? "I'm an only child," she said. *Or at least I grew up believing I was.*

"That sounds great in one way but boring in another."

She managed a feeble smile. "A little of both," she said. "At least we can relax a little, not having to worry about Deluca on our tail every minute."

"And that probably means Mays *was* following Deluca, so we should be rid of both of them."

"Amen and halleluiah," she said.

Smiling to herself, she leaned back in the seat and let the tension drain out of her. In doing so she allowed her mind go over the events at the restaurant and suddenly she sat up straight.

"You kissed me again back there."

"I had to shut you up. I was sure you were going to go into that tirade of being pregnant and your Daddy living in Texas and all that other crap you seem to be able to dredge up on the spur of the moment."

"I'm just resourceful," she replied defensively.

"Well, we didn't have time for it, so that was a resourceful kiss."

"You did that little sucking thing. Was that necessary?"

"Yeah, because last time you said it wasn't much of a kiss."

She sat back and folded her arms over her chest trying to think of a smart reply.

She could see him watching out of the corner of her eye. "I do know how to kiss," he said.

"Well so do I," she snapped.

"Couldn't prove it by me. If you'd wanted to help me out and make if convincing, you could have kissed me back."

"You took me by surprise."

"You mean because I didn't say 'excuse me, we're in a bit of a hurry, so I'm going to kiss you to shut you up.' □"

"Stop the car."

"Why?"

"So I can prove to you I know how to kiss better than you do."

Chapter Ten

He threw his head back and laughed until his belly hurt. "That certainly beats any challenge my brothers ever came up with."

When he looked over to see her grin it put a bit of the devil in him. He took his foot off the accelerator.

"I was kidding, you doofus," she rejoined quickly.

He speeded back up, relieved to see her laugh along with him when he did. There was something about this woman he liked. In addition to being smart and feisty, he found it a constant challenge to keep up with her. Those perky little bumps on her chest were starting to look better and better every time he sneaked a glance at them, and the rest of her literally beamed with vitality, from her pixie haircut feathering a pretty oval face like a dark fluffy cloud, albeit green tinted, to her flawless olive skin he imagined to be smooth to the touch. She had great lips and high cheekbones. He'd had a minuscule taste of those full lips, and if she thought he was going to let that kiss challenge go, she was in for a major revelation.

At dawn, they stopped in Green River for breakfast. In spite of the decreased threat of being followed, Stephen warned about sticking to their routine with parking the car in the back. If Deluca made a guess as to where they were headed, which was highly possible, he could still intercept them at sometime. Especially since they didn't know if the goons had taken down their license number.

For the second time in less than twelve hours they ordered the same meal. This time it was steak and eggs. When Dani offered to drive the next leg of the trip, he shook his head.

"We're already in the grace period on our plate tabs. What if we get stopped again? Your name will sound alarm bells even this far from LA. At least we aren't aware my name has been announced yet."

A frown lined her eyebrows and she looked as though she would comment. They'd gone about ten miles when she launched into another subject. "How long until we get to where the plane is?" she asked.

"It's in the Loveland ski area. My friend's family owns a lodge there."

"This isn't ski season. Do you expect him to be there?"

"No."

She threw her hands in the air with an irritated clucking sound. "So what good is the plane going to do us if he's not there?"

"I'll fly it."

She stared at him for a long moment with wide whisky colored eyes. "You can fly?"

"Why should that be so hard to believe?"

"Maybe because you never mentioned it." she barked.

"There are a lot of things about me you don't know."

She folded her arms over her chest. "Okay, we have nothing better to do right now. Let's have a little getting-to-know-you session."

"Why just getting to know me? How about you?"

"You already know everything about me."

He rolled his eyes skyward then brought them back to rest on her face. "You give out little tidbits then clam up. You call that knowing everything? I told you I have three older brothers and a younger sister in Minnesota. You haven't told me anything about your family."

He could see the rapid rise and fall of her chest. There

was something in her background she was hiding. Either it was too painful or she enjoyed being secretive.

"My parents are both dead. I'm an only child. What else is there to say?"

You said you're father died six months ago. When did your mother die?"

Her hesitancy to answer told him she was struggling with something. She was an only child, so it must be the relationship with one of her parents.

"About seven months before he did," she finally said.

"Is that when you moved to D.C.?"

"Yes." Her answer was blunt. Her jaw clenched and he knew she was ready to clam up again. He was getting close to something she didn't want him to know. She rubbed her sore hand on her thigh as though it itched.

"What happened to your hand?" he asked.

"It's your turn to share," she snapped, clearly telling him the problem with her burned hand was another thing she didn't want him to know, though he didn't have a clue what that had to do with anything.

He shrugged. "I'm an open book. What do you want to know?"

"When did you learn to fly?"

"During college. Some friends of mine were skydivers and half of them were also pilots. When I started skydiving, it just seemed natural to take up flying at the same time. There's something very exhilarating about spreading your wings in the air. My mom wasn't real keen on either idea, so I had to wait until I turned twenty-one."

"You're dad couldn't sign for you?"

He laughed. "And go against Mom? Not on your life. They were stuck together with parental glue."

When she tuned to look out the window he realized his statement had somehow affected her. It made him think maybe life at her house wasn't exactly a bed of roses.

"Weren't your parents like that?" he ventured.

She gave a derisive snort. "They were exactly like that—until she died." She shrugged. "So did you fly in the service?" she asked quickly.

"Yeah, helicopters."

She glanced at him laughing. "You flew a helicopter? What branch of service were you in?"

Stephen suddenly realized she was getting into territory *he* didn't want to talk about. "Special Forces."

She made a low whistling sound. "Well, that explains a lot. I was wondering where you got those ideas like looking at two motel rooms and renting places with escape routes. And I thought I was the one with the special training."

He flashed her a grin. "You were the one who suggested we park the car out of sight where we could make a quick getaway."

"Maybe we make a good pair," she said smiling.

For the next two hours they shared a genial camaraderie telling humorous or embarrassing tales about their early years. They crossed the border into Colorado a little after ten and an hour later stopped at a fast food drive-up window in Grand Junction for lunch. Stephen drove to the back of the parking lot where they got out at a picnic table to eat.

Stephen dug into his hamburger and basket of fries while she picked at the chicken strips in front of her. Slurping noisily on her king-size chocolate malt, she made soft moaning sounds with each mouthful.

"Must be a good malt," he mumbled over a swallow of cola. "I've seen women less enthusiastic during sex."

She contemplated that a moment before replying. "I heard some guy say once that there weren't any frigid women, only incompetent men. Do you suppose that's true?"

Stifling a grin, she gave herself a mental "gotcha" pat on the back when he choked on a French fry. She knew he'd come up with a smart-ass answer if she gave him the chance so she quickly changed the subject.

"Don't you have to file a flight plan or something to

fly?"

He gave her a frosty glare that promised he'd get even later. "I'll take care of that as soon as you tell me where to land. And don't make it too close to the capital. They're a little persnickety about who flies in government airspace."

"I was thinking Bethesda. It's big enough to get a car and near enough to make it to our destination in a few hours. I don't know how fast your plane is or how long you can go until you need gas, so you'll need to handle that part of it."

"Let's get out of here," Stephen said, gathering up his empty food bags along with her ignored chicken strips. "I'll pick up an atlas when we stop for gas. Then I can map out a route when we get to the lodge. We can fly without a flight plan, but I have to make some weather inquiries. The main reason you file a flight plan is so someone can find you if your plane goes down."

"Gosh. That makes me feel a whole lot better." Dani handed him her malt. "You want the rest? I'm full."

"No wonder you're skinny as a rail. You eat like a sparrow, a noisy one at that." Stephen sucked the last of the malt with one long draw and threw the container in the trash barrel along with the rest of the garbage.

"I'm not skinny, I'm slender," she retorted as they walked side by side toward to the restrooms.

He opened the door to the men's room and hesitated long enough to say, "I've heard men get slivers in their peckers making love to skinny women."

The door swung shut behind him before she could comment.

She sent a muttered curse after him anyway.

He was waiting in the car when she got out and they got back on the road heading west in silence. Five blocks later, Stephen looked in the rear view mirror and swore.

Dani whirled around to see a police car with its red lights flashing close on their bumper.

Stephen pulled over. "If he asks for your license, tell him you don't drive," Stephen warned.

"Not a problem. My license is in my jacket along with my badge."

"That's just great," he muttered. "What the hell else is in the damned jacket?"

"My case of condoms. Man, he doesn't even look old enough to shave. I'll bet he's an idealistic deputy fresh out of the academy. We're in trouble."

"Let me do the talking," Stephen said rolling down his window.

The officer wearing a Grand Junction sheriff's deputy badge walked up to the car and leaned in to peruse the inside front to back. "You guys are a long way from home. Do you know your tabs are expired?"

"Yeah," Stephen said. "I know we're hoping to make it back to Minnesota within the grace period."

"That shouldn't be a problem. You still have a few more days. Can I see your license and registration please?"

Stephen glanced at Dani as he reached in his back pocket to pull out his wallet. "Honey, will you check the glove box for the registration."

He gave a slight shake of his head and Dani wasn't sure what he meant. Was she supposed to say it wasn't there? Her heart began an erratic beat as she opened the glove box, pulled out a messy stack of papers, and started going through them on her lap. No registration. Thinking that might be a good thing she found an outdated insurance document that had Stephen's name on it and decided to, play dumb.

"Here it is, sweetheart," she said and smiled past him to the waiting officer. She put her hand on Stephen's thigh near his groin and rubbed it up and down his leg. "We just got married in Las Vegas yesterday. He's been in the service and…well…you know…it was a long wait."

She could feel his leg tense as he sent her a warning glare.

The officer raised his eyebrows. "Were you in Iraq?" he asked Stephen.

"No, Afghanistan."

"Man, I have a brother in Iraq, and according to his letters, it's rough over there. My hat's off to you guys. I'm glad you made it back in one piece." He handed Stephen his license. "Why don't you two just go on your way and enjoy your honeymoon. You don't need me giving you any hassles. Just get those tabs as soon as you get home."

Stephen smiled. "Thank you, sir. I'll do that."

The young officer gave a two-finger salute, touching the brim of his hat, and walked back to his car. Stephen let out a long whoosh that sounded like he'd been holding his breath.

"Shit, that was close," he whispered. He took her hand and put it back in her lap. "You can quit now, you made your point." He put the car in gear, flipped on his blinker and pulled out into the traffic.

Dani gave her own heavy sigh of relief and turned around to wave at the police car.

"What the hell are you doing?" he squawked.

"Just being Minnesota friendly."

"You're crazy, you know that, don't you? What if he'd asked to see our marriage license?"

"Well, honey," she drawled. "I told you I forgot my purse back in that restaurant we stopped at."

"It's disgusting what you sweet-talking good-looking women get by with just fluttering your eyelashes. I don't know why I was worried about you driving."

Dani made a snorting sound. "He wasn't looking at my eyes, he was watching my hand. No wonder women get by with that shit, you men are all alike; you think with your horny heads. And you can be glad I did what I did because there's no registration, just an old insurance receipt."

"Maybe we should steal some plates," he grumbled.

"As an officer of the law, I couldn't allow you to do that."

He gave her a look that questioned her sanity.

She answered with a hoot of laughter.

Chapter Eleven

"This is some spectacular country," Stephen said as they gained altitude climbing into the higher mountains. I've driven to the ski lodge from Denver several times but have never gone farther west than Silverthorne."

Dani gave a wistful sigh. "Yeah, I love this drive all the way from Green River. Both Utah and Colorado have some beautiful scenery and several National Parks."

"Have you been to them?"

"No... I'd have liked to, but it seems I've never done anything just for pleasure."

Stephen glanced at her face trying to determine if she was serious. She was staring out the window as though her mind was going over what she'd just said. "You don't do anything just for the fun of it?" he asked.

"Not since..."

"Your mother died?" he finished for her when she hesitated.

"Something like that," she murmured in a barely audible tone.

Stephen could tell she carried a sour bone where her father was concerned. And it had started after her mother died. He suspected maybe her father remarried quickly, maybe to a younger woman.

He took a deep breath and ventured into territory he really knew little about. "I can only imagine, but it must be tremendously painful to be left behind when a spouse of many years dies. I've seen people do strange things trying to replace what they've lost."

She turned a look on him suggesting she'd swallowed bile and needed a place to spit it. "You obviously didn't know Peter Lovato."

Obviously not. He decided to keep quiet and hope she'd expand on her thoughts. Not going to happen, he realized as she stared out the window apparently satisfied with ending the discussion.

"So," she said after several minutes of silence, "did you come up here skiing with this friend of yours, what's-his-name?"

"His name is Brad. Our whole family did. We grew up in the same neighborhood, attended the same school all the way through senior high. Our parents got together regularly. He had two older sisters and a younger brother."

"Where is Brad now? Do you still get to see him once in a while?"

Stephen swallowed a lump building in his throat. He found it hard to talk about Brad. "Everyday," he said finally, "up to about two months ago."

Dani's whisky colored eyes widened. "Oh my gosh. He's still over there isn't he?"

"Yeah, leaving him was the hardest thing I've ever done, but they wouldn't let me stay. My leg needed healing so they sent me home."

Dani smiled. "I'd bet either he saved your life or you saved his. Is that how you got wounded?"

"Something like that." He didn't know why he was baring his soul when she was so closemouthed about her family. She seemed far more interested in hearing about his life than talking about hers. It was almost like she didn't have a life.

"I guess he's okay with you using his plane then," she said.

He gave her a suspicious look but she didn't appear to have a hidden agenda behind her comment. "I know he is, even when we flew together he always wanted me at the controls."

She reached in the back seat and pulled something out of her backpack. "Probably because you were better at it," she said, unwrapping a chocolate bar.

"Where the hell did you get that?"

She grinned. "Wal-mart. When I bought my clothes. Want a bite?"

The look he gave her when he bobbed his eyebrows and said *yes* suggested it was not the candy he wanted to bite. He might have gotten the wrong idea when she'd put her hand on his thigh to distract the officer. That along with her comment about frigid women and incompetent men might have given him the notion she'd had lots of sexual experiences. She hardly considered two disastrous short-lived relationships experience. Her college roommate was the one who'd coined that phrase one night after Dani had complained about disliking sex. She didn't even know how to flirt.

When she held her hand up so he could take a bite, he grabbed her wrist and shoved the candy and half her hand in his mouth gobbling wolfishly on both.

She rescued her hand but the entire candy disappeared in his mouth.

"Man, this is good," he muttered around a mouth full of *her* chocolate.

"You're a pig," she told him, laughing with disbelief, counting her fingers to see if they were all intact. The sensation of his mouth munching on her had done strange things to her senses.

He reached for her hand. "There's still chocolate on your fingers."

She drew her hand out of his reach. "Forget it, you twisted pervert. I'll lick my own fingers if you don't mind. It was my chocolate."

"I bet a dollar you have more. Women don't buy just one candy bar unless they're dieting." The bold look he gave her challenged her to say she was dieting.

"Know a lot about women, do you?"

He grinned. "Enough. Get the rest of them out."

Passing him a narrow glare, she reached in the back and pulled out two more bars. "Here, unwrap it yourself," she said, throwing one in his lap. She pressed against the door to enjoy her own. When she'd finished, she made a point of licking each individual finger to make sure she hadn't missed any.

She hadn't meant it as a provocative thing, but the look on his face told her exactly what he was thinking. Inwardly smiling, she nonchalantly continued licking and sucking long after the chocolate was gone.

A sudden jerk on the steering wheel brought her out of her playacting. He'd almost hit the ditch on a mountain road.

He mumbled something incoherent under his breath and stared forward, keeping his eyes on the road.

"Did you just fall asleep there?" she asked innocently. "You want me to drive?"

"No," he snapped. "You'll get chocolate on the steering wheel."

For some time after that they sat in silence. Dani looked out her side window admiring the breathtaking snow-capped peaks. She thought about coming here to ski with brothers and sisters and family friends all having a wonderful time together, with a mother and father who loved each other forever and always. But that was stuff of fairy tales when it came to her life. Especially after her mother died and she discovered everything she'd believed in was fake. Small wonder she didn't trust men. She had good reason.

She gave a sideways glance at Stephen. He was one handsome specimen, striking good looks, broad shoulders, even a nice tight rear, but was he a man she could rely on? Most men she'd encountered in her adult life were far more interested in moving on than working on a relationship.

It seemed when the chips were down she always came

up the loser. They said she had the problem, she was lacking. Was it because she could outshoot them on the target range? Or because she could flop them on their asses in defense class. What was she lacking? Big tits? Well, there was that. One boyfriend went so far as to suggest she have them enhanced.

Her mind wandered back to when Stephen had called her skinny. She chewed on her lower lip, giving that some thought. "Can I ask you something?"

"Sure, what?"

"Did your wife have big breasts?"

He turned to stare at her as though she's just asked what size penis he had. Then he laughed. "Here I thought you were working on a strategy to get your crystal from Bethesda to D.C. and instead you want to know how big my wife's tits were. How the hell does that figure into the equation of what we're doing?"

To make matters worse, his gaze dropped to her chest. She quickly threw her arms over it only to have him shake his head and make a gallant attempt to stifle more laughter.

Her eyes narrowed to slivers.

"Sorry," he said. "You just kind of took me by surprise. Now what was it you wanted to know? The size of my wife's boobs? Far as I remembered, she was a 34D."

"I thought so," she muttered.

"I didn't marry her because of her bust size. Although that was a plus," he added, chuckling.

She swung her arm out and hit him on his rock hard bicep. "You men are all so fucking shallow."

"Ouch. I was kidding."

"So why did you marry her?"

"She was smart. Fun to be with. We had a common goal, or so I thought at the time. We graduated from the same law school. And we both went to work at her daddy's firm in Minneapolis. Mistake number one."

"So she's a lawyer too?"

"Yep. And when she took her big tits and moved to LA to marry a stock broker, I was no longer welcome in

Daddy's business."

"Sheesh, that's brutal."

"Sure is, I can still see those boobs."

"All right," she said, rolling her eyes and grinning. "I get the point."

"You ever been married?" he asked after a minute.

"No."

"You have a boyfriend?"

"No."

"Are you a lesbian?"

"Oh, for crying out loud. Just because I've never been married and don't have a boyfriend, I'm a lesbian?"

He shrugged. "I just wanted to know what I'm up against."

"Up against," she repeated.

"Yeah, I mean as long as we're stuck together, no reason why we shouldn't…ah…pursue other interests."

"Typical male. Can't go without sex for…how long has it been for you…a week?"

He didn't answer for some time. When he did, his voice was low. "It's been a lot longer than that."

She gave him a skeptical frown. She wasn't real comfortable with where this was going but she'd ventured this far… "How long?" she asked. "How long has it been?"

"Fourteen months."

She sat bolt upright in her seat. "Fourteen months? Over a year? You expect me to believe that?"

"I'm not the kind of man who cheats on his wife?"

"Even when she's cheating on you?"

"I didn't know that until I got back two months ago. I came to LA to try to patch things up with her and that's when she told me she was pregnant. She'd started divorce proceedings the minute she knew I was coming home." His face hardened as he watched the road.

"So…in two months you haven't found anybody to…lighten your load?"

He laughed. "No, as you put it… I haven't. I'm picky about who I *lighten my load* with."

Now it was her turn to laugh. "And you're choosing *no-tits-Lovato* to help break your fast. Now that's rich."

"Show me the man who said that to you and I'll break his nose."

Again she laughed. "He was thirteen."

"Ouch. Those pre-puberty boys can be brutal."

She gritted her teeth as the memories washed over her. "Not to worry," she said finally. "I've always been resourceful. I nicknamed him Peanut Pecker Paul. It took him two years to shake it."

Stephen gave a low whistle. "Remind me never to piss you off."

Dani passed him a playful glare. "You're just lucky I had another chocolate bar...Rando."

Chapter Twelve

Stephen drove up to the Cessna 180 to check it out and get it ready for flying in the morning.

Dani followed Stephen around as he did his inspection. She had to decide if she should get the Blood Crystal aboard now or wait until morning. It seemed to her that now was a better time. Stephen was preoccupied with oil depths, gas lines, battery conditions, and a number of other things he mentioned as he circled the plane.

When he opened *the hood* he called a cowl and stuck his nose inside to inspect wires and bleed the fuel lines, she made a pretense of readying her own things so she could get the crystal. It nested between the cushions of the back seat just where she'd left it. Even encased in a soft leather pouch, she couldn't chance putting it in her pocket in case it decided to start getting hot from the heat of her body.

She put it in the discarded food bag and discreetly climbed aboard the plane to *take a look around* as she'd told Stephen. It was cramped quarters inside with four seats taking up most of the space. Behind the back seats she found two packed bundles she assumed to be parachutes. A shiver ran down her spine when she thought about actually jumping out of a plane in the air. Not exactly a riveting vision.

She crawled in front and sat in the co-pilots seat where she assumed she'd be sitting when they flew. She wriggled around in the seat trying it out for comfort and size, then looked for a place to stash the crystal.

She discovered a drawer beneath her seat and pulled it open to check the contents. There was a data log stuffed with old maintenance papers, a pair of worn leather gloves, a flashlight, and a set of el-wrenches. She decided to stash the crystal in the back of the drawer where she could get at it easily.

Before she did though, she wanted to look at it one more time. Keeping a wary eye on Stephen she took it out of the paper bag and slipped it from its leather pouch.

At first glance it looked like any ordinary clear crystal other than its human heart shape which in itself wasn't all that unusual. She remembered the first time Deluca had placed it in her hand. Her first instinct had been to wrap her fingers around its smooth oval surface and squeeze. It somehow seemed the natural thing to do in spite of the warning she'd gotten from Bama. It fit so perfectly in her palm just as it did now.

Without thinking her fingers tightened on it. It flickered twice then turned blood red before she could open her hand and release it. Stifling a breathy hiss she flung it on the floor... too late to keep her right hand from being seared. She cursed her stupidity, remembering Deluca's roar of laughter. That time she'd been taken by surprise and hadn't released it as quickly. But still, her hand that had nearly healed was once again enflamed.

She glared at the innocent looking crystal lying by her feet and quickly picked it up by her fingertips and shoved it in its bag, intending to stick it in the drawer just as Stephen popped his head in the door.

"Could you hand me that pair of gloves from the drawer under your butt. And check the flashlight. You can leave it there if it's working."

Well shit, great hiding place. He could probably name every item in that stupid drawer, blindfolded.

Bending forward, she reached beneath her, pulled out the gloves and tossed them back to him. When he disappeared back under the cowl again, she checked the flashlight, found it working fine and tucked it back in the drawer with the crystal behind it. As a precaution, she put the el-wrenches in front of the flashlight for easy finding. And to safeguard it, she was going to sit right there in case he needed anything else.

Stephen came to the door again. "Why don't you slip over in the other seat by the controls?" He handed her a key. "Put this in the ignition next to that red lever and give me just a minute I'll tell you when to turn it."

"What does it do?" she asked.

He grinned up at her. "If we're lucky it'll start the engine."

Her heart did an odd little dance. "Just how long has it been since this thing was running?"

"I'm not sure. Look in the logbook under the seat. That should tell you."

With an exasperated sigh she leaned over and pulled out the logbook and paged to the last entry. The date was two months previous and signed by David Farmer. At least it wasn't fourteen months ago as she'd feared.

She called out the information to Stephen who had his head under the cowl.

"That's Brad's father," he said. "He takes it up for periodic test runs. Okay, turn the key."

She did as instructed and breathed a sigh of relief when the engine puttered to life. Stephen closed the cowl and climbed up motioning her to slide back to the other seat. He flipped some levers and the propeller began to turn. For a second she hung on thinking they were going take off.

Instead he turned everything off and smiled at her. "All systems go."

She took a deep breath and blew out a huff of air that raised the hair on her forehead.

He took off his gloves, put a hand on the back of her neck and pulled her forward. Before she could react he planted a quick kiss on her lips.

"Thanks for your help," he said, then reached down between her legs, rubbing against her thigh and opened the drawer. Her heart about leaped out of her chest as he shoved his gloves inside and snapped the drawer shut again.

"Okay we're done here. Let's go up to the lodge and see if there's any food. Maybe we can order a pizza or something. I can't believe it's only four o'clock in the afternoon and I'm famished."

This was not a good time to make an issue of an impulsive, meaningless kiss. Maybe later when she wasn't sitting on top of a damned crystal that was going to be the death of her if she didn't get rid of it soon. Thinking about Stephen's reaction when he found out she'd duped him was a sobering thought as she climbed down out of the plane and got in the car.

"I hope you're up for a walk in the morning," Stephen said, interrupting her thoughts. It's about a half mile from the lodge to here. I'd like to leave the car in the garage."

"Sounds like a good idea to me. I can walk. I can even run if I have to."

Stephen chuckled. "Oh, yes, I've seen you do that. Let's hope it won't be necessary. Take a look at our baby monitor and see if there's any sign of the goons."

Dani pulled the device from the floor behind her seat and held it steady to check the dial. "Nope. Nothing, but we should take it inside with us just for the heck of it. There's still something fishy about Mays showing up at that last motel. If he was following Deluca, why was he two blocks away? Or does he somehow have his own tracking system?"

"Or did someone recognize us and call him."

Dani rubbed the back of her neck trying to ease the tension. "Who knows?" she said. "I just hope we're rid of the lot of them. Being roused out of a sound sleep every night…or day… is no fun."

"Neither is being shot at."

"I'll second that," Dani said with unenthusiastic

laughter.

Stephen took a left turn into the Loveland ski area. He drove past the main lodge and made a steep climb along the slopes. After a couple of sharp turns they came up to a row of six connected town homes built along the side of the hill. The log structures consisted of two stories with a tuck under garage. He backed the car up the drive stopping in front of the garage door.

"You can wait here or come along if you like. I have to go around back and get the key."

"I'll stay here and keep an eye on the road. In case somebody decides to follow us."

Dani looked back on the spectacular, lofty view. She pictured it bustling in the winter covered with snow and skiers coming down the hills. Skiing seemed like something she'd like to try some day. Sighing, she realized it was probably another fun thing she'd never do.

She was pulled from her thoughts by the sound of a barking dog. The only other home that seemed to be occupied was at the far end where a red firebird stood out front. No other vehicles, no people, meaning no Deluca and no Mays. Maybe they could get some uninterrupted sleep for a change.

The sound of the garage door opening drew her attention to Stephen. He got in the car backed it in and shut off the engine. "We're out of luck," he said. "The hot tub isn't filled."

"Like I'd have a swimming suit anyway." Dani ignored Stephens' leer, got out of the car, and reached in the backseat for her things. "You're sure they won't mind us staying here?"

Stephen tucked the atlas he'd purchased under his arm and searched through his Wal-Mart *suitcase*. "Don't worry about it...ah... here it is." He pulled a cord out of his bag.

"What's that?" she asked.

"The cord to plug in my phone."

"You had time to buy a phone cord at Wal-mart?"

"Obviously one of us had more on their mind than

chocolate."

Dani didn't bother reminding him who ate most of it. "I need to make a call by the way."

He pushed the button to close the garage door. "A private call?" he asked, leading the way into the lower level of the house.

"Yes and no," she said, paying no heed to his curious frown.

They entered a family room large enough to comfortably seat a dozen people, with one corner dominated by a mammoth stone fireplace Dani noted the plush leather furniture, big screen television, and well-stocked wet bar.

She couldn't stop looking around as she followed him up the carpeted stairs. "The guy who owns this place must have won the lottery. Who has their own private popcorn stand for goodness sake?"

Stephen chuckled. "The same guy who owns his own private plane."

"Crimony. You do know how to make the right friends."

"Did you notice anything suspicious outside?" Stephen asked. He set his stuff on the large kitchen table and plugged in his cellular phone.

Dani walked around the kitchen running a hand over the smooth granite countertop and admiring the dark hickory cabinetry.

"Just a red Firebird down in the last unit…nothing else unusual. Oh, and a barking dog."

"That's Gavin Mlynek's car. He owns a restaurant a couple of miles down the road…lives here year round. His dog, Hana, is a great watchdog. She rarely barks without a reason. Of course, to her a stray cat is a reason to bark."

Stephen opened the side-by-side freezer door and peered inside. "Okay…we have a frozen pizza, several porterhouse steaks, bacon, and a couple bags of vegetables. I'm for the steaks. How about you?"

Dani came up beside him. "Wow, that sounds good.

Are you sure they won't mind?"

"Yeah, I'm sure." He took two steaks out and put them in the microwave to defrost. "I'm going out to check if there's gas in the grill, go ahead and make your phone call if you like. I have to check the atlas before I'm ready for it anyway. If you need to use a bathroom or anything, use the one in the master bedroom over there." He pointed to a closed door across the room.

"It's not private, by the way. I'm going to call the LAPD and talk to the guy who was running the camera at that raid."

Stephen stopped at the door and turned to stare at her. "Is that wise? Can you trust him?"

"About as much as I trust anybody I guess. I'm not going to tell him where we are, if that's what you're worried about. I need to know if he has an uncut version of the tape they ran on the air. One that shows I didn't kill my partner. You did say they couldn't trace your phone, right?"

"No problem there. Go ahead."

Stephen disappeared through the back patio door and Dani dialed the number for the station. She was pretty sure she wouldn't find Mays there. He was probably still out looking for them. She glanced at the transceiver on the table. It was still immobile.

"LAPD Carla Mason speaking."

"Can I talk to Byron McDonald Please?"

"Sure, hold on. I think he's still here."

Dani heard a couple of clicks, a phone ringing and then Byron's voice.

"Hello, Byron speaking."

Dani took a deep breath. "Byron, it's Dani."

"Dani! Christ, where the hell are you?"

"I'm sorry I can't tell you that. I want you to know I didn't kill Roger."

"Jesus, Dani, I know that. I was behind the camera. Mays went crazy when you took off. What the hell do you have that he wants anyway? The man is possessed. He confiscated my video and cut it himself before he gave it to the media."

"Do you have a copy of the original?"

Byron chuckled. "Sure do, my camera has an internal recorder. Just don't tell Mays. He'd have my ass in a sling. I'll send a copy to your D. C. post office box address. Just in case something happens to me."

"What do you mean, *in case something happens to you?*" Dani watched Stephen as he came in and sat down at the table to study the atlas.

"I'm telling you Dani. I don't trust Mays. He went out to that raid without waiting for backup, him and Jamison. Like he had it all planned. The only reason I got there in time to video it is because I intercepted the call he made to the station. I was only a couple of blocks from there when it came in. He didn't know I was taping until it was all over, and man, was he livid. I'm telling you, I'm keeping a wary eye over my shoulder."

"Mays is up to no good, I can tell you that much. We both know he killed Roger. Maybe you should get out of there. Take a vacation or something. Where is Jamison?"

"I have no idea. But don't trust him either. Whatever Mays has planned I'm guessing Jamison is in on it. I think I'm safe as long as you're out there and he doesn't know I have a copy of the tape. If anything happens to you Dani, I'm dead meat."

Chapter Thirteen

After Dani related her conversation to Stephen, she left him to map his route and headed for the shower, hoping to scrub some of the green out of her hair.

As with the rest of the house, no expense was spared in decorating the master bedroom, from the imposing fireplace to the king sized log bed and exquisitely framed Degrazia prints on the wall.

Taking care not to disturb anything, she stripped off her clothes and stepped into the two headed granite shower stall. It was large enough to suds up four adults and two English sheepdogs all at the same time. She experienced an overwhelming sense of relief as she laughed at her own outlandish thoughts. Having Deluca and Mays off her back was almost too good to be true. But until they took off with the plane in the morning, they couldn't be sure, and it would be foolish to let down their guard.

At least that's what Stephen said when he recommended they sleep in the same room again. As he pointed out, the master bedroom had a deck, making it the only good escape route to the plane should one of their pursuers show up. After all, they still weren't entirely sure how Mays managed to get within blocks of their motel north of Las Vegas and yet not be at the motel.

At least Stephen had his own weapon now, or weapons, since he had both guns confiscated from Harry and Marty.

Dani stepped out of the shower and toweled off, then donned a clean t-shirt and underwear and put her jeans back on. She touched a comb to her hair, assessing its color, and decided it was now at least a duller shade of green.

The tantalizing smell of coffee beckoned her to the kitchen. She found Stephen still at the table studying the map. The pencil in his hand tapped a rapid dance on the white table in front of him.

"Anything wrong?" she asked as she found a mug on a rack and filled it.

He opened his mouth as though to say something, but stopped and stared at her instead. The tapping slowed and then stopped completely as his intense blue gaze followed her movements. When she sat down across from him he continued to stare at her going from her damp hair to the front of her shirt and back to lock in on her eyes.

"You look good," he said finally.

"Does that mean I passed that inspection?"

He gave her a sheepish grin. "Sorry. I didn't mean to be doing that. Well, maybe I did, but I needed to get my mind off of these figures for a moment."

She looked down at the tablet he'd been writing on. "Do we have a problem?"

"Possibly. We can only make five hundred miles with the Cessna on a tank of gas. And that's with a tail wind. It's close to full now, but we still have to stop twice to refuel."

"And...is that a problem?"

"At the price of fuel, it might be."

"Don't worry about spending your money," she said. "Reierson will reimburse you. I do have a generous expense account."

"My concern is having enough cash without using a credit card. I have a little over six hundred dollars left of the thousand Mays paid me. High-octane aviation gas is nearly a dollar a gallon more than what you'd pay for regular gas at the pumps. At sixty five gallons a pop, that's close to three hundred bucks to fill up."

Dani furrowed her brow in thought for a moment. Not coming up with a viable solution, she dug in her pocket for the money. "Let's check Roger's money. Maybe it's not all counterfeit." She spread eight one hundred dollar bills out on the table and held the first one up to the light. "This isn't even a good counterfeit. Why the hell would Roger accept this crap?"

Stephen picked up one of the hundreds, rattled it between his fingers and held it up to look at. "You're right. These are really bad. He must have been in a hurry when he took them."

They went through all of the bills and came up with nothing spendable. Dani swore. "Marty insisted Deluca wouldn't pass fakes. That leaves Mays. He must have paid Roger off."

"Maybe that explains why Mays wanted you out of the way." Stephen said.

Dani stared at him blinking, thinking. "Maybe it does. He planned to get rid of Roger all along, so he never expected any of the money to be spent. In fact, when they found it on him, they probably planned to use it against him."

Stephen agreed. "And Mays didn't want to have to explain killing a federal agent. That's why he wanted me to get you out of there. But you fouled everything up by grabbing the backpack with both the money and the crystal in it."

"Obviously Roger had the money before we got the crystal."

"How did you get it" Stephen asked.

At some point she'd anticipated that question would come up and yet it took her by surprise. If she told him everything, she'd also have to tell him about the Blood Crystal. If she stuck to the truth as much as possible, there'd be a lot less to explain later...

"Is there some reason you have to think about that so long?" Stephen said, interrupting her thoughts. He had leaned back in his chair, his arms folded over his chest, and his eyes peered at her through narrow slits.

"No. No," she said a little too quickly. "I was just wondering where to start."

"Try the beginning," Stephen snapped. "When you got involved."

She hesitated. "It goes back farther than my involvement. Roger had been working undercover as one of Deluca's grunts. Roger was a large man, broad shouldered, with the look of a professional wrestler. Anyway, Deluca had only dealt in diamonds, gems, even drugs at one time or another, but he knew nothing about crystals. Roger brought me in as his girlfriend. He told Deluca I had a wealth of underground connections dealing with valuable and rare crystals."

"You look too young for that to be believable."

Dani smiled. "That's exactly what Deluca said. I had to do a lot of talking to convince him I knew my business. Of course, Reierson had filled me in on all of Deluca's contacts, so I was armed with that information. Combined with my knowledge of crystals, I could spend several hours just telling you about the healing powers of crystals."

"They actually heal?"

"Supposedly. I haven't seen proof of it, but a lot of people swear by it. Maybe it's the kind of thing where you have to be a believer. I'm too much of a 'show me' person."

"You mean like when you asked me to stop the car today?"

Dani gave him a scathing look. "I'm going to pretend you didn't say that."

"So…you're also an 'ignore it and it might go away' kind of person?"

"Do you want to hear about how I got the crystal or lock lips?"

The look on his face was so comical she almost laughed. Instead of telling him she was kidding, she waited for him to squirm a little. That thought backfired when he gave her a wicked grin. For a fleeting moment, she wondered if he'd forget about the crystal if she went along with the lip thing.

He hesitated just long enough to act like it was a major decision. "The crystal," he said. "Lips later."

Dani rolled her eyes with a dramatic flair and got up to refill her coffee mug. "I don't suppose there's any cream here, but how about sugar?"

"In the cupboard above the microwave."

She searched out a couple lumps of sugar and a spoon, then went to sit down again. "I told Deluca I'd have to see the crystal in order to estimate a price. I already knew about the Smithsonian offer, so I had a pretty good idea what he could get for it on the illegal market."

She couldn't tell him that when Deluca had handed her the crystal she'd stared at it trying to understand its value. Except for its unique shape and smoothness, it looked like any ordinary quartz crystal. He must have seen her confusion because he'd asked her to wrap her fingers around it and squeeze. She did as he asked only to have it turn into a molten rock, scorching her palm. When she'd dropped it on the floor, Deluca's obnoxious laughter filled the room. Roger, ever a Doubting Thomas, wasted no time picking it up and squeezing it himself. Four heartbeats later it landed back on the floor. Nothing Reierson told her had prepared her for what she just witnessed. Surely he knew what it could do and yet he'd kept her in the dark.

Dani took a deep breath. Up to this point she told the truth, but the moment of deceit was at hand. "When Deluca showed me the skull, I was in awe. They're so rare I'd never actually seen one. I told him I knew at least two buyers who'd be interested. Then I told him I'd expect a cut of the profits. He hesitated only a moment before he agreed to eight percent, if I could get the price he wanted. He expected three million. I told him I wanted ten percent and I could get four million, but I had to have it in hand to show."

"Holy shit. Did you really think you could get that much?"

Dani shrugged. "It didn't matter. I had no intention of selling it. I figured by bargaining with him I'd get his attention. It worked."

He turned the crystal over to you just like that?"

"Not exactly. He wanted to know who my buyers were. I told him point blank I wasn't going to expose my contacts before the sale. In the end, he agreed to let me take it as long as Roger and those two other bozos, Harry and Marty, went along.

"I told him that was fine as long as *only* Roger came along in with me when I presented it to my buyer. I gave Harry the address to an old warehouse I'd scoped out earlier. Roger and I went inside while the other two waited in the car. The second we were out of sight, Roger called Mays to tell him we had the crystal and to meet us in the prearranged location then we high-tailed it out the back door. We ran the three blocks to where Mays would pick us up."

"I'd guess the back of that warehouse was where I was supposed to get you in my car."

"More likely just up the street from where we were meeting Mays because Roger stopped there and looked around like he was waiting for something. We wasted a good fifteen minutes there. When I questioned him, Roger said it was to give Mays time to get to the meeting place, but now I suspect Roger was looking for you and was supposed to make sure that I got in your car. To get me out of harm's way he'd have said.

"Now that I think of it, he made a stop in the restroom before we left. He probably called Mays from there."

"That makes sense," Stephen said, "I was almost a half hour late because I couldn't find the address." He chuckled. "I'd make a bet between the two of us Roger and I wouldn't have been able to separate you from that crystal."

"I didn't have it, Roger did. In his backpack. Deluca insisted Roger maintain control of it at all times. I guess he didn't fully trust me, but Roger had been working with him undercover for at least six months. Even longer than Harry."

"Goes to show how elusive that element of trust is."

Dani wasn't too interested in pursuing that subject. "How long until we can eat? I'm really getting hungry."

"I'm with you there. I thawed the steaks in the microwave. I'll go light the grill. See if you can find some canned vegetable or something to go with them.

While Stephen was outside, she searched the cupboards and came up with a can of corn and a box of Bisquick. Even encumbered by her inflamed hand, by the time he came in for the steaks, she had the corn on the stove and was mixing biscuits to put in the oven.

"Looks good," he said. "I love a domestic woman."

"I'm just resourceful."

"I never questioned that. How do you like your steak?"

"Rare."

"Ah, we have something else in common."

Before she could ask him what he meant, he disappeared out the patio door. His comment about domestic women made her smile. No way would she tell him she loved to cook.

After setting the table, she started to walk outside to join him when she heard voices. He wasn't alone. A man and a large golden retriever she assumed was Gavin with Hana had joined him. Probably best, she decided, if she stayed out of sight.

A short while later, the man left and Stephen came in with the steaks. "I'm glad you stayed inside," he said. "The less Gavin knows the better, just in case somebody comes snooping around asking questions."

"That's what I thought."

"Smart lady you are. Domestic and smart. I'm in heaven."

"Schmoozing me won't get you anything. Let's eat."

* * * *

As they finished their meal, Dani noticed Stephen's

drooping eyes. A minute earlier he'd dropped his fork. They were both tired, but she'd gotten a couple of hours of sleep in the car while he drove.

She took pity on him. "Why don't you go take a shower and get some rest while I clean up here."

"Is it that obvious?"

She laughed. "I've been expecting your face to fall in your plate at any minute."

He gave her a smirking grin. "That could really put a damper on my tough-guy image."

"It's wasted on me anyway. Go."

"I'll check the doors first." He got up and locked the patio door then headed down to the lower level. When he came back up he checked the front door and walked toward the bedroom, talking as he went. "Everything's locked up, but I still suggest we stay in the same room tonight. We still don't know how Mays is tracking us."

She'd started to clear the dishes. "No problem. We're both too tired to mess around anyway."

He gave her a look that suggested she was wrong, but even with his brows raised, his eyes hung at half-mass. "You have a lot to learn about men," he mumbled, disappearing into the bedroom.

She shook her head laughing. Give him ten minutes after the shower stopped and he'd be out like a baby.

To be on the safe side she gave him twenty minutes. When she switched the kitchen light off, she thought she heard Hana bark. Pressing her ear against the patio door, she held her breath, listening, but everything was quiet. She shrugged and headed for the bedroom, yawning.

A nightlight in the bathroom illuminated the bedroom. Just as she thought, Stephen was all but passed out, his face buried in the pillow, hair still damp from his shower. Her side of the bed was neatly turned down, but he was spread out on top of the covers clad only in red, white, and blue boxer shorts.

She took a moment to admire his muscular physic. He really was a fine specimen of a man. The only mar in his body was a five inch indent with a knobby scar on the side of his right thigh. It appeared to be healed but was still red, and she suspected it pained him at times because of the limp.

Dani had a peculiar urge to rub her own aching hand over the wound. Moving slowly, so as not to startle him as she had before, she sat down on the bed and cautiously laid her hand on the wound. He made a small moaning sound but didn't stir.

Stroking her hand up and down the reddened area, she was surprised at not only how cool it felt, but how soothing it was to her own scorched hand. She was also surprised at how arousing it was to be touching his skin even though sex was the last thing on her mind. That wasn't her intention when she started rubbing the wound. She just wanted to stroke the place that gave him pain. A smile played on her lips as she imagined what his reaction would be to those words.

Finally she sighed, got up, and went in the bathroom to take her clothes off and wash her face. She left on her underwear and t-shirt, thankful it was long enough to cover her. Then taking care not to disturb him, she slipped into bed beside him.

His hand moved toward her, touching her at the waist. His fingers didn't move, so she suspected it was an automatic reflex. She gently pushed it away from her, but she'd no sooner settled down when the hand returned. Sighing wearily, she left it there, turned over on her stomach and went to sleep.

Chapter Fourteen

"Stephen, will you get down here and take that dog out!"

"Petey died Mom, and call me Randall. You know I'm using my middle name now."

"Fine, *Randall*, but it's not Petey barking, it's Hana."

Hana!

Stephen sat up straight in bed. He looked around, trying to orientate himself. He wasn't at home in the upstairs bedroom he shared with his cousin Quint. And he definitely wasn't a carefree kid anymore.

The bed beside him was empty, but the pillow was rumpled, so she'd been there. It was six a.m. Where was she? He dashed out of bed and checked the bathroom, then slipped his jeans on, grabbed his pistol, and headed for the great room.

The first thing he noticed was the curtains on the patio door waving in the breeze the first hint of dawn filtering through. His heart began a rapid dance. Dani wouldn't have been foolish enough to go out there to investigate a barking dog on her own. He released the safety on the gun and took measured steps toward the open door.

A crash that sounded like a deck chair overturning stopped him. He pressed against the wall next to the door.

"Dani, are you out there?"

Another crash.

"Drop the gun, Douglas, or she's dead."

His stomach lurched when he recognized Mays voice.

"Where is she?" Stephen asked.

"Right here with me. Come on out and join us, without your gun, of course."

"I want to hear her voice first."

"Don't do it, Stephen!" Dani screamed then her voice was muffled.

Stephen glanced behind him and saw a small metal vase on an end table near him. He stuck his gun in his jeans behind him and threw the vase out on the deck, aiming under the table where it landed out of sight.

"Alright, I'm coming out." He put his hands in the air and stepping out onto the deck. Mays was back in a corner with Dani's head pressed to his chest by a hand over her mouth, the end of a Glock revolver pressed against her temple. Her hands appeared to be bound behind her back.

"Okay, good," Mays said. "You know what I'm after, so go get it and nobody gets hurt."

Dani was shaking her head, making frantic sounds behind Mays hand. She kicked her foot against the overturned chair.

"It's not worth your life, Dani," Stephen said.

She made muffled screaming sounds behind Mays' hand.

Mays turned the gun on Stephen. "Settle down, Lovato. He's expendable. I don't need him to get the crystal."

Her eyes grew wide and she stopped fighting.

"Trot in and get the crystal, Douglas, and we'll wait right here."

Stephen experienced a helpless sensation he'd never quite known before. He had to give Mays the skull.

"Alright," he said. "But you hurt her and you're a dead man."

Mays chuckled. "Whatever. Get the crystal. I have no reason to kill either one of you as long as I get what I want. I'll just let the authorities hunt you down. She's wanted for murder and you're an accomplice. You can screw each other until the cows come home for all I care. Now get the crystal before I change my mind and put a little hurt on one of you."

Stephen's hands worked into fists. He wished he had them squeezed around Mays' throat. All in good time, he thought.

"I'll get it." When he turned to leave, he heard Dani's muffled protests and another flying chair.

He found the backpack and dug out the skull. Pulling it out of its velvet bag, he turned it over in his hand and considered replacing it with another object, but was pretty sure Mays wouldn't be fooled by that. One thing Stephen knew for sure, Dani's life was worth a hundred crystals, although she might not agree with him at the moment. He didn't see any other options though. Maybe they could get it back.

He carried it back out to the deck and stood by the patio door probably twelve feet from where Mays was holding Dani. They hadn't moved, but the approaching daylight showed a murderous glare in Dani's eyes. And it was directed at Stephen. Well, hell, what did she expect him to do?

Stephen held it out. "Here it is. Let her go and you can have it."

"Take it out of the bag."

Stephen had expected that. He undid the tie, slipped the skull out of the bag and held it up for him to see.

"Alright, good. Now set it on that table over there and back off."

"Release Dani first. You have me and you have the crystal. Let her go back in the house."

Mays laughed. "Not on your life, buster." He pressed the gun into her temple. "Set it down and be gentle about it."

Stephen's mind wrapped around an idea he hoped he wouldn't live to regret. Gripping the crystal in his hand, he lofted it in the air toward Mays, where it would miss him by at least two feet. As Stephen hoped, Mays swore, shoved Dani aside and leapt to catch the skull. To do so he had to also drop his gun. He made the catch and charged to retrieve his weapon, but Stephen was on top of him with the speed of a flying cat. In another two seconds, he put a sleeper hold on the older man, who collapsed to the deck like a limp dishrag. The crystal skull dropped out of his hand, rolled to the edge of the deck, and disappeared over the edge. He knew it was at least an eight foot drop to the grassy slope.

Stephen turned to look at Dani who had struggled to her knees. She was breathing hard as she stood up and came toward him.

"Turn around," he said. "I'll untie you."

While he did so, she mumbled, "I can't believe you gave him that crystal."

"What did you expect me to do, let him kill you?"

"He wouldn't have killed me. At least not until he had his hands on the skull."

"Yeah, and then?" He turned her around to untie her hands and discovered handcuffs. "Where's the key?" he asked.

"Try the chain around his neck."

Stephen yanked the chain free, undid the handcuff, and in turn snapped them on Mays' wrists. "Let's get him inside. Bring his gun."

"We can't shoot him. He's a cop. Even if he is a rotten one."

"I wasn't planning to shoot him," Stephen retorted, dragging Mays heavy body into the lodge. She picked up Mays' gun and followed Stephen inside. He gave her an incredulous look. "Aren't you even curious to see if your crystal smashed to smithereens out there?"

Her hand flew to her mouth, eyes wide. "Oh my gosh. How could I forget?" She raced outside and returned a moment later with the skull cradled in her fingers and the bag to put it in.

"It seems to be okay," she said, turning it over in her

hands. "By the way, that was a pretty stupid thing to do to a four million dollar crystal, throwing it in the air like that. What if he hadn't caught it?"

"Then he wouldn't have had any reason at all to kill us." When she snorted, he added, "Besides he's gone to some pretty extreme measures to get his hands on that thing. You really think there was a chance he wouldn't let go of you to save it?"

"I guess," Dani muttered.

"I hadn't even bargained on him dropping his gun. That just shows you how desperate he is."

Dani gave the subject of their conversation a scathing look. "How long will he be out?"

Stephen was already searching the drawers in the kitchen for a roll of duck tape. "Not long. Ah, here it is." He came back from the kitchen with the tape and proceeded to wrap it around Mays' feet.

She slipped the crystal in its nesting bag. "I'm going to put this back in the knapsack and get some clothes on."

"Good idea," Stephen said. "What were you doing walking around half naked anyway. And why were you out on the deck?"

"I'll fill you in on that later."

"Okay, I'm going to check his pockets."

Two minutes later she came out with her jeans on. "What did you find?"

"Not much. Wallet, car keys, and his badge."

"Any money in the wallet?"

"Three hundred-dollar bills, a couple of twenties, and a few small bills." Stephen gave her a mock frown. "Are you suggesting we steal it?"

Dani stared at him with wide eyes. 'I'm a federal officer, Stephen. I couldn't do that—but we could exchange those three big ones with some other bills we have."

Stephen jumped to his feet, laughing. He grabbed her face and planted a kiss on her lips. "That's why I love you, honey. You're so damn clever."

When she winched he noticed the bruise his left hand

covered. He turned her face to the side to examine it closely. It was dark red and already starting to swell. Hot rage surged through him. "What the hell did he do to you? We have to get some ice on that or you won't be able to see out of your eye in a couple of hours."

Stephen sat her in a chair, grabbed a towel and pulled a tray of ice out of the freezer. He dumped the ice in the towel, wadded it up and pressed it to her face. He pulled her hand up to keep it in place then headed for Mays.

"What are you going to do?" she asked.

"Kill him."

"Stephen!"

Ignoring Dani's protests, Stephen grabbed Mays by the arms and hoisted him up into a recliner. He walked back to the kitchen poured water in a large glass and started back toward Mays. "I need to get some information out of this bastard—no offense to his unfortunate mother—and I hope he doesn't come easy with it because I'm going to enjoy this."

He splashed the water in Mays' face. Mays shook his head struggled with his binding, swearing. "You better untie me, Douglas; you're in enough trouble already. Assaulting an officer of the law will put you behind bars for a long time."

"Is that so? Well it seems to me that you are the one in trouble here. You entered my home uninvited, and from what I know of the law, you have no authority whatsoever in Colorado while Dani as a federal officer, whom you assaulted, has the power to arrest you anywhere in the states. Feel free to correct me if I'm off base."

"Oh, you're off base all right, asshole. She's wanted for murder and you are guilty by association."

"Are you forgetting that *you* hired me to pick her up and protect her?"

"Try proving that, buster."

Stephen chuckled. "You might have a little trouble explaining why I'm out of jail driving a car rented in your name."

"There's no record of you ever being in jail," Mays sneered.

"Huh, I guess you did something right then."

"And I reported the car stolen," Mays added.

"Enough chit-chat," Stephen said. "I want to know how you found us here."

"Screw-off, Douglas. I don't have to tell you anything."

Stephen wasn't aware that Dani had walked up behind him until she spoke.

"I think you do have to answer him if you want to leave here intact."

That's when Stephen realized she was holding a large butcher knife. He decided to keep silent, trusting she knew what she was doing. Her face had an ominous look as she pressed the knife between Mays' legs against his crotch.

Mays tried to press back against the chair. "What the hell are you doing, Lovato? Have you lost your mind?"

"More or less," she said, giving the eight inch blade a twist.

Mays made a frantic sound, swearing profusely.

Stephen grimaced. "I think she means business. Maybe you shouldn't have hit her. You better start talking."

"Crazy bitch! A dimwit could have known you were coming here."

"That explains why *you* found us." Dani said. "But I still want to know how."

Mays laughed. "It wasn't too hard to find out he owned a plane here."

"He doesn't," Dani said, "his friend owns it."

Mays scoffed "Like hell. It's registered in his name."

Chapter Fifteen

Dani turned to look at Stephen, waiting for him to deny it.

He didn't.

She yanked the blade from Mays' crotch with a white knuckle grip on the handle.

Stephen held up his hands, retreating a step. "Take it easy, Dani. I can explain, but I'd rather do it when we're alone."

"What else have you been lying about?" she asked.

Before Stephen could answer, Mays let loose with a roar of laughter. "He's a worthless bum, Dani. Forget about him—he's a loser. Tie in with me. There's enough money in that crystal for both of us. I'll split fifty-fifty with you."

Dani whirled back to face Mays. "You mean like Roger? Is that the deal you gave him? Or were you just promising him fake hundred dollar bills. Of course, he didn't even have to know they were no good since you killed him."

"I didn't kill Roger."

"Are you forgetting I was there?" She threw the knife on the floor dangerously close to Stephen's feet and stormed into the bedroom.

She started gathering her things together.

Stephen followed at her heels. "What are you doing, Dani?"

"Getting ready to go. Wasn't that the plan?"

"Yes, but—

"Just tell me one thing. Did you know about the crystal before you picked me up in LA?"

Stephen stared at her as though she'd lost her mind. "Of course not."

"Why did you lie about owning the plane?"

"Because I wanted the truth from you first. I have family. Coming here was getting too close to involving them."

Dani stared at him breathing hard. Stephen throwing that skull had renewed her suspicious that he knew it wasn't the real crystal. Finding out he lied to her didn't help matters any.

She was angry, but she also knew she needed him and *his* plane. "Let's get out of here," she said. "If Mays found us, so could Deluca."

"I'm with you on that." Stephen said. He wasted no time throwing on a shirt and stuffing his own things in a duffle bag he'd pulled out of the closet. Grabbing his shoes he said, "I better run down and start up the Cessna to make sure he hasn't sabotaged it. Can you handle Mays until I get back?

"No problem. I'll take care of the money exchange in the meantime."

"Good." At the door he stopped and turned back to her. "Sorry, for lying to you," he said, then he was gone, taking his duffle bag with him."

For some reason, his apology didn't sit well with her. It reminded her too much about her own secret, but—she reminded herself—that was business, not personal.

Dani suddenly had the sinking sensation that he could just take off and leave her, but she shrugged it off and went out to check on Mays.

Mays had struggled himself onto the floor, but that's as far as he got. She noticed that Stephen had picked up the knife she'd used and placed it on the counter.

Making sure Mayas didn't see what she was doing;

she picked up his wallet from a side table and walked back in the bedroom with it.

She exchanged his hundreds with three of them from the backpack, yanked out the four credit cards he had along with his California driver's license and stuffed them in her hip pocket.

When she came back out, Mays, from his prone position, tried once more to reason with her, offering her even more than he had before if she threw in with him.

She ignored him and searched the pantry for food they could take with them. She found an unopened box of crackers, a bag of marshmallows, a couple of cans of sardines and even a can of spam. She stared at the spam in surprise. It was something she'd never purchased in her life and wasn't even sure what it tasted like. Shrugging, she put everything in a sturdy cloth environmental bag she discovered on a hook and added some bottled water and sodas she found in the refrigerator. As an afterthought, she took a twenty out of Mays wallet and left it on the counter.

Stephen still hadn't returned so she started tidying up, trying to ignore Mays constant badgering as she walked around him on the floor.

"He's a worthless bum, Dani. The only thing he has to his name is that ten-year-old Cessna. He hasn't held a full time job since he graduated from college."

She finally went into the bedroom and had just finished making the bed when she heard Stephen call from the other room.

"Dani? You here?"

She hurried out to meet him.

"Plane fired right up," he said. "All we have to do is get rid of him." He nodded toward Mays.

"He hasn't shut up since you left," she said.

"I figured as much. I don't want to leave him here so let's put him in his car and handcuff him to the steering wheel."

"Do you know where his car is?" she asked.

"No, but he's going to tell us because if he doesn't,

and I have to find it, I'm going to lock him in the trunk. Either way works for me. So...where's the car?" he asked Mays.

Mays snarled like an angry dog. "I want my keys and my badge and wallet back."

"All in good time," Stephen said. "Where's the car?"

"Down at the end of the road that turns up here. It's not too late," he turned to Dani speaking rapidly, "you can still ditch this jerk and come with me..."

He was still trying to convince her when she tore off a five inch strip of duct tape and slapped it over his mouth. She stuck his wallet in his back pocket. He mumbled something that sounded like *what about my keys and my badge*.

"I'll mail them to you," Dani said.

Stephen undid the tape on Mays' ankles and shoved him out on the deck. Dani followed carrying her backpack and the food bag. Stephen glanced in the bag, gave her a crooked grin, and locked the door behind them. "You can leave your stuff here," he said. "We'll pick it up on the way back."

They found Mays's Audi right where he'd said it would be. Stephen cuffed him to the steering wheel, then opened the hood and yanked out a few wires. Before he'd even finished, Mays had his gag off and was swearing copiously.

Stephen and Dani hurried back to the lodge. She grabbed her bags and they continued past the lodge toward the plane. When she stumbled going up the hill, he gave her a hand up and reached for the backpack.

"Let me carry some of this."

"I can do it. You have a bad leg."

"I'm not exactly a cripple. Or don't you trust me to carry your precious crystal?"

She handed over the backpack with a small laugh. "I shouldn't after you threw it across the deck."

"Pretty clever, I thought." He hoisted the pack over one burly shoulder and started climbing again. "For some reason, my leg feels really good today. It must have been the dream I had last night."

"What dream?" she asked.

"I dreamt you were rubbing it with some magic balm—my leg. I mean."

They had reached the summit and she stopped to catch her breath. "Do you just make this stuff up as you go along?"

"Nope, God's truth. Of course, I also dreamt my mother was hollering at me to get out of bed and walk the dog." He stopped alongside her. "Beautiful sunrise, isn't it? Should be a good day for flying."

Something Dani was not looking forward to. She could see the plane below, glanced at the brilliant sky line and remembered words her father often quoted, *red sun in the morning, sailor take warning*. She hoped it wasn't true.

As they descended the hill in silence, Dani switched her food bag to her right hand. When she did she realized it wasn't hurting any more. She put the bag back in her left hand and opened the palm of the right to examine it. Strange, the redness as well as the pain had disappeared.

CHAPTER SIXTEEN

"You do realize that knob you're gripping is the skydiving eject handle?"

Dani released the knob with a frantic shriek. "Why are you laughing?"

"I was kidding. Just trying to make you relax."

"By telling me I'm trying to launch my non-flying body into space?"

"Why don't you grab that wheel over there and I'll let you fly. Maybe that will boost your confidence."

Dani gave him her best *are you crazy* glare. "Is there an eject button for your side?"

Stephen threw his head back and laughed. "Have you even looked out the window? It's beautiful up here. When all this mess is over with, I'll take you up skydiving so you can experience the thrill of flying like a bird."

"Do you have any barf bags?

"Just relax and enjoy the ride."

"What's that smoke smell?"

"Just a little oil spill on the engine. Nothing to worry about."

"Nothing to worry about! We're flying over mountains for Pete's sake."

Stephen snickered. "For your information, Ms Lovato, I can land this rig just about anywhere, anytime—with or without power." When she gave him a skeptical glare, he added, "By the way, my motto is, *Trust Me*."

Dani gave an indelicate snort. "Mine is, *never trust a man who says trust me*."

"Well, I think that statement is half right anyway. And you can relax, we're just about past the mountains."

"That's a relief, I think."

"Maybe we should get your mind off of flying."

"I'll second that. Did you get a look at Mays' car when we took off?"

"Yup. I couldn't see any sign that he'd gotten out. Gavin should be driving by there pretty soon to go down to his restaurant. It'll be interesting to hear what kind of an explanation Mays gives for his predicament."

Dani chuckled. "I'm betting he won't mention us."

Stephen reached over and touched her swollen cheek. "What did he hit you with anyway?"

"I'm not sure, I think it was his fist, but it knocked me out cold. I woke up about thirty seconds before you appeared."

"How did you end up out on the deck with him?"

"I heard Hana barking, so I got up to check it out."

"For god's sake, why didn't you wake me up?"

Dani shrugged. "You needed your sleep, besides I certainly didn't expect to find Mays there."

"Was he inside or out?"

"I'm pretty sure he was inside. I walked up to the patio door and listened for the barking, but it had stopped. I hadn't switched any lights on, but there was enough morning light to tell the patio door was unlocked. I didn't even have time to think about it because that's when my head exploded from whatever hit me. The next thing I knew, I was outside and my wrists were cuffed. He was shaking me, asking about the crystal. I'm thinking he dragged me outside so he wouldn't wake you up. What woke you up anyway?"

"I must have heard Hana barking the same time you did, but I was in the middle of a dream and in such a deep sleep I didn't wake up right away."

"The same dream as the other one?"

"You mean when you were rubbing me? No, that was much earlier, seemed like when I first fell asleep."

Okay, Dani thought, *on to a new subject.* She chanced a curious peek out the window. "You're right the mountains are gone. Where are we?"

"Northeast of Denver. I avoid the big cities—too much commercial air traffic."

"How fast can this thing fly?"

"About 160 miles an hour." He reached forward and snapped his finger on a little round gage.

"What are you doing?"

"Gas gage seems to be stuck. What did you bring for breakfast, I'm getting hungry?"

She reached behind her seat and pulled out the green food bag. Searching through it, she said, "You have a choice of Crackers with sardines or cracker and Spam."

"I love spam. I can make a great Egg McMuffin if you have biscuits, eggs, and cheese in there."

"Along with a stove?" She quipped pulling the strip top off the spam.

"Oh yeah, that too."

She glanced at him. "Can you eat while you're flying?"

Stephen let loose with a belly laugh. "You're making jokes. That's good. It means you're relaxing." He tapped the gas gage again."

"If you don't quit doing that, I'm going to stop relaxing," Dani said, staring at the contents of the Spam stuck in its container. "Huh. I guess I should have brought a knife or a fork."

Stephen bent sideways, pulled a jackknife out of his pocket and handed it to her.

Dani shook her head. "You're such a—*man*."

"That didn't sound like a compliment? Is it just me or do you have a beef against all men?"

"Pretty much all of them," she said matter-of-factly, trying to clean the knife blade on her t-shirt.

"Gee, that makes me feel a whole lot better."

Dani slathered a chunk of spam on a wheat cracker and handed it to him. He popped the whole thing in his mouth, cheeks puffing as he chewed around it. She did the same, then took out a bottle of water and a can of diet Coke. She held both up for him to choose. He pointed to the Coke. She handed it to him then opened the water for herself. He settled the Coke in a holder between them. Seconds later, he turned to her frowning, staring at her hand.

"What?" she asked.

He reached over wrapped his fingers around her left wrist and pulled it toward him. "Open your hand," he demanded.

She complied, confused.

He looked up at her face. "Yesterday your hand was red and sore."

It was her turn to frown. "It wasn't *that* sore."

"Hell it wasn't. I saw you grimacing last night in the kitchen whenever you used it."

She hadn't realized he'd noticed. "So?"

"So, why isn't it sore today?"

"I-I don't know," she said honestly.

"Okay, what made it hurt to begin with?"

That took her off guard. She opened her mouth but didn't speak. His gaze was fixed on her face, waiting.

The Cessna chose that moment to make a sudden burping sound and then it was quiet. Too quiet.

"Holy crap," Stephen yelled. "We're out of gas!" He was working some buttons and levers as the plane slowly descended.

Dani couldn't breathe. And then she could breathe, but too much. Little daggers of panic squeezed her brain making her head swim. She was hyperventilating.

Stephen glanced over at her, reached out to touch her. "It's okay," he said. "We're fine. Trust me."

His touch had calmed her, but his words made her breathing race. He searched behind his seat and brought out a little white paper bag. He blew into it to puff it up all the while they were getting closer to the ground. "Here, breathe into this."

She took the bag and pointed toward the ground. He grinned. If that was supposed to reassure her, it didn't work. She'd have slapped him if she were able.

He went back to the controls.

The plane tilted. She squealed, gripping the lever at her side. Then remembering his joke about it being an eject handle, she ripped her hand away from it and grabbed the edge of her seat. They were still descending straight toward a grove of trees.

She heard the wheels clip the tops of the trees then they dropped lower over a hay field full of large round bales.

Dani closed her eyes, breathed into her barf bag and prayed. When they touched down in the field, the wheels bumped and bounced like wayward rubber balls, catching the ruts and jerking the plane first this way, then that way. Each hit brought another round of shrieks from her. She opened her eyes in time to see them joggling straight at a stack of bales that was nearly as high as the plane.

About ten feet from the stack, everything went silent.

Stephen looked over at her. He wasn't sure if she was going to kiss him or slug him. "You okay?" he asked.

She nodded slowly, dropped her breathing bag, laid her head back against the seat, and closed her eyes. He squeezed her knee with no response.

"You handled that well," he said. Her eyes popped open and stared at him. "I'm going to see if I can figure out what happened."

Stephen opened the cowl and boosted himself up to inspect the fuel line. It looked fine, but he could smell gas. He followed the line back to where it connected to chassis of the plane; everything seemed intact. From there, he heaved himself down and crawled underneath. There he found a snip in the hose. It was a clean cut just deep enough to allow the gas to seep out slowly.

No doubt in his mind. Mays.

One of two things must have been his intention. Either he'd hoped the plane would drain out of gas and wouldn't start, or he expected it to run out in the air and they'd crash land. Stephen was guessing on the first option because he'd have known the crystal would be on board. If the later were true, he might have planted a honing device to find the downed craft.

Stephen was royally pissed at the man. This plane was his baby. Right now he wished he had done Mays some bodily harm, like maybe a broken leg. He was, however, even more teed off at himself for ignoring the gas dial. Problem was it had malfunctioned before. He usually judged his gas by the number of miles he flew.

"What are you looking for?"

Stephen jumped when she spoke. He hadn't even heard her alit. He explained what he'd found and that he was looking for a possible transmitter. "They can be really small, like finding a needle in a haystack, if you'll excuse the pun."

Dani looked around at the field surrounded by trees. "Do you have any idea where we are?" she asked.

"Somewhere in Western Nebraska, I think."

"This looks like the middle of nowhere. I can even smell the fresh air. There must be a farm around here. I think I saw some cows before we hit those trees"

"We didn't hit them. We skimmed them. I had to get low enough to land so I wouldn't hit the bale stack."

"You really scared the crap out of me," she said. "But I have to admit you did a good job landing."

Stephen stopped what he was doing and looked at her. "Did I actually hear you say that?"

"Oops. What I meant to say is, couldn't you have found a better spot. This was kind of bumpy. And how the heck are you going to take off. There can't possibly be enough room here to launch an airplane."

Stephen had gone back to inspecting the crevices and

underbelly, seeking out any place large enough to plant a transmitter. "We'll figure it out. The first thing we have to do is fix the gas line and then get gas, or we won't be going anywhere. And if Mays planted a bug on us, we have to do it before he gets here."

"Oh my gosh. I hadn't thought of that. I guess it's possible though."

Stephen grunted as he opened yet another hatch. "Sure is. What are the chances he had a spare car key and an extra key for the handcuffs?"

Dani moaned. "Most likely he had both. Maybe we should start walking?" Dani murmured not very enthusiastically.

"First I'm going to fix the gas line. Would you be a sweetie and get my jackknife?"

"Well, as long as you put it that way." She climbed into the cabin calling to him. "Do you want anymore crackers and spam while I'm in here?"

"Yeah, great. I'm still hungry. And bring that roll of black tape under your seat. I might not have enough hose to cut and mend this thing."

She climbed back down, cut the rest of the meat and handed him his knife.

While he worked, she stuck his food in his mouth and in her own alternatively.

"Have you ever been stranded like this before?" she asked.

"Lots of times. When I learned to fly, my instructor actually shut off the engine and made me practice finding a landing spot. Same thing with skydiving. That's why you carry a reserve chute."

"I can't believe I work with undercover gun-toting thugs and you live a more dangerous life than I do."

Stephen laughed. "My oldest brother, Virg, says I have a guardian angel watching over me. Having two brothers and a live-in cousin all older than me has set me up for a lot of ribbing."

"Sounds like you give as good as you take."

"I do, but there's three of them."

"Do guardian angels ride painted ponies?" she asked suddenly.

Stephen looked up. He heard the approaching horse before he actually saw it. A small black and white Shetland pony with an equally small bareback rider coming at a full gallop. The kid, appearing to be about twelve, reined his spirited pony up beside them. The animal did a sidestepping dance with wild eyes trained on the airplane.

"Wow," the kid said, sticking to the prancing horse like he was glued on, "that's the coolest thing I ever saw, landing an airplane in the middle of a field. Grandpa told me to wait for him because he said you'd probably all be dead."

"Your grandpa's coming then?" Dani asked. "With a car or a pickup?"

"Yup, he's right behind me. He's too slow, though. You know how old people are. And I haven't never seen no dead bodies."

Stephen snickered. "Sorry to disappoint you son, but you won't find any here."

"Well shucks! I guess that's okay, though. You must be a really good pilot, huh?"

"Must be," Stephen said, giving Dani a puffed up peacock look.

"Is that how you hurt your eye?" he asked looking at Dani.

She fingered the bruise on the side of her face. "I guess. What's your name?" she asked the inquisitive kid.

He leaped from his pony, dropping the reins. "Gary, and my horse is Lucky. Can I see inside?"

Stephen shook his head grinning. "Sure, why not." To Dani he whispered, "You could learn something about enthusiasm from Gary."

Dani rolled her eyes. "Keep it up. He might get to see a dead body after all. Or I could just tell him you gave me this black eye. Is it turning black?"

He stepped toward her and turned her face this way

and that to examine the bruised cheek. It had a bluish purple hue not really close enough to the eye to give her a shiner. "Could be. Maybe I'll have to kiss it and make it all better." He glanced to see Gary sitting in the pilot's seat. "Don't push any buttons or monkey with any levers in there," Stephen called out to him. "How far is the nearest airport where we can get gas?"

Gary stuck his head out. "Ogallala isn't very far. But grandpa has lotsa gas on the farm. Man, are these parachutes? Can I try one on?"

"No. You have to be eighteen."

"Here comes Grandpa," Dani said, staring across the field where an obnoxiously loud John Deere tractor was puttering in their direction.

"We're Mark and Robin Martin," Stephen whispered.

"And we just got married in Las Vegas and we're going to see my daddy—"

"Don't start," Stephen warned. "And let me do the talking."

"Okay, Marko, I'll follow your lead."

The tractor stopped near the rear of the Cessna. A man wearing striped bib overalls and a scruffy grey beard that made his age indefinable stepped down.

"Howdy folks. I see you got a little dilemma there. Gary, what the heck you doing up there? Git yerself down here." He extended his hand. "Name's Harold Flinn."

Stephen shook the proffered hand. "I'm Mark Martin, this is my wife Robin. You're right we have a problem. Apparently the fuel gage isn't working and I think we ran out. We need to get to an airport where we can get aviation fuel. You know where the nearest place is?"

"Probably Ogallala. It's about twenty-five miles to the north."

"Nothing closer?" Dani asked.

"Don't think so, ma'am. There's some landing strips, but they aren't manned and I doubt you'd find the kind of gas you need."

"Any chance you can take us there? Stephen asked.

"We'll be more than glad to pay you."

"I would, but my wife is sick. I can't leave her. But I have an old pickup you can use."

Stephen smiled. "We'd be much obliged, Mr. Flinn."

Flinn looked around the field scratching his beard. "How you gonna take off here anyway. I can't even figure out how you got landed."

"He's a good flyer," Gary supplied. "I saw him land." He made an elaborate swooping motion with his hand. "Except the lady bumped her eye."

"I can't take off," Stephen said." Not enough space, and even if there was, it's too bumpy and rutted to get any speed. I need at least five hundred yards or more. Any chance you can tow me to a road?"

"Sure, you can use my driveway. It's not far. I always carry a chain on the tractor so I'll back up to the front and you show me where we can hook 'er up."

* * * *

It took half an hour of bouncing over bumpy fields until they were at the farmyard facing a little over a quarter mile of gravel road. It looked short to Dani, but Stephen announced it sufficient. She discretely tucked the Blood Crystal in a zippered pocket of her backpack and carried it from the plane.

A few minutes later, they were on the way to Ogallala in a 1975 F-150 Ford pickup.

"Man, this thing is a classic," Stephen told Dani. "I love these old trucks."

"You probably love baby ducks and warm wooly mittens too."

Stephen gave her a lopsided grin. "It might surprise you to know I love adventures like this. I mean not the part about being chased by bad cops and gun wielding thugs, but getting in and out of predicaments is my specialty and has a satisfying value of its own."

Dani gave a deep sigh. "I guess it was kind of fun meeting that old farmer and his grandson. They were so nice. And him giving us his pickup...you just don't see that kind of thing very often in big cities."

"Sure you do. You just have to be desperate enough to find it."

"I take it you've had some adventures in your life."

Stephen laughed. "I spent a month bumming my way through Europe on a very tight budget."

"Interesting," Dani said. "That's what Mays called you—a bum."

"At one point in my life that wouldn't have been far off. I used to be a pretty carefree happy-go-lucky spirit. Afghanistan changed all that, and a bad marriage didn't help. I don't think I'll ever be the same again. I guess that's why I'm actually enjoying this venture. It reminds me of my younger days. We just have to stay in one piece until we get that crystal home to its owner."

"Right on," Dani agreed, patting her backpack.

"Once we get back in the air we'll be set as Jell-O. With the extra three hundred from Mays, we might just have enough for gas money unless Flinn charges us an arm and a leg for the truck and towing. The only way they can catch us after that is with a faster airplane"

"Oh crap."

CHAPTER SEVENTEEN

"What?" Stephen looked over at her waiting for her to go on.

She didn't.

Stephen gritted his teeth. "Don't tell me Deluca has his own plane!"

"Okay, I won't."

"Shit. Well, that puts a new wrinkle in our smooth-assed plan. How big is it? How fast can it fly?"

"I haven't a clue. I only know about it because Roger told me he had a ride in it."

Stephen breathed deeply, willing himself to remain calm. What did it matter if Deluca had a plane? Even—given all his wealth—if it was bigger and faster.

"We still have the edge," he said. "He might know we're going by air and he likely knows our eventual destination, but it's a big sky. This delay might turn out to be in our favor. He'd never expect us to make a stop so soon after taking off."

"I guess it's to our advantage to get back as quickly as we can and get in the air."

"That's my girl. I'll make a pilot out of you yet."

* * * *

Dani experienced yet another bout of fear when they took off on the rutted gravel road. She glanced at Stephen a bit, reassured by his nonchalant attitude, as he fiddled with the dials and buttons on the panel in front of him paying little attention to the road. His face had a look of utter bliss. The man loved to fly. She waved out the window to Gary racing beside them on Lucky trying to keep up.

The Cessna lifted off just before the end of the road and they were once again airborne. Stephen turned and buzzed over the farm, dipping the wings from side to side in what he said was a goodbye. Even the ailing grandmother had come out to see them off.

"I can't believe he didn't charge us anything, even for the use of his truck."

Stephen nodded. "Like the man said, he gets a good feeling by helping people and that feeling wasn't for sale. I'll have to remember that line. I like it."

"I'm glad we at least filled the pickup with gas when we stopped at the grocery store."

"Me too, and, speaking of gas. Twenty gallons isn't going to keep us running very long. I'm going right back to Ogallala to fill up. It's a few miles out of our way, but they didn't seem to recognize us, so we shouldn't have any hassles."

* * * *

"It looks like rain up ahead. Is that going to be a problem?" Dani asked staring out at the dark sky. She was just getting used to the idea that flying with Stephen was safe.

Stephen shrugged. "Not unless it gets real heavy and windy. Problem is, by the time it's too bad, it's hard to find a place to land. With this headwind we're pushing, we'll be ready for fuel again in half an hour, so it might be a good idea to land somewhere for the night. Take off again first thing in the morning."

"I'll second that plan. Maybe we can actually get a full night's sleep."

The look he gave her suggested something on his mind other than sleep. He had the sexiest grey eyes she'd ever seen. No man had ever made her melt inside with just a look. She tore her gaze away from him and watched the approaching storm. They appeared to be heading straight into it and it was coming on fast.

His soft chuckle had her wondering if he'd read her mind. "I could use some more of that magic balm you used on my leg last night too," he said.

Dani gave an unladylike snort. "I didn't rub you with magic balm."

"What did you use?"

"Nothing. You said yourself it was a dream."

"Are you saying you didn't rub my leg last night?"

"What I'm saying is that storm is coming up mighty fast. Shouldn't we be looking for a place to land?"

"That storm is still seventy miles or more away."

"But we're going toward it at a hundred and sixty miles an hour."

He glanced at the sky and sighed. "Get the atlas from my bag in the back and see if you can find a town in eastern Iowa that's not too big but large enough to have an airport—at least ten thousand people."

Dani turned in her seat and reached for his bag. In doing so she noticed her backpack. The crystal was still in it since she didn't have an opportunity to put it back in the drawer under her seat. She wished she could slip it in the pocket of her jeans but it wasn't safe since she didn't know what made it get hot other than squeezing it. A sudden shocking thought struck her. Magic balm!

She opened the atlas forcing her mind from magic balm. "How far into Iowa are we?"

"Maybe thirty miles. We crossed I-29 about twenty minutes ago."

She spent a few minutes studying the map and town sizes. "Can you find Storm Lake, that shouldn't be very far?"

"That's an actual town?"

"Uh-huh. Right here." She held her finger on the spot.

"Hand me the map. I need a couple of reference points." A minute later he turned the map back to Dani. "Okay, hang on; we're going to turn toward the southeast.

When the plane dipped its right wing, Dani did hang on, literally, but she was proud of herself for not making any panicky sounds. Looking out the window on her side made the ground easy to view. She saw a small river following a highway and a town.

"That's Orange City," he told her.

She found it on the map. "Yes, I looked at that one. It was too small and so is Cherokee."

The plane leveled off again and Stephen looked at her smiling. "You're a good navigator...and you didn't even pull the eject handle."

"Can you actually skydive out of this plane?"

"You bet. Not while I'm piloting, of course."

The black cloud was now approaching them from the left side and was too close for Dani's level of comfort.

"Are we going to make it?"

Stephen waggled his eyebrows at her. "Trust me."

She gritted her teeth.

"Why don't you follow along on the map?" he said. "That'll give you something constructive to do."

She glanced down at the map, put her finger on Orange City, the last check point, and traced it in a straight toward Storm Lake. At Cherokee she saw a river. Looking ahead she spied the narrow winding steam. "That must be the Little Sioux River. When we cross that we're half way there." She quickly calculated the distance remaining. "Only thirty more miles," she said, grinning.

Stephen burst out laughing. "Pretty soon you'll be ready to take the controls."

She went back to studying the map, mumbling under her breath. "I may not fully trust you, but I definitely trust you being over there more than I would me."

Laying her head back on the seat, she closed her eyes and willed her body and mind to unwind. The hum of the engine had become a familiar and welcome sound. Being in the company of Stephen Douglas gave her a likewise feeling. She really had no reason not to trust him. He didn't have to be here risking his life to help her do her job. From the time he'd picked her up outside that warehouse he'd done nothing but try to protect her. He'd been willing to face Deluca alone while she escaped. Add to the mix that he was the most upbeat person she'd ever known. Did that come from being raised in a large loving family?

When the crystal was back in Bama Kendu's hands and their mission was over, would he disappear back to his family? That thought left her with an empty ache in her chest.

When she heard the first splatters on the windshield, she looked up, frowning. Then she looked down to see if they'd crossed the river. They had. She saw a small town below them but it was too small to be Storm Lake. Alta, she hoped. That would make it only five more miles. It was only five-thirty, but the sky was getting ominously darker by the minute and the rain, though still light, was coming down with drops the size of saucers.

A gust of wind griped the plane and it blew sideways. Stifling panic, her gaze flew to Stephen's face looking for any sign of alarm. He brought the plane back under control with amazing ease without batting an eye and appeared as calm and confident as Gary riding Lucky at full gallop across a rutted field.

Seconds later, the engine gave a mighty roar and banked into a sharp right hand turn, circled to the left and started dropping altitude. Before she could figure out what he was doing, she felt the bounce of solid earth beneath them. She swallowed the lump in her throat and gulped in a monstrous breath of air.

Stephen wasted no time taxiing to the fuel pumps. "Might as well take care of business," he said. Leaning over, he pulled her forward by the back of the neck and pressed a firm, moist kiss on her lips. "Thanks for being a trooper. You can wait here I'll get us fueled up, tied down, and see if we can find a ride into town." He grabbed a rain slicker from the back and then hopped out into the rain.

* * * *

The Drop Inn motel, less than a mile from the airport,

was clean, quiet, and more than adequate. A plus was the attached restaurant that advertised food from Grandma's Kitchen.

Stephen came out of the bathroom, drying his hair with a towel. Dani stood by the window, staring out at the rain. Something was bothering her. And he was pretty sure it wasn't the king sized bed he'd requested because she'd barely spoken three words since they'd landed. He pulled his damp t-shirt off, threw it on a chair along with the towel and walked up to stand beside her.

"Man," he said, "it's really pouring buckets out there."

A flash of lightening streaked across the sky followed closely by room-shaking thunder.

She turned to give him an accusing stare. "You can't fly in this weather, can you?"

"Hell no. If you do it once, it's unlikely you'll live to do it a second time."

"That's what I thought. So, I'm wondering why you didn't suggest stopping until I pointed out the darkening sky. You were flying straight toward it like you were totally oblivious to it. Why didn't we stop sooner?"

"That's what has your tail in a twist?"

"If you must put it that way, yes." He reached up and pushed the hair from her bruised cheek. He half expected her to back away from him but she stood her ground. "You believe that, after all we've been through, I'd deliberately do something to endanger your life?"

"I don't know. You're, by your own admission, a daredevil. Just set my mind at ease and explain why you were flying into that storm with no inclination that you were going to stop."

"Actually, that's an excellent question. But let me explain something else first. It's true I was a daredevil. I took a lot of chances, but that was all before Afghanistan. I was a twenty-eight year-old kid when I went over there. But there's something about watching your friends get maimed and killed that makes you grow up. I gained an appreciation for life. I still took chances, but they weren't daredevil stunts, they were survival tactics."

He saw her gaze flick to his wounded leg and then back to his face. "I can sympathize with that, but it doesn't explain you flying into that storm."

"I wanted to get as close to the weather as possible."

Her eyes widened. "For God's sake, why?"

"If Deluca is behind us with a faster plane, I don't want him to catch us. I guess you might as well know that when you fill fuel they write down the numbers on your plane, so if he had enough connections, he could possibly follow us. It's still a big country, but with the storm coming, he would have stopped long before we did."

"So…you weren't just taking a foolish chance?"

Stephen smiled. "With your crystal on board…never."

She gave him a playful swat on the bare chest. "You're such a brat. Why didn't you tell me?"

"At first I thought you were sleeping, but rest assured, when I'm flying, I'm always aware of the lay of the land ahead of me. My mind flicks from one potential landing spot to next without even thinking about it."

"What about in the mountains?"

"Especially there. Plus, I've flown that particular route many times, so I know the terrain. Of course, in an emergency I can always skydive to safety."

"Oh, that must be a wonderful comfort to your passengers."

He gave a deep throated chuckle. "Not to worry, my sweet. My chute is equipped with a piggy back attachment."

"I don't even want to know what that is."

He grinned and pulled her into his arms, relieved that she didn't resist. When her arms came around his waist, he buried his faced into the softness of her hair. She had the scent of woman with a hint of lavender.

"Dani, Dani, Dani. I've been living under a heavy cloud for over a year. You may not realize it, but you brought the sunshine back in my life."

"There's a drenching rainstorm over our head," she

whispered, her breath tickling the hair on his chest.

"Ah, but the sun is shining in here."

They stood like that quietly for a moment, their arms wrapped around each other. "I'm really hungry," he said finally. "Would you like to go eat or do you have something else in mind?"

"Eat," she said, pulling away from him with a husky laugh. "We better go eat before I have to put my sunglasses on."

The restaurant seated about thirty people, but the only other customers were a couple with two toddlers and three farmers having coffee.

After placing their order, Stephen pulled out his cell phone. "My brother Hunter has a lot of resources. I'm going call and see if he can find out what kind of plane Deluca has. What's his first name?"

"Ambrose."

"Huh. That's a new one," Stephen said, pushing speed dial. Three rings and Hunter's wife, Nicole, answered.

"Hi, Nicole, it's Stephen"

"Stephen. We've been worried about you. How are you?"

"I'm fine. How's the baby?"

"Little Kevin is doing great, but he's hardly a baby. He's going to be a year old next week."

"I bet Shanna and Kyle are enjoying that little tyke. How're they doing?"

"Kyle started first grade this year. He talks non-stop about his uncle Rando, the war hero. You really should have stopped in here before you left for California. Your family misses you."

"I'll be home soon, I promise. I do need to talk to Hunter. Is he handy?"

"Yeah, I'll go rescue him. He's trying to change Kevy's diaper."

While he waited for Nicole to get Hunter, Stephen reached across the booth and played with Dani's fingers resting on the table top. He got the feeling that she enjoyed listening to him talk to his family. Obviously something she lacked in her life.

Hunter's voice came booming over the phone. "Yeah, Rando, I'm glad you called. What's going on? How's the leg?"

"Almost good as new. I know somebody with a magic balm."

"I hope you're taking care of yourself."

"Don't worry, big bro, I'm over the wench. My life's back on track. I need some information and I was hoping you could help."

"Does it have anything to do with your new girlfriend? Ava was it?"

"Really, Hunter, you and Virgil are worse than a couple of gossiping old ladies."

Hunter chuckled. "Yeah, how does it feel to be on the receiving end for a change?"

"Wonderful. Just wonderful. Don't get mushy on me, but it's great to be back in God's country."

"I'll bet. What do you need?"

"A man by the name of Ambrose Deluca owns a small plane. I want to know what kind it is."

"That shouldn't be too hard. Where does he live?"

The jovial waitress who looked old enough to be somebody's grandmother set a hamburger with fries in front of him and chicken fried steak in front of Dani.

He picked up a fry and stuffed it in his mouth. "Los Angeles?"

"Are you still out there?"

"Nope. I gave up that scene along with the lovely, big-breasted Nadine."

Dani, chewing around a bite of chicken, rolled her eyes at him.

"I'm glad," Hunter said. "You finally realized that was the only thing she had going for herself. What's the new woman's bra size?"

"She's right here. You want to ask her?"

"No!"

Dani looked up at Stephen expectantly. "What does he want to ask me?"

"He's concerned about your bra size."

Dani stared at him with her mouth hanging open. Then she laughed. "You men are so superficial. Tell him to think fried eggs."

Stephen winked at her then talked back in the phone. "I hope you heard that, brother dear."

Hunter was laughing. "What I'm hearing is that you're back to normal. If she's responsible for that, she's okay in my book. I'll call you when I have some info for you."

Stephen closed his phone and dug into his food.

"What did he say?" Dani asked.

"He said you're okay in his book."

"Because of my bra size?"

"Nope, because you helped me get my life back."

"How many kids do they have?"

"Three. Shanna and Kyle were Nicole's sister's kids. Kyle is in first grade so Shanna must be in third. Kevin is a year old. I've never seen him"

Dani's brow furrowed. "That's so sad. You've missed a lot being gone so long, haven't you?"

He shrugged. "Some."

"Do you have any other nieces and nephews?"

"My younger sister Corinne and her husband Billy have a two year old. And my cousin, Quint, who's like a brother to me, is married to Jamie LeCorre, the NASCAR driver."

"Oh my gosh. You have a celebrity in your family."

"She quit driving when she got pregnant, which was almost immediately after they got married. I think she's due in another month."

"Have you seen any of them since you got back?"

"Just my parents and Virgil, the brother you talked to on the phone. They are the only ones still living in New York."

"How many kids does Virgil have?"

Stephen laughed. "None that I know of. He's the

oldest and the only one who's never been married."

"It must be so great to have a large loving family."

Stephen devoured his last French fry. "Most of the time it is. I suppose being an only child, that's something you would have liked to have."

Dani nodded. "Most of the time," she said, smiling.

Somehow her smile didn't reach her eyes.

Mrs. Jovial brought their check to the table, set it in front of Stephen, then made a point of glancing from Dani's bruised eye to frowning at Stephen.

"I swear, I didn't do it," Stephen said, trying to stifle a grin.

Dani slipped out of the bench seat shaking, her head. "You are one unusual man, Rando. Most men would get upset about an accusation like that."

"So would I if I was guilty."

Chapter Eighteen

They walked back to the room under the protection of the five-foot overhang that connected the row of rooms. It was still raining though it had settled into a slow, steady drizzle.

"As long as this weather keeps up we can sleep in peace tonight." Stephen said, slipping an arm around Dani's shoulders.

She in turn wrapped her arm around his back. "I sure hope you're right."

When they reached the room, he glanced around, saw nothing unusual, and opened the door. Nothing out of place inside either.

It seemed so natural that she turned toward him the moment the door closed behind them. He took her in his arms and their mouths met with a searing, hungry kiss. Stephen pushed her up against the door and aligned his hard frame with her soft, yielding one. She complied by stretching her arms around his neck and giving as good as she got. He throbbed for her in a way he'd never before experienced.

When they finally separated enough for him to put his hands on the sides of her face, he looked down at her in all seriousness. "Honey, do you want this as bad as I do, or am I coercing you into something you aren't ready for."

Dani looked up at him, pressing her lower body toward his rigid manhood.

"I want you, Stephen Rando Douglas" she said her breath coming in short gasps. "I'll never be more ready, trust me."

His body shook with laughter even while he reclaimed her mouth. "That's my line," he murmured.

He reached down to her waist and pulled her t-shirt up over her head and she did the same to him. The rest of their clothes followed in a flurry and the next minute they were sprawled crosswise on the king-sized bed.

He moaned softly and deeply as he slipped an arm under her neck and a leg over her lower body, cradling her against him. "Sweetheart, you feel so good."

Dani ran the palm of her hand over his muscular shoulders, trailing her fingers along his equally solid upper arms, enjoying the texture of his skin and the taut muscles that covered his body. His hand roamed her curves as well. From her breast to a rounded hip. He broke the kiss and moved his mouth to her nipple.

She gasped, gripping him by the hair, moaning as he suckled on her. He moved over her, taking her with him until she was on her back. His talented mouth moved to her other breast all the while his hand manipulated her most erogenous places. Swimming in a sea of pleasure, she cried out and pushed her body up to meet his probing fingers as they stroked and caressed.

For a moment he separated himself from her and reached for his jeans. She had the sinking feeling he was going to stop. Then she realized he was putting a condom on. "Sorry," he said. "I had to take care of business."

He opened her legs and moved between them. "Are you ready for me, sweetheart?" His husky words were barely above a whisper.

"Yes, yes, please," she pleaded.

Dani wasn't a virgin, but the sensations she felt when he entered her it were like nothing she'd ever experienced or imagined. He didn't thrust into her, he moved slow and easy. And even after he'd entered her, he didn't draw out and slam into her. He just stayed there, pressing deeper and moving slowly against her, bringing her to a climax so violent that her brain cells launched into space like tiny skyrockets and she felt herself losing consciousness. Her heart hammered and her breath came in loud rasping gasps as she fought to regain her lost air.

He stopped moving and rose to his elbow, his face buried in her hair. "Dani? Honey? Are you okay?" he asked, his voice coming in a breathless but concerned whisper.

She nodded weakly, unable to speak.

He rolled to his side, bringing her with him so as not to lose their connection.

When she opened her eyes, she saw him watching her. She'd been so wound up in her own release she realized she didn't even know if he'd had his. As though he knew what she was thinking, he took her hand and placed it over his heart. It had a resounding beat that matched her own.

She reached up and pushed the hair back from his forehead. Though he'd seemed to barely exert himself, he'd broken out into a sweat.

He gave a soft chuckle. "I don't know what just happened here, but I'm amazed I survived it."

"I don't know either, but I feel like I just took a *beam me up Scottie* trip to outer space and back."

Stephen gave her a squeeze and a smile. "Me too." He nuzzled her hair and placed a kiss on her ear. "I just have one question?"

"Lucky you. I have a million questions. What's yours?"

He pushed his groin against her. "Do you exercise those muscles in there? You had me in a vice so tight I was afraid I'd never get out. On second thought, maybe I was afraid I would."

Somewhere she found the energy to laugh. "You are one crazy nut."

He laughed with her. "If I have to do that again, I'm

going to need some of your magic balm."

They laid together in comfortable silence for a time, but Dani's mind was anything but resting. Was it possible there was a connection between her hand healing and his leg feeling better? She already knew what she wanted to do. The idea had been festering in her head like a fast growing germ.

What if it was true? What if the crystal really had healing powers? It would be priceless. There was only one way to find out.

"Speaking of magic balm," she said. "How is your leg feeling?"

His hand tightened where it lay on her waist as though he'd fallen asleep. "Mmmm. Much better. Did you notice I barely limped today?"

Yes, she had noticed.

She waited until his breathing evened out and she knew he slept. Quietly, she slipped out from under his embrace, picked up her backpack, and headed for the bathroom. Once inside, she closed and locked the door and switched on the light. It would be easier to explain the locked door than what she was about to do.

Zipping open the pocket that encased the Blood Crystal, she carefully lifted it out using her fingertip and set it on a towel. From there she shook it out of the paper bag then undid the leather tie holding it in its velvet bag. Her heart pounded as she upended the bag and let it slip to the towel. It was the first time she'd actually had a chance to examine it without interruption. It looked so ordinary, so innocent.

She wasn't looking forward to scorching her hand again, but it was the only way to find out. Sitting on the toilet seat with the towel in her lap, she cautiously pressed her index finger against it. Nothing happened. Then she squeezed it between her index finger and her thumb. Still nothing.

Thinking maybe it had lost its ability to get hot, she picked it up and wrapped her fingers around it prepared to release it quickly if it heated up.

It turned to molten fire almost instantly.

Stifling a screech, she dropped it back in the towel but not before it had done its number on her hand. Her palm was bright red and burned like the fires of hell. Worse than she remembered it before. She ran cold water in the sink and held her hand under it. As she did she stared in mixed wonder at the translucent pale crystal nesting so innocuously in the towel on her lap.

She gritted her teeth against the pain in her hand and wondered how she was going to explain it to Stephen if the magic balm trick didn't work. Using the fingertips on her good hand, she quickly slipped the crystal back into its bag, put that back in the paper bag and returned it to the zippered pouch, all the while groaning that the whole thing had been a stupid fantasy idea. This was the twenty-first century after all, and she was a grown woman with an adult brain. None of that, however, explained the crystal getting hot in the first place though. Well, there was only one way to find out.

She stood up, glancing in the mirror as she unlocked the door. The bruise on her cheek had darkened and was still sore when she touched it. She stared at her image for a moment then reached up and pressed her enflamed palm against the bruise.

She held it there for a good minute, rubbing it as she had with Stephen's leg. She could feel the heat from her hand, but the palm continued to burn, her face was still bruised with no change whatsoever. There was only one thing left to try.

Knowing she had to do it while he slept, she walked quietly to the bed carrying her backpack. She left the backpack on the floor and crawled into bed beside Stephen. He was on his side facing away from her and still naked with his injured leg exposed. She took a moment to admire his beautiful muscular body. If she hadn't *handled* the crystal she could have lain down against him and gone to sleep, but sleeping was out of the question the way her hand throbbed.

Remembering that first night when she'd wakened him and he all but attacked her, she was amazed at how relaxed he'd become.

Moving slowly, she placed her hand on his thigh holding her breath when he moaned and shifted his weight a couple of inches. She remained still for a moment, letting her hand rest on him. His skin felt cool to her hot touch as it had the first time she'd ministered to his leg. Slowly she started rubbing. Her hand felt better, but she attributed that to the coolness of his leg. His breathing suddenly increased and his fist on the pillow clenched and unclenched several times. Finally he sighed, mumbled something in his sleep, then laid still while she rubbed her *magic balm* over the rough surface of his wounded thigh.

Her last thought before she fell asleep was maybe she could tell him she scalded her hand in the shower when the water got too hot.

CHAPTER NINETEEN

"Wake up, sugarplum. Our baby-faced driver will be here in twenty minutes. If his daddy lets him use the car, that is."

Dani stretched, giving him a sleepy laugh. "He wasn't that young."

"It seems like the older I get, the younger these kids look. I'll use the bathroom first. Won't take me but a few minutes." He first walked to the window and peeked out, presenting her with his totally bare backside, then went into the bathroom.

Dani swung her legs over the side of the bed then realized she was naked too. She glanced at the bathroom door feeling a bit odd. Waking up nude with a man beside her was a first, but then, so was having the kind of experience she'd had with Stephen. A warm flush flooded her face and she smiled at the memories.

She heard the toilet flush and knew she better get clothes on quick. This was not the time to think about what their night of terrific sex meant in the long run. He was fresh out of a bad marriage and she certainly had no thoughts of going in that direction.

Slipping her t-shirt on, she wished she had something else to wear. Who was she kidding though, until this was over and that blasted crystal was back in the right hands, she was cursed with it and all the problems it brought.

Her hand!

She opened her hand looking for the telltale redness. Nothing. A surge of adrenaline raced to her heart. Her gaze tore to the bathroom door. Had he been limping? She couldn't even ask without bringing suspicious questions about magic balm.

Stephen came out of the bathroom dressed in jeans. His feet and upper body were bare. Dani grabbed up her backpack and headed through the door.

"You have ten minutes," he called after her. "I'm going to run over to the restaurant and see if they have some muffins or something to eat we can take with us."

She answered, "Okay," from behind the closed door. Once again with more light, she examined her hand thinking there had to be a logical explanation. There was no time to come up with one now. Hopping into the shower, she spent five minutes there then got out, dried off, put her t-shirt and jeans on, brushed her teeth, and ran a comb through her wet hair.

Seconds later, she heard Stephen come back in the room saying it was time to go, their ride was waiting. It was barely daybreak, but he didn't need to remind her of the urgency. She couldn't imagine how Deluca, or Mays for that matter, could continue to find them, but they had before so…

* * * *

From inside the cockpit, Dani watched Stephen walk around the plane readying it for take-off. He worked quickly with the confidence of having done the same job a million times. It was impossible to tell if he limped.

Within minutes, he jumped in beside her and had the engine running. That's when she realized she wasn't afraid. Maybe she was starting to trust him. He must have read her mind because he looked over at her and grinned.

"Looks like you're ready," he said. Then before he buckled in, he leaned over and gave her a long unhurried kiss. He said in a low husky voice, "Did I mention that you were terrific last night?"

She felt her face grow warm even as a knowing smile spread over her lips that now tingled from his touch. "No, I don't believe you did. I guess, Rando, that means it was as good for you as it was for me."

"Uh-huh. That nickname sounds a lot better coming from your lovely lips than from my brothers." He gave her a wink that jump-started her pulse then put the Cessna into motion, giving her a further adrenaline rush.

The skies were clear and blue as they headed into the sunrise. Dani reached for the paper bag he brought from Grandma's Cafe. "What kind of muffins did you get?"

Poppy seed and Bran. You take your pick, I like them both." When she handed him the bran muffin, she noticed him watching what seemed to be the tail end of the plane. "Is something wrong?" she asked.

"Not yet," he murmured, taking a bite of his muffin.

She frowned at him. "What exactly does *not yet* mean?"

"Hunter called while I was up at the café. He found out Deluca owns a helicopter which we don't have to worry about, but he also has a Cessna 210. It's a six passenger and can run 220 miles per hour."

"Lordy. You said we can only go a hundred and sixty."

Stephen grinned. "But he has to find us first. I just want to keep an eye to the rear so he doesn't sneak up and surprise us."

"Do you have a plan for what we can do if he does catch us?"

"Well, we have the crystal so he can't exactly shoot us down."

Dani stared at him, her brain going at the speed of light. Stephen cut into her thoughts before she could speak.

"You know Deluca better than I do. What do you think he'll do to get his hands on a four million dollar crystal that you stole from him?"

Dani drew in a breath of air. Then another. "He'll go to any lengths to recover it. And by now, he's provoked

enough he'd shoot us down and give up the crystal before
he'd let us get away with it."

"My thoughts exactly. Keeping that in mind, we can
rest assured he knows exactly what kind of aircraft we have
and he's barreling down our ass at full throttle. I hate to be
a spreader of doom, but you may as well know he can fly
5000 feet higher with his Cessna. With the sky as clear as it
is, he can cover a lot of territory looking down from that
height?"

Dani looked out the window realizing she could easily
see another plane a long way off, and if he was a lot higher,
he could see for miles and miles. "I guess it would be better
if we had some clouds," she muttered.

"Yeah. I'd say you're right, and on the other hand,
there's always the chance he doesn't know about my
plane."

Dani made a rude sound. "The odds on that are slim to
none. He has enough contacts to know everything you've
owned since birth."

"Wonderful!"

Dani rubbed a weary hand over her eyes. "And I don't
believe for one minute Mays has given up either. One way
or another, he'll show up again."

"Who do you know in this whole mess you can trust
anyway?"

"My superior, Bob Reierson."

"When's the last time you spoke to him?"

"When I left D.C. two weeks ago."

Stephen took another bite of muffin, thinking.
"So…why didn't you call him right away when you got the
crystal?"

Dani hissed out a huff of air. "I didn't have control of
it until five minutes before I jumped in your car. I was
going to call him when Roger and I ran out the back of that
office building, but Roger had the cell phone. Deluca took
mine away because he said I don't need one since Roger
had his. Roger didn't want to waste time calling Reierson,
said he'd call Mays to pick us up and we could call

Reierson then. Well, you know how that turned out."

"That was three days ago. I'm just really curious. You could have used my phone. We've been on the run for three days and you never tried to call him to help you out."

Dani nibbled on her muffin. "I don't want to turn the crystal over to him. It belongs to Kendu."

She could hear Stephen grinding his teeth. "I guess what you're saying is you don't fully trust Reierson either."

She shrugged. "I'm not sure. He's the one who sent me to Mays."

Stephen ran a hand through his unruly coffee-brown hair, his lips moving in what she knew was a volley of silent curses.

He was silent for some time. She knew by now where the speedometer was and could tell they were going at full throttle.

"Take hold of that wheel in front of you," he commanded, startling her.

She stared at him as though he'd asked her to pick up a snake. "Why?" she asked suspiciously.

"You're going to learn how to fly this plane."

"Why?" she repeated.

"So you have at least a clue if something happens to me."

"What's going to—"

"Just do it, Dani."

He seemed pretty determined, so she put both hands on the wheel. When he let go on his side, she swallowed the bile racing to her throat.

He gave her a confident smile. "Don't worry. Nothing's going to happen I don't want to happen. Just get the feel of it. Turn a little."

She did and the plane listed to the left. She turned the other way and it listed to the right. Nothing surprising. When she righted the wheel the plane leveled out. He started pointing out the gages and dials on the dash between them, explaining what they were for. When she asked questions, he explained further.

Her stomach started to settle until she asked, "What about landing?" He gave her a look that that told her she wasn't ready for that. Still, he explained as well as he could.

"When we do the next fuel stop, I'll give you a briefing so you can at least follow along and get the idea."

She expected him to retake the controls when he seemed to have explained everything, but he didn't. Instead he sat back and watched her. Then he pulled out the map and started studying it.

Dani's hands froze on the wheel. Every once in a while he looked up then went back to the map. She thought about relaxing but was afraid she'd go into a nose dive or something worse, though she couldn't imagine anything worse. She did notice he glanced toward the rear every few minutes.

"Relax," he said. "This thing pretty much flies itself."

She wiggled her fingers, willing them to ease up on their grip and shifted around in her seat to get comfortable. His chuckles put her at ease more than anything, until he pointed to the altimeter and said, "Pull back a little; we're getting too low. Bring it up to 5500 feet. East bound traffic flies at odd numbers and westbound at even numbers—so you don't collide."

"Lovely thought," she grumbled, following his instructions while watching the gage, then leveled off again.

"Good girl," he said. "Now just keep it around that altitude. I forgot to mention that you should be watching for other small planes—it's mostly see-and-avoid on these small rigs. How's our fuel doing?"

She sent a frown in his direction then glanced at the gage. "A little under half," she said.

He went back to the map. "I think we'll stop at Kokomo, Indiana for fuel."

Dani surprised herself. She was starting to enjoy the feel of being in control of an airplane. It wasn't a lot unlike driving a car, and in some ways, a lot easier. You didn't have to keep your eyes on the road every second and there were no ditches. Of course, she was only playing at it since she knew Stephen, even though he acted nonchalant, was watching every move she made. She actually did spot another plane coming toward them at a much lower altitude. Once again she was both amazed and disturbed at how far away she could see it.

Stephen suddenly threw the map in the back and took the wheel. "Don't look now, but we have company."

Chapter Twenty

Dani whipped her head around to look but saw nothing but empty sky. Before she could comprehend what was happening, a shadow fell across their plane. She looked up and saw the wide intimidating wingspan overhead.

Her heart pounded in her chest, threatening to break free. "Oh my god," she said. "It's huge."

It's not that much bigger than this plane."

He'd barely gotten the words out when the shadow lifted and seconds later the Cessna 210 was beside them on the left. She saw Deluca himself holding a microphone up to the window.

Stephen held his course and gave her a wary look. "This is your party, Dani. You want to talk to him?"

She swallowed back a lump to clear her throat. "Might as well."

Stephen lifted the mike, handed it to her, and dialed in the frequency. "Press the button to talk, release to listen."

She took a deep breath and depressed the talk button. "What do you want, Deluca?"

His raucous laughter came through the airwaves. "Your head on a platter, that's what I want, Ms. Lovato. But I'll settle for my crystal. Your choice."

"It's not yours and we both know it."

"Take a look at the window behind me."

Dani leaned to look around Stephen to the window. The large barrel of a very large gun was pointed at their plane.

"Do you think I'm bluffing?" Deluca growled.

"How do you expect to get it if you shoot us down?"

"I can afford to lose the crystal. Can you afford to lose your life?"

Dani looked at Stephen, he shrugged. "It's your game."

"What do you want us to do?" she asked into the mike.

"Land at the next small airfield you see. Turn over the crystal and you can be on your way. And don't even think about calling the cops. You're wanted for murder. Who do you think they'll believe if I tell them you stole it from me? They'll haul you off and guess who'll have the crystal then?"

"He's really starting to piss me off," Stephen said.

Dani agreed. She'd come too far, she couldn't let Deluca win without a fight. "Is there any way we can get away from him?"

"Sure. Tighten your seat straps."

Before she could think about what he was saying, the plane banked sharply to the right and her side was literally pressed against the door. A small sound escaped her as the sky swirled around her. Moments later, she was sitting upright again, working at keeping her stomach intact. She could now see Deluca's plane below them.

"Don't get sick on me, Agent Lovato," Stephen ordered. "You have work to do. Get Mays' gun from your backpack."

Reminding her that she was a federal agent did it. She scrambled to get the gun and had it cocked and ready before he could say another word. "What's your plan?"

"You told me you were a good shot. I want you to do a little showing off. Open your window and aim for the center of his wing on your side. Fire as many rounds as you can quickly then we'll move to the other side and do the same thing to the other wing. We'll only get one chance, because once he realizes what we're doing, the fun's over. We'll be in his blind spot so he won't see us."

"My god, won't it blow up?"

"Unlikely...this isn't a Bruce Willis movie. But rather him than us. Keep in mind the speed we're traveling."

Dani breathed deeply, willing her hands to stop shaking and told herself this was no different the target practice—and she saw a large red O in the center of the big Cessna's wing. *Ready or not, Deluca, here I come.*

"Okay now! Before he banks."

Stephen's command spurred Dani into action. Bruce Willis and Kippy-I-A ran through her head as she took aim and fired four rapid direct hits into the right wing."

Her side of the plane tilted skyward and righted again, giving her a long shot at the left wing. She shot twice but only hit once before the plane dove away from them.

Stephen veered sharply the other direction and opened the throttle.

"Wow! Fantastic shooting," he said. "I had hoped for one hit. You must have gotten three in the right."

"Four," she replied. "But only one into the left. What damage did I do?"

"Their fuel tanks. There's one in each wing. I don't how full he was, but he'll probably have enough to chase us down before he has to land."

Dani stared at him. "And then what?"

"Then we'll find out if he was bluffing."

It took a good five minutes before Deluca appeared behind them again, coming at full speed. Stephen let him get close then reared skyward and banked to the right.

Pressed back in her seat by the sudden up thrust, Dani hung on, reminding herself to breathe and telling herself she trusted Stephen. He knew what he was doing. If he didn't, he was certainly doing a good job of faking it.

When they leveled off again, she opened her eyes— she hadn't even realized she'd closed them—they were once again above and behind Deluca.

She readied the Glock to get another shot off but they

never got close enough. Deluca made a wide turn coming up behind them in less than three minutes this time.

Dani glanced at Stephen's face. He seemed to be on the ready, waiting. If she didn't know better, she imagined she saw rapture on his face. Could he actually be enjoying this cat and mouse chase?

She wasn't sure but she thought she heard gunfire over the noise of the engine. A second later they were in a dive. It looked to her like they were headed straight for the ground. Maybe they were hit. Again she glanced at Stephen, expecting to see horror on his features, instead she saw concentrated determination. They leveled off just above the tree tops and then they were turning again.

This time, she realized, she hadn't closed her eyes. "Were you a stunt pilot in another life?" she managed to ask.

He gave her a look with a hint of a smile. "Nope, not another life. In this one. I'm proud of you, Dani. You haven't even asked for the barf bag."

She returned his smile, grimacing, and held up a hand with the bag crushed in her fingers. Laughing, he reached over and squeezed her knee as they crossed the wide span of a river or more likely a reservoir.

She pointed out at the treetops they were barely skimming at a hundred and sixty miles an hour. "Maybe you should keep your eyes on the road."

This time Stephen full out laughed. Okay, I'll watch the *road*, you look back and see where Deluca is."

She looked out and sure enough there he was. "He's not very close yet but he's coming down aiming right toward us. Did he shoot at us?" she asked.

"Uh-huh. Didn't hit us though. Not yet anyway."

She gave him a skeptical glare for the last comment. Keeping one eye on Deluca, she said, "He's not going to give up, is he?"

"Not until he runs out of fuel."

Dani glanced at their fuel gage. It was under a quarter of a tank. *Or until we do.* "We can't just land either," she said as much to herself as to him. "If we were on the ground, he could fire at will because his precious crystal would be safe."

"Okay, time to Rock and Roll. Hang on."

Stephen pulled back on the wheel and their plane rose into the sky. This time Dani didn't close her eyes, instead she looked back to see what Deluca was doing. He was ascending too, but at a much lesser angle. "I guess his pilot didn't go to the same stunt school you did."

Stephen laughed as he brought the plane out of the rise and banked sharply to the right. "You're making jokes. Does that mean you're having fun?"

"No. It means I'm delirious."

Deluca was well behind them now but still doggedly after them. "He's going to be ready for you this time," she said.

"Yeah, but even if he is, he can't turn as sharp as I can."

"I didn't even know a plane could do what you're making this thing do."

"Hah, you wanna see me do a rollover."

"No!"

"Here he comes. He's staying slightly above us and looks like a tenacious pit-bull baring his teeth. I think he's after blood this time."

His choice of words reminded Dani why they were here in this predicament. *Was the Blood Crystal really worth all this?*

She didn't have time to continue her thought as the plane went into a sudden dive again. As they expected, Deluca anticipated the move and dove beside them.

This time, as close as the two planes were, there was no mistaking the sounds of rapid gunfire. Dani wasn't sure, but she thought she felt the plane give a couple of jerks. Had they been hit? She glanced at Stephen and found him frowning heavily. Dani was afraid to ask any questions.

They must have been hit because Deluca's plane was descending. Was he was going down to get ready to pick up the pieces, or more specifically the crystal, when they crashed?

Stephen let out a loud whoop bringing her close to jumping out of her skin. Except, he was laughing. Was he delirious too?

"They're looking for a place to land. That means they're either near to or out of fuel."

"We're nearly out too," she reminded him.

"I know. Pull out the map and let's figure out how far we are from Kokomo. We got off track with all this monkeying around we've done. Remember the big water we crossed? See if you can locate that and get our bearings. If you can't, you can take the wheel and I'll look."

While Dani was looking, Stephen fiddled with some gauges. "Keep in mind he said we need an airport that's manned, so best if there's at least 50,000 population."

She looked up at him. "We were hit, weren't we?"

"Yeah, I'm pretty sure we were. That's why we need a larger airport. I need someone to give me a visual on my landing gear. I think that's what they were aiming at. My guess is they didn't want to bring us crashing down, but they wanted to make damn sure we wouldn't take off again."

"And since he probably knows where we fueled up he knows we need to stop again soon."

Stephen grinned at her. "You're catching on real quick."

"So…if he's tracking us by fuel fills, he won't be able to if were grounded."

"First we have to get on the ground in one piece."

Dani swallowed thickly and went back to the map. "If the water was a dam on the Tippecanoe River and Deluca went down shortly after that, Kokomo should be straight south. Marion is east and not out of our way, but it's only thirty thousand."

Stephen got on the radio and tuned in Marion, Indiana. He had an answer in less than a minute, explained his dilemma and got permission to fly overhead to get a visual read on his landing gear.

By the time they sighted Marion, their fuel gauge was on empty. Stephen grumbled about it taking a lot of fuel to play games with Deluca. He flew in low over the Marion airport, dipped his wings at three guys standing in the small runway, and depressed the listening button on his radio.

"Your left wheel is hanging sideways. You'll have to circle around and make your approach on the left side of the airport cause you're gonna drag heavily in that direction. Try to keep her leaning to the right as long as you can before you touch down. Do you think you're skilled enough to do it?"

Dani made a sound through her nose. She'd have liked to answer that. *Is Jesus skilled enough to turn water into wine?*

Stephen gave them a thumbs-up answer and then turned to Dani. "I hope that was a snort of confidence and not an are-you-kidding-we're-gonna-die reaction?"

"What's to worry about? That sounds so easy I could probably do it."

He started the turn toward the runway then took his hands off the steering column. "Go ahead give it a try."

She gave him a wild-eyed glare and stuck her hands behind her back. As he laughed and continued the turn, a sudden silence filled the cockpit and Dani realized the engine had quit.

"Are you doing this without power for a reason?" she asked hopefully.

"No! Brace yourself we just ran out of fuel."

Dani forced herself to breathe in from her mouth out through her nose as she'd been trained and gripped anything she could grasp her fingers around as the ground closed in on them. She heard a deafening grating sound as the airplane jerked to the side. She guessed they were still traveling at least fifty miles an hour. The plane left the edge of the runway and plowed into a grassy knoll. They were swiveling like a wobbly top finishing its spin. Just as it stopped, the left wing dipped toward the ground, then righted itself.

Breathless, she stared at Stephen who let out a huge woof of air. "Well," he said, in a hoarse whisper. "That was...invigorating."

Dani covered her face with her hands and started laughing. It wasn't a this-is-funny kind of laugh. More like nearing hysteria. She felt Stephen's fingers tighten on her shoulder.

"Dani, are you okay?"

He had taken his seatbelt off so she was able to throw her arms around him. "I think I was all right until the engine quit. I thought—I thought—"

He smoothed a hand over her hair. "We're safe, honey." She felt him unbuckling her. "Let's get out of here. Don't mention anything about Deluca, okay?" He took the Glock she had stashed next to her seat and stuck it in her backpack.

She nodded and gave a short laugh. "I'm fine," she said. "And no, I won't. That would mean we'd have to explain who we are."

A big red fire truck pulled up beside them. And suddenly there were people swarming around them with congratulations to Stephen for a job well done. There were several hands there to help her out of the tilted plane. Stephen was explaining how he might have damaged his wheel on a take off in a rutted field. Even skirting around the truth, he was very convincing.

All was going well until he asked how long it would take to fix it.

A sandy haired man with the name, Dustin, monogrammed on his shirt answered. "Oh, we'd have to get parts out of Fort Wayne. Take a couple of days, another day to do the work and you'll be good as new."

"I have a deadline. Is there someplace I can rent a car?"

"Sure thing," Dustin said. "The Ford dealer in town rents. Would you like a ride into town?"

Dani looked at Stephen in alarm. You needed a credit

card to rent. Stephen, apparently having read her mind not for the first time, gave her shoulders a squeeze. "It's okay, honey. Everything's under control. Let's get our stuff out of the plane."

Dani was thankful she'd left the crystal in her backpack when someone handed it down to her. Stephen took a few minutes to make the arrangements to get his Cessna fixed, then they were squeezed into the front seat of a pickup with her in the middle next to Dustin. If he thought it strange she insisted her backpack stay on her lap, he didn't say.

Stephen slipped an arm around Dani's shoulders saying. "My wife and I are really grateful for your help, Dustin."

"Hey man, it was worth it watching you bring that baby in. You're one hellova pilot. We haven't had so much excitement here since the air show last July. I heard there was another plane went down with engine trouble about fifty miles north of here. Landed on a busy strip of highway."

"Anybody hurt?" Stephen asked.

"Don't think so, but I hear tell the owner read his pilot the riot act." Dustin chuckled. "Likely some rich dude who doesn't know beans about how to fly a plane himself."

"Most likely," Stephen muttered, giving Dani a squeeze.

"Well, here we are. You just go in and talk to Tommy. His dad Jim owns the shop. I think one of the guys called ahead and explained why you'll be needing a car right quick."

Dani gave him her brightest smile as they got out of the pickup. "Thank you for everything," she said. As soon as he drove off, she turned on Stephen. "How can we rent a car without using a credit card?"

"First of all, I don't think it matters any more. We haven't used a credit card yet and nobody seems to have a problem finding us. Besides, my name hasn't been used anywhere. If you're worried about it though, we can always use my plane as collateral. Let's go talk to Tommy."

She put a hand on his arm stopping him. "Why are you doing all this, Stephen? Why haven't you just dumped me to take care of my own problem?"

He bent down and kissed her on the nose. "Damned if I know."

CHAPTER TWENTY-ONE

Heading south on sixty-nine toward Interstate 70 with Dani asleep in the seat beside him, Stephen had time to think about the reason he had championed her cause and was still with her.

A week ago, he was sitting in an LA jail cell with a splitting hangover headache contemplating the events that had brought him there. He was pretty sure he'd never loved his wife, but they'd had a good time dating, and when his guard unit got called up to serve in Afghanistan, she suggested they get married. At the time, having someone back home waiting for him seemed like a good idea. Most of his life he'd done things on impulse, so it was nothing new when he ignored the advice of his family and got married by a Justice of the Peace ten days before he shipped out.

When he'd told Dani he was a lawyer, it was more of a dream than reality. His brother Virg was a lawyer and he'd always looked up to his oldest brother. He did spend four years in law school where he met Nadine and then moved with her to Minneapolis to do an internship in her father's law firm. At that point, he still wasn't sure if that was really what he wanted to do with his life.

After six months dodging bullets in a war torn country, he wrote Nadine a letter, confessing that he was thinking of going in a new direction when he got home. He just hadn't decided what that direction was going to be. She'd written back that her daddy was very unhappy with Stephen's thought process and maybe he had better do a little more thinking on it. He didn't know if that was the catalyst that started her running around or if she'd already been doing it. It didn't matter though. She was his wife, and if she loved him, she'd have stuck by him.

He'd come home a hero not because he really believed he was one, but because things just worked out that way. He'd done what he had to do, and his habit of acting on impulse for once paid off. It was the first time in his life his family had actually been proud of him. Having them find out he'd landed in jail would have put him right back to square one. It wasn't too hard to jump at the chance to get his record cleared.

He looked at Dani sleeping so peacefully beside him. She was as different from Nadine as day was from night. He smiled when he thought about her transformation from fear of flying to stomaching all the wild dips and turns he'd made trying to avoid Deluca. And in the midst of it all she took Mays' Glock and fired ace hits into that beautiful Cessna 210's fuel tanks.

Recalling both Virg and Hunter's words of wisdom about transitional women after a divorce gave him a good laugh. Dani Lovato was one hell of a transitional woman.

When she'd asked why he'd championed her cause, he'd lied and said *dammed if I know.* But he did know. She and their little escapade had given him his life back.

The next question was how did he feel about her?

His answer, *"damned if I know."*

* * * *

Dani woke up stretching and yawning feeling more rested then she had in a long time. "Man, how long have I been sleeping?"

"Almost three hours."

She looked into the darkness and then glanced at the clock in the dashboard of their rented Ford Taurus. "It's seven o'clock."

"Uh-huh."

"Why didn't you wake me up?"

"I figured you needed to rest. We've had a busy couple of days."

She ran a hand through her short hair and laughed. "More like a week. I've lost track of time. I don't even know how long it's been."

"Are you hungry?"

"Famished. Where are we?"

"I-70. About twenty miles from the Ohio border. Cambridge City is coming up. We'll stop for a bite."

"How far do you suppose we are from D.C.?"

"I'm guessing around six hundred miles."

Dani took a deep breath and let out a long sigh. "And then it will be over."

Stephen turned on his blinker to exit the interstate at Cambridge City. "I've been thinking," he said. "I didn't mention this before, but yesterday I specifically flew north farther than I should have just to throw Deluca off if he was following us, and yet, there he was right behind us. I'm wondering if we have another bug."

"Where?"

"Maybe we should get another backpack and ditch the one you have. It has all kinds of little pockets and corners where a bug could be planted."

"Could be possible. Let's do it. There's a trucker's café," Dani said, quickly pointing to his left.

"Might as well gas up here," Stephen replied, pulling up to a pump.

He filled quickly, went in and paid, then drove into the café's large parking lot. Grabbing the atlas, he got out of the car while Dani reached for her backpack. He gave her an amused look as though she was being foolish by clinging to that thing like it was her only supply of oxygen. She didn't care. The crystal was not getting out of her sight. Well, at least not out of reach.

They walked inside and took a seat in a far corner where they could keep an eye on the car. Except for three men hunkered over the counter, and a waitress with cleavage to spare leaning over them, the place was empty. The waitress left the men and brought two cups and a coffee pot.

"Coffee?" she asked. They both nodded. As she poured coffee, she asked if they needed menus.

"Yes, please" Dani said, avoiding the display below the tag that named her as Lani.

Lani then leaned past Stephen, affording him a generous view, and plucked the menus from a holder at the end of the booth.

She handed one to each of them. "I'll be back in a minute," she said with a wide smile.

Stephen glanced at the menu and appeared not to have noticed until he said, "I'll bet she can run a three minute mile with that set of lungs."

Dani's foot connected with his shin.

"Ouch," he howled. "What was that for?"

Dani pursued the menu. "Sorry, Rando, my foot slipped. I think I got a cramp sitting in the car so long."

Stephen gave her a charming pout. "And just when my leg was starting to feel good as new."

That got Dani's heart beat racing. "Really, good as new?"

"Uh-huh. I don't even think I limped today. You rubbed more magic balm on me after I went to sleep last night, didn't you?"

Without thinking, Dani glanced at the palm of her hand. When she looked up, she caught Stephen frowning at her. A warm rush settled in her cheeks.

Thankfully, Lani came toward them with a pad and pen in her hand. "You all decided yet?"

They placed their orders and when she left, Stephen laid the map out on the table.

Dani was just relieved he let the magic balm thing slide.

"I figure we can drive another couple of hours tonight," he said, "and get an early start in the morning. We just need to find some place with an all night Wal-mart."

"You bought the atlas at Wal-mart. Look in the back, you'll find the location of every Wal-mart in the country."

He glanced up at her with raised eyes brows then flipped though the atlas and found it. "Woman, you are a genius. I could kiss you."

Dani just shook her head laughing. "You don't get out much do you?"

"Guess not. Wow, it even shows all the exits within two miles of the freeway." After a moment of studying the list, his eyes lit up. "Here we go, Englewood. It's just about the right distance, and we can stop for the night, ditch the old backpack, and pick up anything else we might need. And while we're at it, we'll go through that damn thing and get rid of everything that belonged to your partner that has even a remote possibility of carrying a bug."

Dani had a mild jolt of alarm even as she nodded her agreement. She had to get the crystal out of the backpack before Stephen went through it with a fine tooth comb.

Lani came rambling around the corner with their food. She set it down smiling and hesitating, then said, "Bucky over there,"—she gestured to one of the truckers—"is from Minnesota. He thinks you're that Douglas fella who came home a war hero. Is that right?"

Dani stopped with her fork in mid-air while Stephen glanced at the trucker with a small wave. "Nope. Sorry. Not me."

"Aw shucks," Lani said. "And here I was all set to ask for your autograph."

After she left, Dani rolled her eyes. "I think she'd like more from you than your autograph."

"Ya think?" Stephen said, grinning. He cut off a bit of his hamburger steak, popped it in his mouth, chewed a moment, then said, "You know, my mother had small breasts. She nursed all five of us kids."

When he didn't go on, Dani sighed in exasperation. "Is there a point to that story?"

"Sure," Stephen said. "When I was about six, I heard

Dad telling my older brothers that more than a mouthful was a waste. I was twelve years old before I realized he wasn't talking about nursing babies."

Dani burst out laughing and nearly choked on a cherry tomato she'd been about to swallow. She downed a healthy swig of water. "You are such a nut. I thought you were going to tell me that her nursing you with small breasts gave you a boob complex."

Stephen grinned. "It might have if I could remember it. Mom insists my brother Hunter recalls everything since birth. I'll have to ask him about that sometime."

"You have a crazy family," Dani said almost wistfully.

That's an understatement," Stephen replied. "Being the youngest boy, I got the crazies handed down to me from all sides."

You've mentioned your brothers Virgil and Hunter and your sister Corinne. Who is the fifth one?"

"Diana," he said after a long moment. "I never knew her because she died the day I was born."

"Oh, how awful for your parents. How old was she."

"Five. The same age as my cousin Quint. His parents were killed in the same accident so that's how he became a member of our family. He's been around since I was born, so I've always considered him a brother. In fact, the two of us shared a room when we were growing up, so I may be closest to him."

"I can't even imagine what it's like to have so many people who care about you."

"Yeah, I guess not. If you were an only child and your parents are both gone, that pretty much leaves you on your own, doesn't it?"

Dani looked out the window, thinking a moment before she said, "Uh-huh. I don't even have any cousins."

* * * *

As they walked out to the car after eating, Dani asked if he wanted her to take over driving.

"I'd love that," he said, "but I don't think we should take a chance. You have no driver's license, and even if you did, your name could set off all kinds of alarms we can't afford right now."

Keeping a wary eye on the rearview mirrors as they crossed the border into Ohio, Dani studied the map while Stephen calculated how much cash they had left and would need.

With hotel rooms, aviation fuel at two hundred dollars a pop, gas and meals, plus other things they'd bought, he had less than two hundred dollars left of the thousand Mays had given him—which thankfully wasn't counterfeit. They needed gas for six hundred miles, food, and one or two nights lodging. Luckily, he'd been able to con Tommy at the Ford dealership out of the car by putting the Cessna up for collateral. The more he'd thought about it, the less he liked the idea of exposing a credit card.

He guessed that after they were rid of the crystal, credit cards would no longer be an issue.

"I have around a hundred and eighty dollars left," he said. "I know you have three bills from Mays, do you have anything else?"

Dani set the map aside and shook her head. "Just a few dollars. But Reierson will reimburse you for our expenses," she said.

Stephen wasn't sure why but he had a bad feeling about Bob Reierson. "I don't think we should turn the crystal over to him. Why can't we take it straight to Kendu, the owner? You said you knew where he was staying."

"Yes, I do and he knows me, but Reierson would be pissed big time."

"Now why do you suppose that is? My guess is either he wants in on the credit for returning it, or he doesn't intend to return it at all." Stephen watched a car that seemed to be in a hurry approaching from behind. He held his breath and his speed until the car passed. It had an Ohio license plate. Taking a deep breath, he went on. "How well do you know this guy anyway?"

"I don't. As I mentioned before, I met him when I came in on the case."

"So who recommended you for this job? Who knew about your knowledge of crystals?"

When she didn't answer, Stephen turned to look at her. She seemed to be holding her breath, thinking. A sudden queasy feeling took root in his gut. Her hesitation brought up a volume of suspicions he couldn't even began to name, but he decided to wait and see what she came up with for an answer to what should have been a simple question.

"Someone my father knew," she said finally.

Ah, the mysterious father resurfaces. "Does this someone have a name?"

"Tony. Just Tony."

No last name... Just Tony...oookay. Stephen mulled that over a few seconds.

"Look Dani, I'm not trying to pry into your life. If he's an old boyfriend or even a current one, I can handle that. I'm just trying to get a grip on who we can trust. Reierson's tie to Mays sets warning bells off for me. How much to you trust Tony?"

"More than I want to."

This was getting nowhere fast. "Obviously he's not someone you want to expose. So...let's play twenty questions. If you don't want to answer just say so." She didn't comment one way or another, so he continued. "Is Tony the man—I'm assuming Tony is a man—who got you into the agency in the first place?"

"Yes."

"And your father knew him?"

Dani gritted her teeth. "Yes."

"A friend of your father's then?"

She didn't answer, so he let that one pass assuming Tony was not a friend of Peter Lovato.

Stephen watched another car speed past them, wishing he had his brother, Hunter's brain. Hunter was good with riddles. But if she kept answering, maybe he could figure it out. What he really wanted to know was if Tony was a love interest.

"You told me you moved from LA to Washington after your father died. Did you do that because of Tony?"

"Yes, but he wasn't, isn't, nor ever will be a sexual partner if that's what you're getting at."

"Huh, in that case, Tony must be gay."

"It isn't my place to divulge that kind of information."

Acceptable answer he thought with an internal smile, but it didn't explain why she'd follow him to D.C. And, if she was telling the truth, he wasn't even a friend of the father she seemed to despise and care about at the same time. If her father had at one time, pursued a sexual relationship with Tony, it might explain a lot. Unless... "Is he your grandfather?"

Dani threw her head back and laughed. "I remember a song way back when titled *I Am My Own Grandpa*. So unless there's some weird quirk going on I don't know about, he not my grandfather. He's only three months older than I am and I'd rather not talk about him anymore. This little game brings up a depressing phase of my life I'd just as soon forget."

Stephen reached over and ran his hand down the side of her face. "Sorry," he said, "I guess I just want to know everything about you. Maybe someday when you fully trust me, you'll tell me about him. I do have one more question and then I'll let it drop. It should be an easy one."

She threw her hands in the air. "Go ahead. Shoot."

"Is Tony someone you like?"

Dani gave him a sad smile. "Yes. More than I want to."

At least that convinced Stephen—if they ran into trouble they could call Tony, whoever he was. The number of men Dani admitted to trusting was a mighty short, almost nonexistent, list. What he didn't understand was why she wouldn't tell him the story on her father. He was about to ask when she popped in with a question of her own.

"When Virgil called on your cell phone, he mentioned your mother having issues. Is she ill?"

Apparently, she'd rather talk about his family. That was a never-ending subject. "Yeah," he said chuckling. "She's sick all right. Homesick for her grandkids. Since Quint and Jamie moved to Minneapolis, all the grand kids are in Minnesota and she's in New York. She told my dad if he won't move with her, she'll go alone."

"She'd leave him? Do you think she's serious?"

"Ma's pretty stubborn."

"What do you think your dad will do?"

"I don't know yet. Virgil's working them over. He's the only one left in New York."

A car came up behind them, tailgated for a minute, then whizzed around them. Shit. He chastised himself. He was becoming paranoid. Dani was so concerned about his parents she hadn't even noticed.

"Do you think he'll be able to do something?" Dani asked.

Stephen shrugged. "I hope so because dad doesn't even know how to use a can opener."

Dani smiled. "Your family sounds like so much fun. What are your parent's names?"

"Hank and Delta."

While she thought that over a road sign announced one mile to Englewood.

"You were all named after stars." she said.

Laughing, Stephen turned his blinker on to exit at the Wal-mart. "Not too many people figure that out," he said, slowing down, keeping an eye on the off ramp behind them until he was satisfied they weren't being followed. "My mother got that from my grandmother. My uncles all had strange names."

"Your extended family must be huge."

"Yup, they rent a hall once every three years for reunions." He gave her a rundown on cousins that lasted until he turned into the shopping center parking lot.

"Get whatever you need. I'll grab a backpack and meet you inside the front door in a few minutes."

"Right on. I need to get a lightweight jacket with large

pockets to carry my Beretta."

He knew she was a federal agent familiar to carrying a gun, but for some reason, it was unsettling. Too remindful of the volatile situation they were involved in.

Thirty minutes later, they pulled into a gas station with a Motel-6 next door. Stephen filled gas and went inside to pay. When he came back out, Dani was moving stuff around in the back seat. She saw him coming and hurriedly returned to the front.

"I just had a thought," he said, looking around. "Why don't we leave the car parked over here behind those semis and walk to the motel?"

"Good idea," she agreed.

"I'll take my duffle bag and check in. You can bring the rest of the stuff when you see me coming out of the office. In the meantime, keep an eye out for any suspicious looking cars. If Deluca is following us, he'd be in a rental car. We'll dump the backpack after we've emptied it in the trash container on the far side of the lot. If it does have a bug, he'll find it and think we just stopped for gas." He tossed her the keys. "Here, you wanted to drive. You can park over behind that Werner Freight truck where you can watch for me."

Dani knew he'd been watching for cars tailing them even though he'd been discreet about it. She doubted if he knew she'd been on the alert too. It didn't take a genius to know that Deluca would not give up until he had his hands on the crystal or until they had it delivered to Kendu. Getting rid of the backpack should be the last possible chance he had of following them.

Pulling the car over to the side, she quickly went about finishing what she'd started before Stephen had shown up quicker than she'd expected.

She pulled the Blood crystal out of her backpack and quickly stuffed it in the crease of the back seats as she'd done in his Cadillac convertible.

That finished, she breathed a sigh of relief and slipped

on her new nylon jacket specifically chosen in the sports department for its multiple pockets. Her Beretta fit nicely in the large inside zippered pouch. She'd barely finished when Stephen waved at her from the end room closest to the car, but across the grassy divider.

She hesitated, thinking about the crystal. It would easily fit in one of her pockets but…what if it got hot if she accidently put too much pressure on it or if Stephen dug in her jacket for whatever reason? No, she decided, it was safer left where it was. Crossing the grass, carrying the backpacks, she smiled to herself. Stephen wouldn't need any magic balm if they did a replay of last night. Just the thought made her female hormones heat up.

When she stepped into the small room, Stephen reached for her bags and all. Drawing her into his arms, his lips found hers in a hungry pent up lock.

"Oh sweetheart, I've been waiting all day to taste you," he whispered into her mouth, his voice soft and husky.

Her bags dropped to the floor as her arms slipped around his neck. His hands grasped her behind and pulled her again him. The need in her swelled to match his. She wrapped her legs around his waist, gripping him as tight as she could.

Stephen groaned. "Honey, you're going to have me unloading in my jeans like a teenager in another minute."

"That would be a waste," she muttered against his lips. "Maybe we should get rid of all these clothes."

He stopped kissing her and buried his face in her neck. "I fully agree, but we need to take care of business. Let's get rid of that damn backpack first. I don't want anyone tapping me on the shoulder while I'm making love to you."

She sighed and dropped her feet to the floor. "I second that motion. Let's do it."

He gave her another quick kiss, moved away from her, and picked the backpack up from the floor, taking deep sighing breaths as he did so.

When Dani laughed at him, he gave her a wolf-like

leer that had her melting clear down to her toes.

"I'll take the stuff out, we'll determine what to keep, and you can put those items in the new bag," Stephen said. He took out Mays' Glock and checked the magazine. "There are only five rounds left. You might as well keep it in there. I still have both of the goon's guns in my duffle. Do you have your Beretta?" When she padded the side of her jacket, he grinned. "I should have known. Here, you can check this."

He handed over a sack of toiletries. She took a quick look, announced them okay, and put them in the new bag. When they started on the small pockets, the first thing he pulled out was her red see-through nightie. "Ooowee. Where does this come from?" Dani squealed when he attempted to put it up to his nose and snatched it out of his fingers.

"Hey, if that belonged to Roger, we should check it for bugs."

"Later," she said, trying to stifle the hot flush she felt cresting her cheeks. "You can check it while I'm wearing it."

"Is that a promise?"

"If you behave," she said, stuffing it in her bag.

"Ouch, that's gonna be tough."

She shook her head laughing. "You're such a brat. What's left in there?"

"This." He held up the velvet wrapped skull.

Dani froze for just a second before she reached for it.

"We better check the bag," he said. He slipped it out and examined the skull while she held her breath. Then handing the skull off to her, he searched though the bag, turning it inside and out.

While he did that, she experienced a moment of panic. What if the bag with the real crystal had a bug? That would, in fact, be the most logical place Deluca would have planted one. Damn. Double damn. She'd have to come up with an excuse to take care of that later.

"Looks clean to me," Stephen said, handing the bag to

her.

She put the skull inside, pulled the tie shut, and put it in a side pocket of her new backpack.

"All that's left is your partner's passport, badge, and travel papers, oh, and five hundred dollars worth of scrap paper."

"I'll keep the badge since I don't have one anymore,"—she gave him a mock glare—"and you can leave the rest in there to throw away."

He checked the badge for bugs then tossed it to her. "I'll just keep these for now," he said sticking the counterfeit bills in his hip pocket. "Never know when they might come in handy."

"If you try to spend them, I'll have to arrest you," she quipped.

"Ooh, will you frisk me."

"Every inch," she said giving him a bodily leer.

He stuck his tongue out, lolling it like a panting dog.

She stared at him a moment and said, "You keep that up and we'll never finish."

He started coming around the bed toward her, his gray eyes smoldering. "Okay, let's finish it."

Now she full out laughed. "Not that, this!" She pointed to the emptied backpack. "We need to get rid of it."

"Oh, fine, first things first". He reached for the pack but she grabbed it away from him.

"I'll do it, you can take a shower." She knew that sounded odd, but she really needed to get back out to take care of the crystal.

"I was thinking I'd take it across the street to the other service station so it's not in the same parking lot as our car. You start the shower and I'll be back in six minutes or less to join you."

The kiss he gave her was deep, all consuming, a hungry promise. It weakened her knees and her hold on the bag. She collapsed to the bed, watching him race out the door before she could even catch her breath. She pressed her hands to her heated face amazed at when he could do to her with a simple kiss. Granted, that kiss was anything but simple, even if it only lasted ten seconds. Since she knew there was no way to get to the car and back before he returned, she had to come up with another plan. But first, she needed to take a shower.

Their lovemaking was even more exquisite than the first time, if that was even possible.

"I saw a laundry down by the office," Dani said. "I'm going to throw a load of clothes in the washer."

"Do you really need to do that?" Stephen murmured half asleep, tightening his grip on her waist.

"I slept so long in the car I'm not tired," she lied. Their rowdy lovemaking had left her exhausted. "Plus, I want to wear my cargo pants. I love them."

Stephen chuckled sleepily. "I like you better in your tight jeans."

"I think you like me better in nothing."

"True." He started to get up. "I'll come with you."

"No!" she said a bit too loudly. "You need your rest. We have a long way to go tomorrow if we're going to make it to D.C. I won't be long and I'll take my Beretta."

"Okay," he said, getting out of bed. Her heart sagged when she saw him reach for his jeans.

"Really, I can go by myself," she insisted.

"I just want to be ready if I hear any shots coming from that Beretta." He zipped up, pulled Harry's pistol out of his duffle, along with a pillowcase containing his own dirty clothes. "As long as you insist on washing, you may as well do these." He tossed her the pillowcase, put the gun on the nightstand, and laid back down.

"I'll take my key, so don't shoot me when I come back in."

"You got it, Babe. Hurry back."

Dani grabbed her backpack, let herself out and raced to the laundry to drop her bundle of clothes in the washer. She bought some soap, put the quarters in the washer and pushed the knobs for the quickest wash. Dani imagined her mother standing over her shoulder chastising about mixing colors. "Sorry, Mom," she muttered. "I'm in a hurry."

Making tracks, she passed their room and ran over the grass divider to the car. She used the keys from her pocket to open the door, thankful she hadn't had to con them out of Stephen. All the while, she kept an eye out for suspicious vehicles. If Deluca was following them, he'd be in a rental car, unless he got his plane repaired and flew, which was unlikely.

Taking the Blood Crystal from its nesting place, she dropped it out of the paper sack, removed it from its leather pouch, then taking care not to squeeze it, dropped it back in the sack and stuffed it once again between the seats.

Now all she needed to do was find a place to discard the leather pouch. The pouch itself was beautiful. Made of soft golden leather and woven with intricate bead designs. Probably hand made in San Delta. Any one of the fifty or so beads could have been exchanged for a bug. It was impossible to tell, plus she didn't have time or sufficient lighting. While contemplating what to do with it, she spotted a highway patrol car parking behind the coffee shop attached to the service station. Dani leaned back out of sight and watched as two officers got out and walked into the cafe. A gem of an idea hatched in her busy mind. Crouching down, so as not to be seen, she inched up to the patrol car, opened the cover accessing the gas cap and tucked the pouch in the cavity behind the cover.

She hurried away, grinning, imagining Deluca following a bug hidden in a police car.

Walking past their room, she noted all was dark and quiet inside. Stephen was getting his much-needed rest. From there she hurried back to the laundry to wait for the clothes.

It took ten minutes for the load to finish. Plucking them out of the washer, she moved them to a dryer, deposited two quarters and turned it to high heat. She then glanced out the window while she waited. She was able to see the Taurus from her vantage point, but their room was out of her view as was the registration office. The parking lot out front remained quiet except for an older couple who'd been registering when she'd returned from the car.

Leaning her head back with a sigh, she tried to remember what things were like when her life was normal. Then she realized her life hadn't been normal since her mother died and her father turned Dani's life upside down. When he died a year ago, she'd been very angry at him. It was so much more rewarding to hate him when he was alive. Maybe hate was too strong a word. Maybe it was just major disappointment.

The only saving grace in the whole mess was Tony. He was nothing like she'd expected. She'd been prepared to hate him too, but no matter how much she wanted to, it just didn't turn out that way.

She was just starting to rebuild her life when Tony introduced her to Tom Reierson who offered her a chance to help an impoverished dying country. Bama Kendu turned out to be the sweetest man she'd ever met. How could she not want to help him?

Never in her wildest dream had she imagined meeting someone like Stephen Rando Douglas. The sad thing was, when this was over, Stephen would go back to his family and she'd go back to studying and working with crystals and gemstones.

An annoying buzzing interrupted her musings. She got up and pulled the clothes from dryer, folded everything and put Stephen's clothes in the pillowcase. She arranged hers in her backpack.

She slung the backpack over one shoulder, picked up the pillowcase, and headed back to the room, thoughts of spending the night sleeping next to Stephen swirling like delicious chocolate through her head.

Humming quietly as she rounded the corner to the room, she stopped short and froze. A large figure hunkered at the edge of the building just a few steps beyond the door. A muted light glowed through the drawn shades.

Her heart did a hammer dance as she stepped back to the protection of the corner. She was only five rooms from where he stood in the darkness. A sudden glow from a cigarette lighter pulled the man's face from the shadows and she recognized Marty. Her stomach lurched even as she drew her Beretta from her jacket. She fought to still her breathing and willed her hands to stop shaking.

A plan! She needed a plan. Stephen was in the room. Probably with Deluca and Harry and who knew how many others. There'd been four people in their plane, but there was a good chance the pilot stayed with it to catch up to them after it was fixed.

Whirling around, she ran back to the laundry where she went out the back door. She faced another row of rooms that backed up to those on the other side. If she could come around the other side, she might be able to come up behind Marty and disarm him without alerting whoever was in the room.

Swallowing the fear mounting in her chest, she made it to the end and peeked around the corner. She could see Marty's shoulder as he leaned heavily against the building, probably off balance due to his injured leg. She set her bags down and pulled out the heavy Glock. Making sure the safety was on, she held it by the barrel, stalked toward Marty and slammed the butt end into the back of his skull. When he slumped forward, she grabbed his arm and maneuvered him to the side so he wouldn't fall into the window. He dropped to the ground at her feet, blood oozing from the wound. She considered hitting him again but he seemed to be out.

She pulled his gun, a 38 Smith and Wesson, out of his belt and stuffed it in the back of her jeans under her jacket. Next she yanked off his belt, drew his arms behind his back and quickly wrapped the belt around his wrists, securing it as Tony had trained her to do.

That finished, she pulled in a breath of air that maxed her lung capacity and released it slowly as she stepped over Marty's body and moved toward the door. She couldn't see anything through the pulled shade and curtains. That meant she'd have to charge in blind and be ready to fire her gun, to kill if necessary. Knowing Stephen was in there with them gave her courage.

The door was locked so she used her key, and holding her Beretta with both hands, she swung the door open and charged in.

Deluca and Harry were going through Stephen's duffle bag, dumping the contents on the bed. She didn't see Stephen. Both men whirled to face her, shock widening their eyes. Neither one held a gun in his hand.

"Freeze!" she shouted, aiming her Beretta straight at Deluca's heart. "Either one of you reaches for a gun, you'll be the first one dead, Deluca. Hands behind your heads!" Harry looked at his boss as though waiting for permission."

"Do it." Deluca said. "That double-crossing bitch is crazy enough to shoot." He took his time raising his hands and Harry followed suit. "You aren't going to get away with this, Lovato."

Keeping an eye on Harry, Dani stepped behind him grabbed him by the back of his belt and jammed her gun into his spine. That's when she saw Stephen unconscious on the floor behind Harry, blood seeping from a head wound. For a brief second, she had to war with herself not to pull the trigger.

Choking back her fear and fury, she barked at the man responsible. "You better warn your man that if he makes one move I don't like, you'll be pissing in a bag the rest of your rotten life." To drive her point home, she increased the pressure of the gun on his backbone enough to make him wince.

"You fire that gun, Lovato, and you'll have police crawling all over this place. Are you sure you want that?"

Dani did another jab on his back.

"At this close range by the time this little Beretta slug goes through your backbone and your belly, it won't make a whole lot of noise. Of course, it might cause a little more commotion when I have to drop Harry." She noticed a gun on the bed on the side where she stood and guessed it belonged to Deluca.

"Where's your gun?" she asked Harry.

"I don't have one," he snarled. "You took it, remember?"

"Yeah? We also took Marty's and he seems to have found another one. Take your jacket off."

When he hesitated, she rammed the Barrette into Deluca's back with all the strength she had. The action brought a howl of pain from him. He swore at Dani through gritted teeth and then at Harry. "Dammit, Harry. Do what she tells you."

Harry took his jacket off and tossed it on the bed. It exposed a holstered weapon under his arm.

"Unbuckle it and toss it on the bed," she ordered, hoping her voice didn't reflect the fear squeezing at her throat or short gasps emitting from her lungs. The only thing keeping the adrenalin rush at bay was surging anger each time she looked at Stephen.

Harry glanced at Deluca, did as he was instructed, then put his hands back up behind his head. Dani eyed the drapery cords thinking they'd make good bindings. She shoved Deluca toward a chair and ordered him to sit. When he sat down she removed the gun from his spine and he turned on her with the speed of a cobra. She dodged his fist but his hand wrapped like a vise around her gun wrist. From her position behind him, she tangled her free hand in his hair, yanking back on his head while holding a death grip on the little Beretta and trying not to squeeze down on the trigger and fire a wild shot.

Out of the corner of her eye she saw Harry dive for his gun, and at the same time, his legs went out from under him. He landed hard on the floor with Stephen on top of him. When Stephen's fist connected with Harry's face, he howled and backed against the wall, holding his blood spouting nose, swearing and moaning in the same breath. In the next instant, Stephen charged at Deluca, grabbing the arm that held Dani's wrist captive.

Dani took the opportunity to reach behind her back for Marty's Smith and Wesson. She brought the stub nosed 38 down on Deluca's head. With the poor leverage she had, she didn't get a good hit. He barely flinched. She hit him again, harder this time. He stumbled but still didn't fall. On hands and knees, Harry went for his gun again only to be stopped short by Stephen's bare foot connecting with his bleeding face. Harry collapsed to the floor motionless.

When Dani brought the 38 down a third time on Deluca's head, the huge man finally released the grip on her wrist and went down to his knees. Stephen leaped on him with the same sleeper hold he'd used on Mays.

Deluca slumped to the floor with Stephen on top of him. For a moment, neither man moved.

"Stephen!" Panic edged Dani's cry.

Stephen raised his head slowly. He wiped the blood that had run in his eye. Are you okay?" he asked, his voice raspy.

She nodded, her throat too tight to speak, but not to think. Racing for the bathroom, she grabbed a clean washcloth and hurried back to press it against the gaping two-inch wound on Stephen's temple. He stared at her but hadn't moved.

Stephen's head pounded and the last thing he wanted to do was move, but he knew it wasn't a choice. He put his hand up to replace hers and said, "Let's get out of here."

Dani nodded her agreement and hurried to the bed to rake Stephen's things together along with the two guns and shove them in his duffle bag. Numbly, Stephen watched her work, periodically brushing tears from her eyes. For a moment she froze, and in the next instant, she had the knife in her hand Stephen had taken from Harry back at the service station. With it, she cut the drapery cords, and pounced on Harry like a steer wrangler and had his hands tied behind his back in record breaking time. When she moved toward Deluca with the second cord, Stephen rolled away to give her access to the man's hands. After Deluca was secured, she took the bed sheet and ripped three four-inch strips swiftly, using two to bind the men's feet. The third she wrapped around Stephen's head to hold the washcloth in place. Tears dripped on his fingers as she worked.

When she finished with him, she cut one more strip from the sheet, then went through both Deluca's and Harry's pockets and quickly deposited everything she found in his duffle bag Pausing over Harry, she held up a set of car keys, a triumphant smirk on her face. She then slung his duffle bag over her shoulder and started for the door.

"I'll take the stuff out to the car and come right back. Wait here."

Stephen stared after her in awe, thinking he had grossly underestimated this woman when he called her a rookie. Judging by her actions, she'd obviously had training from a master.

Stephen's head pounded and his chest ached with guilt for allowing Deluca to get the upper hand on him. He'd heard them come in, but since they used a key card they'd likely bribed from the manager, Stephen thought it was Dani, and didn't realize the mistake until it was too late. When he'd gone for Deluca, Harry hit him from behind. He'd blacked out and woke up moments before Dani charged into the room like the Calvary in a blaze of glory.

She was phenomenal.

When Stephen tried to get to his feet, a wave of dizziness hit him. Being weak and vulnerable didn't sit well with him. Cursing, he gritted his teeth and forced himself to crawl to the bed and drag his body up on it. From there he made it to the bathroom to examine the gash in his head. It didn't appear to be very deep but it was gapping. He probably needed stitches.

He'd washed most of the blood off when he heard Dani call his name. "I'm in here," he said.

She appeared at the bathroom door with a t-shirt in her hand. "I realized when I got to the car I didn't leave you a shirt." He raised his arms while she helped him slip it over his head. She then went in the other room and reappeared with his shoes.

"I'll put 'em on in the car," he said. "Let's get out of here."

"Good idea, Marty's stirring." Dani drug his arm over her shoulder and lead him to the door.

"Marty?" he said finally.

"Yeah, he's right outside—and so is our car."

Stephen was still shaking his head in disbelief when he saw Marty's prone body as Dani helped him into the passenger side of the car. She ran back in and came out with a bed pillow pulling the room door shut behind her.

Laying the pillow on his lap, she started the car, put it in gear, and backed out. Seconds later they were back on the interstate heading west.

"You're going the wrong way," he muttered.

"I'm going back to Wal-mart to get you some bandages."

"Good thinking. While you're in there, get some peroxide, needles and white thread. Oh, and a pair of scissors."

She turned to stare at him. "I hope you're not thinking what I'm thinking."

"I need stitches. We can't go to an emergency room. There'd be papers to fill out."

He watched her opened mouth clamp shut as she absorbed that information. A colorful expletive escaped her full pouting lips. "I'm not trained in first aid."

"I am. I'll step you through it."

* * * *

When Dani got back in the car with her shopping bag fifteen minutes later, Stephen had his head propped against the window on the pillow. There didn't seem to be any more bleeding from his wound, so she decided to get back on the road and put some distance between them and the gruesome scene they'd left at the motel. She'd have to stop soon though to take care of the gash in his head. The thought of putting stitches in an open wound, even with the topical tooth ache stuff she'd bought, had her stomach tied up in knots.

They probably didn't have to worry about Deluca following them anytime too soon. Without his wallet, he'd have no money, no credit cards and no ID. And without keys, he'd have no car. She was glad she'd remembered to grab Marty's wallet too when she picked up the things she'd left around the corner. Deluca had enough resources to find a way to get back on the road, but it would take some time. She wished she'd known where their car was parked so she could have punched the tires because they could likely break in and hotwire it, but they'd still need money for gas eventually. The real question was how they found them again! Did they locate Roger's backpack and head for the nearest motel? The highway patrol car was gone, but she didn't know when they'd left in case there really was a bug in the crystal bag.

Just past Springfield she saw a motel advertised and decided it was a good place to stop. Stephen woke up when she put the blinker on. She wasn't sure she dared to let him sleep much longer anyway in case he had a concussion. He looked pale and weary.

"How are you feeling?" she asked.

"Great. Except for this freight train parked on my head."

"Are you nauseous?

He gave her a lopsided grin that appeared forced. "No. I don't think I have a concussion if that's what you're thinking. I took the hit on the side of my head."

"I'm sorry I wasn't there."

"Don't be. We'd probably have been in the final round of a terrific sexual encounter and he'd have had us both. As it was, you charged in and saved my ass."

"More like you saved mine when you took out Harry and grabbed Deluca's arm. That was on nasty kick you gave Harry by the way. Where did you learn that?"

"I have friends in low places."

Laughing, Dani turned into the Relax Inn five miles outside of Springfield. She stopped the car near the registration office and sighed. "This looks like as good a place as any to get you fixed up. I'll go in and get a room."

She got a room at the far end of the motel, helped Stephen out of the car and into the room even though he grumbled he wasn't an invalid. She brought the bags in they'd need, then parked the car in an unlit parking lot behind the motel.

When she came back in the room carrying her backpack, Stephen was in the bathroom examining his wound. It was longer than she thought, at least two and a half inches, but only about an inch of it was wide enough to require stitches. Stephen poured some peroxide in a plastic cup and used one of the gauze bandages she'd bought to disinfect it.

"Why don't you sit down and let me do that?" she said.

Stephen handed her the cup and sat down on the bed. "Be my guest. Soak about fifteen inches of that thread and the smallest needle in peroxide."

She did that then finished cleaning the wound. Trying not to think about what she was going to do, she scrubbed her hands then doused them with peroxide. She threaded the needle and walked back in the bedroom. Stephen had laid down on the bed with his cut exposed and ready for her ministration. He had his eyes closed, or so she thought.

Dani swallowed hard trying to down the queasy feeling in her gut.

"Don't think about it," Stephen said. "Just go ahead and do it. Four stitches should be enough. Pull them tight even if I cringe a little. Rambo I'm not."

Dani nodded, hoping her fingers didn't shake too much to do the job. Dani spread the Ambesol on the surface.

"What's that?" Stephen asked.

"Something my mother used when I was a kid when I had a tooth pulled. It numbs it a little. I don't know if it will work, but it's worth a try."

Stephen nodded and closed his eyes. She saw him

clench his teeth and wished there was something she could do about her squeamish stomach.

When she stuck the needle in, he flinched, but made no sound. She pushed the needle through, breathing deeply, and pulled the wound together tightly as he'd instructed. After tying it off, she snipped the end and did the second one. Stephen never moved after the first flinch. As she worked, she remembered her father pulling slivers out of her finger and knew how badly even that hurt. Stephen's stamina was incredible.

She prided herself on keeping her stomach intact as she finished the last stitch.

Stephen let out a long slow breath as though he'd been holding it throughout. "How does it look?"

Dani smiled shakily as she dabbed at the spots of blood left by the needle punctures with sterile peroxide gauzes. "Not bad considering I can't even sew on a button."

Stephen groaned. "Now you tell me."

"Don't move," she said, hurrying into the bathroom and coming out with some butterfly bandages. She applied them intermittently, leaving space for air in-between, explaining what she was doing as she worked.

"And you told me you didn't know anything about first aid."

"When I was a kid, I was a bit of a rebel, so I spent many hours in emergency rooms getting stitched up. It all came back to me, like my life flashing before my eyes. Of course, I never had to suffer thorough it without anesthesia."

"Huh, you a rebel? Why is that not difficult to imagine?"

Dani laughed, rocked her head from side to side and rolled her shoulders, working the tension from her body. "I'm sure I was no more of a rebel than you were."

"Lord, I wonder what our children would be like."

Dani stared at him laying there with his eyes shut, resting as though he hadn't just made a heart-stopping statement. Okay, she thought, just ignore it and take it for the flippant comment it most likely was. He was probably a little delirious from pain anyway.

"Would you like some pain killer?" she asked.

"Only if you have something that can derail a freight train?"

Dani laid a hand on his forehead to check his temperature. It was cool. "I wish I had. I feel so responsible for this."

"Please don't," he said, reaching for her free hand. He kissed her fingers and held them close to his lips. "Just keep rubbing my head. That feels so good."

His words shocked her like a dash of ice water to the face. Her mind raced. Did she dare? If she tried the Blood Crystal and it didn't work, she'd be driving with a raw, aching hand when they left. She continued to rub his head, pushing his short dark hair back from his forehead, trying to work up the courage to do it.

When his breathing evened out and she knew he was sleeping, she decided it was now or never. Withdrawing her hand from his grasp, she walked to the door, opened it, and stepped outside. With one last glance to make sure he stayed put, she pulled the door shut and raced to the car.

Her hands shook as she pulled the crystal from between the seats and dropped it into her palm. Thinking she must be crazy to be doing this, she steeled herself for the pain and squeezed.

She squeezed lightly hoping she could drop it before it fully burned her. But it didn't get hot. She tried two more times and still it stayed cool to the touch. The fourth time she squeezed down on it firmly and it turned instantly blood red. She let out a short screech and tossed it to the seat.

Now she was convinced that each time it burned faster and hotter. It made three pulsing beats and returned to normal. Her hand was so badly burned she could hardly open it. This was really a ludicrous idea, and she suspected she was losing her grip on reality. She needed to get back to the room and put ice water on her hand.

She stuck the crystal between the seats, locked the car, and hurried back to the room. She opened the door cautiously in case Stephen had awakened. Thankfully, he was lying exactly as she'd left him.

In the bathroom, she ran cold water over her hand, but it did little to ease the pain. It was worse than it had ever been before. She shoved a chair under the door, looked out the window to the parking lot. Nothing seemed to be disturbed.

Easing herself onto the bed behind Stephen, she laid down and slowly opened her hand, gently placing it over his bandaged wound. Nothing seemed to be happening and she hoped it wasn't because it wouldn't work through a bandage.

The coolness of his head did ease the burning when the cold water hadn't, so she just laid there, not intending to fall asleep. Knowing that it was already two a.m. made her realize how tired she really was.

CHAPTER TWENTY-TWO

When Dani next became aware of her surroundings, she was alone in the bed and the shower was running. It was still dark outside. No wonder, she thought glancing at the clock; it was only six a.m.

Taking a deep breath, she pulled her hand out from under the covers. It still had a tint of redness and was tender to the touch, but it wasn't burning any more.

For a moment she laid there, thinking she must be dreaming. Could the crystal really heal? Was it possible? Many people believed in healing crystals. But she never heard of one doing it by getting hot like the Blood Crystal. Plus, she'd already experimented on herself when Mays had hit her in the face. You couldn't heal your own body with it. That was totally out of line with what crystals were believed to do.

Stephen's phone ringing brought her out of her musings. She sat up, trying to locate where the sound was coming from and found it in his jeans lying on the end of the bed.

Glancing toward the shower, she shrugged. What the heck, he'd let her answer it before. She took it out of his pocket and checked for an ID number. It was listed as unknown. Flipping it open she said a timid hello into the receiver.

"Dani? Is that you?"

Dani's heart rate accelerated. It was Tom Reierson. "Yeah, it's me. How did you get this phone number?"

"Did you forget I work for AI?"

"No but—"

"Obviously you did since you haven't called. Where the hell are you and why aren't you answering your own cell?"

Dani rubbed a hand over her weary head trying to decide how much she should tell him. "The first thing Deluca did was confiscate my phone."

"No surprise there. Why didn't you call on this one since you're answering it?"

"I—I didn't know if it was secure."

"Trust me—it is. You need to keep in touch and remember I'm here for you."

I'm here for you. Her father's favorite saying. *I'd never do anything to hurt you, honey. You're my favorite girl.*

Reierson voice jarred her from her errant thoughts. "I even called Tony and he said he hadn't heard from you either. We were both worried. Especially with all the news flashes out of LA. And don't let any of those charges distress you. We'll take care of it."

"You called Tony?" she asked.

"Yeah, when I didn't hear from you, I was getting concerned."

"What did he say?"

"He said to leave you alone, you knew how to take care of yourself. And it turns out he was absolutely right. Where are you, Dani?"

"Ohio."

She heard a sigh of relief. "Do you have the crystal?"

"Uh-huh."

There was a hesitation on the line. "Can you talk? Are you alone?"

He'd just given her an out. "No," she said, "I'm not."

"I understand. I'm assuming you're still with Douglas. Can he hear me?"

"No"

"Where in Ohio are you?"

"Classified."

"Good. Listen Dani, you've done a fantastic job. I couldn't be prouder of you. You were so new to the department, I had my doubts about putting you on this project, but so far you've come through with flying colors. Excellent work. I'll meet you in the lobby of the Capital-Lex Hotel where Kendu is staying. I have to tell you he's more than a little anxious. I've been trying to keep him informed, but up to this point, I haven't had anything to tell him. He'll be happy to hear the news. So—you're driving, right?"

The man worked hard at schmoozing her, too hard. "Uh-huh."

"Good. Then if all goes well, you should make it here today yet. You know my number. Call when you get within a hundred miles and I'll be there for you... Oh, and get rid of Stephen Douglas. He's bad news."

Reierson hung up just at the Bad News Boy walked out of the bathroom in naked splendor. The man oozed sexuality. His body, hard all over, had muscles on his muscles. A two day beard enhanced his appeal. A heat surge shot through her like the streak of a rebellious lightning bolt.

Right now he had a questioning look on his strikingly handsome face.

"Reierson," she explained, handing him his phone, her gaze going up and down his very male body.

"He called you on my phone?" Stephen gave a short laugh. "I guess I don't have to ask how he got the number."

"Nope."

"What did he have to say?"

"Among other things, he said I should ditch you, you're bad news."

Stephen's brow shot up. "Did he have any other words of wisdom?"

"I think he said you should get in this bed and screw

my brains out before I get rid of you."

Stephen dropped the towel he had in his hand and covered the four steps separating them. "Well…he's the boss. I think we better accommodate him. So, get your clothes off, baby cakes, we're burning darkness."

Laughing, Dani stood up to undo her jeans. "You do know how to romance a lady." Both her jeans and underpants barely hit the floor when his firm body came against her. He pulled her into his arms and brought his mouth down on her lips with a need so hungry it stole her breath away. She ran her hands greedily over the taut skin on his back and arms. His body was warm and smooth and she couldn't get enough of touching him.

He stepped back long enough to pull her t-shirt over her head, then laid her back on the bed. He was between her legs in an instant, reaching down to touch her.

"Dani, Dani, you are so ready for me. I love that about you. Someday we won't be rushed and I'm going to take my time making love to you." When he pressed into her, filling her with his rigid member, she gasped with pleasure. He started moving against her then stopped, suddenly motionless.

Her heart raced even faster than it had been. She thought he heard something. When he pulled out and reached for his jeans, she panicked.

"What is it?" she whispered.

"I forgot the condom."

She drew her hands up and ran them through her hair. "Oh my gosh, you scared the daylights out of me."

He had the little packet ripped open and he hesitated looking at her. "Would you rather have a baby? Say the word."

"Will you just get that damn thing on and get back here. We can talk about procreating another time."

Stephen chuckled and was back on top of her in three seconds. Then he was back inside of her, moving slow and easy, driving her out of her mind.

He kissed her eyes, her mouth, her cheeks, and worked

his way back to her lips. "Oh honey, you feel so good. You're so tight. So hot. You must have a furnace inside you."

He continued making love to her with his body and his words. She wrapped her legs around him and drew him tighter and closer while his deliberate easy motion brought her to the verge of ecstasy and held her there for longer than seemed possible. She heard herself begging him to end it. His hands came under her, gripping her buttocks and crying out her name over and over when he found his release. The sound he made finally took her over the edge with him.

Her breath was coming in wild frantic gasps, he rolled off of her, giving her air to breathe. "How do you do that?" she managed to whisper.

He moved to his side top look at her. "Do what?"

"Bring me so close and know how to keep me from coming. You're a tease."

He laid back down, his body shaking with laughter. "I have no idea what you're talking about." He reached over and cupped a breast in his hand, first one and then the other. Then he leaned over and kissed each one in turn. Her nipples hardened under his ministrations.

"What are you doing? I can't do this again. My heart won't take it." Even though she said the words, she didn't try to stop him from playing with her.

"I've neglected them," he said. "I didn't want them to get the idea that just because they're small they aren't beautiful, and lovely, and soft, and even when I'm not touching them, they turn me on something fierce."

She could feel them bouncing up and down as she laughed. "You are crazy. You know that, don't you?"

"So I've been told." He bent over and kissed each one quickly followed by a short kiss on the lips. "I hate to boink and run, sweetie, but we need to make tracks before we get company."

She dragged herself out of bed and made for the bathroom, talking over her shoulder. "You are a master lover, Rando. How did you learn your skills?"

"My cousin had a farm in upstate New York and we used to go up and watch the cows do it."

She looked back to see him grinning at her. She picked up his towel and threw it at him. "Reierson was right, you are a Bad Boy. I'll be done in a minute." She left the bathroom door ajar as she took care of business so she could hear him.

"When we get to driving you can tell me the rest of his story."

She peeked out the door talking past her toothbrush. "By the way, how's your head."

He reached up to touch the bandage. "Wow. It feels so good I forgot about it. Of course, I did have a lively distraction. I just remember you rubbing me when I fell asleep. You do have the magic touch."

Dani looked at her hand and then faced herself in the mirror. She didn't want to believe what she was thinking. Maybe the wound wasn't as bad as it looked and that's way he felt so good. And maybe his limp was gone because of all the exercise they'd have. And maybe those cows he watched boinking gave chocolate milk.

* * * *

"Maybe I should drive," Stephen said, watching her get into the driver's seat.

"Absolutely not. You could still have a concussion."

"Okay, fine, boss lady. Be that way."

She pulled out, heading for Interstate 70. "We don't need gas yet. I thought we'd drive an hour or so then stop to eat. We can fill up then."

Stephen glanced in the side mirror and nodded. "Sounds like you've got it under control." He sat back then started sniffing the air. "Is something burning?"

Dani's hands froze on the wheel. Now that he mentioned it she smelled it too.

There was a distinct burnt cloth odor. "I don't smell anything," she lied. "Maybe it's coming from outside. Somebody might be burning trash."

"I don't think so." Stephen continued to sniff the air. He turned around. "I think it's coming from the back seat," he said.

She watched helplessly while he unbuckled his seatbelt, knelt on the seat and search for the source of the smell.

"Here it is," he said, reaching between the seats. "Looks like a cigarette burn that started to get out of control. How the heck did that happen? It's not warm, so we don't need to worry about it." He turned around and rebuckled.

"Now that you mention it, I think I smelled that yesterday when we first got in the car. I was so tired I didn't think anything of it."

"Huh. Funny I didn't notice it then." He shrugged. "Oh well."

Dani allowed herself to breathe slowly so as not to call attention to erratic gasping, which is what she wanted do to.

For the next couple of miles, her mind went over the night before when she'd dropped the crystal on the seat. The burn proved one thing—the crystal had gotten hotter than before. It was the fourth time she'd handled it and this last time she'd had to grip it tighter to make it get red. Was it losing its power or did it react differently because the same person had used it so many times? That was bizarre thinking. It was an object. It couldn't know how many times she personally had squeezed it.

"Do you see that black car behind us?"

She jumped when Stephen spoke. Fortunately, he was looking out the mirror and didn't notice.

She looked in the mirror frowning. "Yeah?"

"It's been following us at a distance since we left the motel."

She turned to stare at him upset with herself for not noticing. "Are you sure?"

"Positive."

"It could be coincidence. Should I slow down and let it catch up?"

"No. You're going the speed limit. Just continue as you are. We'll see what he does when we exit for gas."

"Deluca?"

"Or Mays. Considering the time we wasted running out of fuel and landing in the field and then stopping early because of the rain." He shrugged. "If it didn't take him long to get loose and he had a cell phone in the car, which I didn't check, he could have caught up with us."

"How? How can he know where we are? It wouldn't be by chance that he'd be right behind us."

Stephen shook his head. "I don't know anymore. We got rid of everything that could have had a bug."

"Did he follow us from the motel or after we got out on the interstate?"

"The motel."

"You mean he was out there when we were…"

"Boinking?" he finished for her, grinning.

She felt a rosy flush creep up her cheeks. "If he was there, why didn't he break in?"

"I wish I knew."

Dani took a deep breath and blew it out in a huff. "Maybe it's just someone who stayed there the night and took off the same time we did."

"Yeah. Maybe."

When he laid back to rest his head, she wondered if it was hurting him. He stayed that way for all of two miles before he sat up again. "You were going to tell me about your conversation with Reierson."

Dani made a sound of derision. "First he chastised me for not calling, then he buttered me up big time, telling me what a great job I'd done. He wants me to call him when we're within a hundred miles of D.C. and meet him when I get there in the lobby of Kendu's hotel. Oh yeah, and I need to get rid of you."

Dani didn't tell him about Reierson calling Tony. That would bring up too many questions.

"What are you going to do?"

The fact that he asked her what she wanted to do

endeared him to her like nothing else would have. How many men would allow her make the decision about something so important?

"I haven't decided yet, but I'm thinking, how bad it can be to meet him in the busy Capital-Lex Hotel lobby. Maybe he is on the up-and-up and his only fault is being a sap wanting to take credit for recovering the crystal. I don't care about the credit; I just want to make sure it ends up in the right hands. Anyway, I still have four hundred miles to think about it"

Dani noticed Stephen intermittently staring out at the side mirror as she talked. "Still there?" she asked.

"Uh-huh. He's tuned in to your exact speed. How about we stop on the other side of Columbus for breakfast? It's a big city, maybe we can lose him in the traffic."

"Good idea," she agreed. "I'm glad you're on top of it. I've been a little preoccupied thinking about Reierson's call. You choose when you want me to exit."

They were just about through Columbus when he gave her the go ahead to exit. He turned to watch the ramp behind them a moment then shook his head "I'll be damned, the car whizzed right past without even slowing down."

Dani exhaled a sigh of relief, laughing. "Apparently they're just fellow travelers."

"It would appear so." His words agreed with her but his tone remained doubtful. "Pull in to the Perkins over there." He pointed to a large American flag flapping in the breeze.

Inside the restaurant, they sat at a window where Stephen could keep an eye on the Taurus. Dani had her backpack on the booth beside her. They placed their order, and while they waited for the food to come, Stephen reached across the table and took both of her hands in his.

"I don't know what you're going to do when we get to D.C.," he said. "But I'm behind you all the way. It's been one hell of a ride. And I'm not talking about the 'B' thing this morning."

Dani smiled. "Well...there is that too."

Stephens's penetrating gray eyes settled on her face and he gave her an x-rated, heart-stopping grin. "Have you thought about what you want to do when this is all over?"

Dani felt her face grow warm. She averted her eyes and tried to shrug nonchalantly. "Take a vacation, I guess. Then finish my training."

"With Tony?"

Dani's gaze shot to his face. "I never said I was training with Tony."

Stephen squeezed her hands and released her as the waitress set two plates of omelets in front of them. She refilled their coffee cups and left with only a mildly curious glance at Stephen's bandaged head.

Stephen picked up his fork and stabbed it into his Mexican omelet. "You didn't have to. Somebody gave you intensive expert training and Tony is the only person you've talked about with even a hint of affection. Didn't take much to put two and two together."

Dani avoided his gaze, dumping two packets of sugar in her coffee. "Good with math, are you?" she commented dryly.

He concentrated on his food, taking a moment to answer her. "I'm even better with reading...people. Although," he added, "you are harder than most folks to read."

"Should I be flattered?"

"It's a good asset for being a government agent."

With the subject of Tony behind them, she was becoming amused. "That sounded like a compliment."

Stephen laughed. "You have lots of other assets that have nothing to do with being an agent. You want me to list them?"

Dani rolled her eyes, intent on turning the subject away from her assets. "When we get back to the car, we should check how much cash Deluca and his boys donated to our cause. His wallet was an inch thick."

Stephen smirked. "Does it bother your conscience to

appropriate funds the way you do?"

"Ooh. Big lawyer word."

"Stephen's gaze lifted to her without raising his head. "I'm not really a lawyer," he muttered.

Dani made a tsking sound. "I never believed you were."

At that statement his brows drew together in a frown. "Why not?"

"You aren't..." she shrugged, "suave enough."

"Well, missy, it might surprise you to know that I took all the schooling. I just haven't taken the bar exams."

"Yeah, well, don't bother. You don't have the killer instinct it takes."

Stephen threw his head back and laughed. "Oh, that's rich. I can't wait to tell that one to Virg."

"Jeez, I suppose he is a lawyer."

Stephen was still laughing. "Uh-huh. I can tell you one thing, he's suave enough. He has the kind of looks they put on those romance covers. Women drool over guys like him."

"And I suppose you're going to tell him what I said."

"The first chance I get."

CHAPTER TWENTY-THREE

Stephen was still laughing when they got back to the car. He could tell Dani was trying her best to make him forget the last part of their conversation. It gave him a sudden desire for her to meet Virgil and the rest of his family. With her sense of humor she'd fit right in, and there was little doubt they'd all love her as much as he did.

That thought gave him pause. It was too soon after Nadine to think about loving someone. The word transitional woman came to mind. Is that what Dani was—a transitional encounter?

Wanting to get his mind off that idea, he reached behind him, pulled his duffel forward, and fished out the three wallets Dani had *appropriated*. She watched with interest as he opened Deluca's fat wallet. Sucking in a soft whistle he counted out eighteen hundred dollar bills, three fifties and six twenties, plus a number of fives and ones.

"Holy crap," was all Dani said as he tallied it up.

"Two thousand, ninety six dollars," he announced when he'd finished.

"That doesn't surprise me," Dani said. "With the kind of business he's in, I'd expect nothing less. And I doubt he'd want to leave the kind of trail credit cards provide."

"You're right, no credit cards, just a driver's license and a bunch of business cards. Now this is interesting. His license shows his name as Samuel Morris."

"Not too surprising. I'm sure the man has several aliases."

"I can believe that. He's only forty-nine years old. I thought he was much older."

"Living a life of crime ages you," she said. "Check the other two. I'm curious to see how well he paid his thugs."

"Marty has four twenties and six ones—he's only twenty-one, by the way—and a couple of credit cards. Harry has two hundred and ten dollars—he's twenty-six, no credit cards. I wonder if Deluca knows Harry's license is expired."

"Anything else of interest?"

Stephen, for lack of anything better to do, listed other items he found. As he talked, he pulled two big bills out of Deluca's wallet and stuck them into Marty's.

"What are you doing?" Dani asked.

"Marty's underpaid. Harry gets nothing for beaning me on the head.

Dani burst out laughing. "You're a nut case, Stephen Rando Douglas."

"Hey, I'm just showing you my sensitive side."

When Stephen's phone rang, he tried unsuccessfully to shush her before he opened it. A code came up indicating it was Virgil.

"Hey, bro. what's up?"

"Not my dick, that's for sure. This family shit is wearing me out. All the rest of you leave and I'm left here to deal with these two teenaged senior citizens."

Stephen laughed. "Uh-oh. What's new on the Ma-leaving-Pa front?"

"I took care of it, but just remember, you all owe me big time."

"What did you do? Promise Pa a good looking live-in maid if Ma leaves."

"Huh, I never thought of that. She'd never have left him then."

"See, just cause I'm the youngest son doesn't mean I don't have good ideas. What did you come up with?"

"I bought them a cabin in Minnesota on Sturgeon Lake just a mile from Hunter and Nicole's place. That way they can spend a couple of months in the summer there and have a place to go whenever they visit. I think if Dad gets used to the idea, and does a little fishing out there, he'll start liking it.

"Wow, Virg, that's genius. Ma's good with that scenario?"

Virg chuckled. "So far, but if I hear one word otherwise from her, I'm going to propose your plan."

"Good man."

"I didn't mention the other plus side. If I want to get away from them, I'll just spend some vacation time out there alone. And here's another side. I know that you don't have a place to live when you get back, so you can stay there until you find something. I'm sure it would even be okay if you did it while the folks were there."

"Oh yippee."

"I'm always thinking of you, little buddy. How's it going out there anyway? You still in LA?

"Nope, I'm in Ohio."

"Let me guess—with Ms. Dani Lovato. Or is it Ava?"

Stephen griped the phone, not sure if he wanted to answer that. Virgil interrupted his thoughts.

"One of my business partners just got back from LA. He happened to see your mug shot on TV. Are you in need of a legal counsel?"

"Not at the moment. Don't believe everything you see on television."

"Is the infamous Ms. Lovato there with you?"

Stephen glanced at Dani who he could tell was trying to keep up with the one sided conversation."

"Yup. She's right here. Would you like to speak to her?"

Dani's eyes widened and in the next instant she glared a warning at Stephen. "I can't. I'm driving."

"I hope you heard that," Stephen said, grinning. "She's a real stickler for the law."

"So I've heard."

"Don't believe everything you hear. By the way, if you hear from Nadine, tell her the car is safe at the lodge and I'll get it back to her."

Virgil sent a burst of laughter though the phone. "She already called and said you can keep the piece of crap, but you owe her for a broken window. Oh…and where should she send your girlfriend's jacket?"

Stephen shook his head. "You know, just when you think the worst of somebody, they come around and truly surprise you."

"Neither one of you were ready for marriage. Don't make the same mistake again."

"Oh? Is this advice from the marriage expert?"

"My mission statement is—avoid it at all costs. I gotta go. Take care of yourself, Rando, and watch your back."

When Virgil hung up, Stephen was still shaking his head. He related most of the conversation to Dani. She smiled when he talked about the problems with their parents.

"It must be nice to have a family that sticks together like that."

"We do tend to look out for one another. Although I have to admit the others have been doing a lot more looking out for me than I have for them."

"I suppose because you're the youngest?

"Corrine's a year younger, but she's married with a baby and has a bully of a husband to look out for her."

Dani laughed. "They all sound so interesting. I'd love to meet them someday."

"Maybe you'll get the chance. Didn't you say you were going to take a vacation after this was over?"

"I don't think we're ready for that. Sharing family stories is one thing, meeting them is another."

That reminded Stephen of something. He glanced in the mirror and, satisfied they weren't being followed, decided to broach a subject that had been wearing on him for some time.

"Speaking of sharing family stories," he started. "Don't you think it's time you told me about your father? It's clear you had a love-hate relationship with him from the time your mother died. I'd sure like to understand why."

Dani gripped the steering wheel with one hand and ran the other through her short hair. She inhaled deeply, and by the time she exhaled, he could tell she was ready to talk.

"It's difficult for me, but I guess you've earned the right to hear it all. I'll try to start from the beginning so you can understand my feelings. My parents had a wonderful loving marriage. My father was gone a lot because he did some undercover work, and there were times he couldn't even call home and we couldn't contact him for up to a week at a time. There were some years he was even gone for Christmas and other holidays. We worried about him, but we understood that's how it had to be. She knew he was a cop when she married him, and we had such special times together when he did come home that looking forward to it carried us through."

When she hesitated at that point, Stephen realized the rest was going to be painful for her and he waited for her to go on. She swallowed hard, obviously choking back tears. He wished he'd been the one driving, but maybe that gave her something to focus on.

"A week after mom died, he took me aside and told me he was getting married. I was in shock. I said things to him I wouldn't dare repeat to another human being. By the time I'd finished, I was exhausted, but I'd force the whole truth out of him." She took a deep breath and went on. "He was actually already married. He'd lead a double life for twenty of the twenty-two years he'd been married to my mom. He said he couldn't help it; he loved both women equally."

Stephen stared at her as she wiped tears from her eyes. "That's polygamy. How did he get by with it?"

"The other marriage was done by an Indian shaman. She was Native American. It wasn't a legally recorded marriage, until mom died and then he went through the real ceremony with her. He expected me to accept her as my stepmother."

Stephen leaned back and blew out a long slow draft of air.

After a bit she looked at him. "I can't even begin to tell you how angry I was. How betrayed I felt."

"Your mom didn't know?

"No. But *she* did!"

Stephen could see her hands shaking on the wheel. He wanted to ask more questions, wanted to know if Peter Lovato had children with this other woman, but sensed she had maxed out her ability to talk on this subject and drive safely at the same time.

"Why don't you pull over and let me drive?" he said softly.

"No I'm okay. I—I'd just rather table this subject right now, though."

Stephen smiled. "I'm good with that. I do appreciate you telling me. It explains a lot and I'm glad you trusted me enough to share it."

She gave him a soggy smile. "It actually felt good to get it off my chest. But right now, I need to get my mind on something else."

It had become an automatic reflex for Stephen to eyeball the side mirror every few minutes. This time when he did, he gritted his teeth. "Well, I know just the thing that'll do it."

"What?"

"Our company's back."

Dani's gaze flew to the rear view mirror. "How did they do that?"

"I'd say they know exactly where we're headed and just drove ahead and waited for us at the top of an entrance ramp."

"If you had to make a guess, who do you think it is?"

"Maybe it's your buddy Tony keeping an eye on you."

"Oh, for crying out loud, that's ridiculous. Your head

must be hurting."

"Nope, in fact it feels amazingly good." He touched the bandages on his temple. "I don't understand it either. The bastard hit me hard enough to knock me out. I don't know for how long, but by the looks of the room, they'd had time to go through it. I've seen guys with similar injuries take pain medication for a week." He turned to grin at her. "The only explanation I can think of is you sewing me up with your magic fingers."

"Maybe your brain's too numb to feel pain."

Stephen chuckled. "I have to tell you it really turns me on when you make naughty little comments like that. I suppose it would be too distracting if I kissed you while you were driving."

Dani was unable to hide the smile on her face. "You better busy yourself with something else before we have to pull over and put on a show for our rear view guests."

Grunting, Stephen looked out to confirm that they were still there.

They were. He was thinking he should have some defensc handy.

His duffel still nested at his feet and he reached down to dig out Deluca's gun. His breath caught in his throat. "Holy shitmobile! This is a gold plated Desert Eagle 50 Action Express. That's one rare and expensive weapon. I'll bet he's really pissed.

"You know what?" he said looking at Dani. "If anything, this convinces me it's not Deluca behind us. I don't think the guy who owns this gun would have the patience to hang behind when we bested him at the motel, tied him up, and took what has to be his prized possession. Ordinary Joe Blow thugs don't own gold plated Desert Eagle 50AE's. I've never even seen one outside of a magazine. Throw into the equation the factor that we have the crystal he thinks he owns—this is not a man who would sit back waiting, doing nothing, while we get closer to D.C. where he wouldn't have a chance of getting either back."

Dani sucked her lower lip into her mouth and looked

at him with amused whiskey colored eyes. "Do you realize that sounded like you were giving a closing argument in a court case?"

He gave her a sideways glance. "You think I have the killer instinct after all?"

"No, I think you could have passed your bar exam anytime you wanted to."

He looked at her for a long minute then turned to stare out at the pavement clacking monotonously beneath the car. Finally he said, "I went to school with Nadine for two years. We graduated together and got married four months later. I thought we knew each other pretty well by then. She believed I didn't take the exam when she did because I was afraid I wouldn't pass."

Dani shook her head. "I think you were afraid you *would* pass."

"Unless you're real hungry, I have an idea," Stephen said, looking up from the map he'd been studying. "It's just about noon. Exit at Cambridge like we're going to stop for lunch. Instead of stopping, we'll hop right back on the interstate and get behind our elusive follower. Maybe we can figure out who it is. We should switch places then too. You've been driving since before dawn. I'm perfectly capable of taking over."

Dani's neck and shoulders were aching, so his suggestion sounded like a good idea, at least the switching drivers part.

She eyed the rare canon lying across his lap, chastised herself for the sudden wayward thought, and asked, "What do you propose we do when we catch them."

"Excellent question." He sat thoughtfully for a moment, then said, "If it's Tony, we do nothing." Dani rolled her eyes at that. "If its Mays, we call 911 and report him as a drunken driver. That'll get him off our tail at least. I'd put my money on him. He's basically a chicken-shit coward and just wants to make sure he's there to get his cut when we turn the crystal over to Reierson. To me, that would confirm Mays is in with Reierson thick as fleas on a mangy dog.

"I don't believe it's Deluca, but if it is, you can shoot a tire out. All the more reason to switch places. You're a far better shot with a pistol then I am."

"You trained in special forces. Why would I be a better shot?"

"I'm skilled with big guns. Give me a 50 BMG and I can take the eye out of an elephant at five hindered yards. Of course you wouldn't find hide nor hair of the elephant afterward, but if you did, he'd definitely be missing an eye."

Dani was still laughing when she exited the interstate, pulled over, and dashed around the car to change places with Stephen. He took off, squealing tires, before she had her door fully closed.

"I need to catch him before he exits to wait for us. Get your Beretta in hand— just in case"

She pulled her windbreaker forward and zipped the Beretta out of its pouch. After checking it over, she looked up to see Stephen whizzing past cars at a speed that couldn't have possibly have been within the limits of the law. She glanced at the speedometer noting he was going in excess of ninety miles per hour. She kept an eye on the rearview mirror expecting to see flashing red lights at any given moment.

"There they are!" she bellowed when the black car came in sight. Adrenaline kicked up her heart rate as she gripped the handle of her gun, trying to still the shaking in her hands. Hitting targets, even moving ones, in no way prepared her for shooting out tires at ninety miles an hour. She swallowed hard remembering the Cessna she'd filled with holes. If she could do that expecting the plane to burst into explosive flames, she could do this.

When they got within five car lengths of the black sedan, Stephen slowed down.

"See if you can get a license plate number," he said.

"We're too far away."

She could see Stephen take a deep breath. "Okay, get ready, I'm going to pull up beside him. Catch the license number if you can before we pass."

He'd no sooner got the words spoken when an arm came out the driver's side window. She saw a quart jar size object placed on top of the car, before the arm disappeared back inside. For a heart stopping moment, she'd thought he was going to throw it at them.

Seconds later a red light flashed on the object, a loud siren sounded and the car sped away from them.

Chapter Twenty-Four

They both stared after the car dumbfounded.

"What the hell," Stephen muttered.

"I'll second that," Dani said when she found her voice. "It's an unmarked patrol car. We can't chase after that."

"Certainly can't," she agreed, and then whispering, "Maybe it *is* Tony."

Stephen gave her a hard look. He dug his cell phone out of his pocket and tossed it to her. "Call him."

She hesitated only a second before opening the phone and punching in Tony's number. It rang five times before his voice mail answered asking her to leave a name and number."

"There's no answer," she said. "What's the number to this phone?" She held the cell toward him while he rattled the number off. She repeated it slower, gave her name, and then snapped the cell shut.

"Is there anyone else besides Mays, Deluca, and Reierson wanting to get their hands on this freaking crystal? If there is, I'd like to know about it right now."

His attitude annoyed her but she shared his frustration. "All I know is the Smithsonian offered an undisclosed amount of money for it before it left San Delta. Five men were in charge of bringing it here: two International Affairs agents and three of Kendu's guards. They were all found murdered. The first time it resurfaced was when it leaked out that Deluca was looking for a buyer. I was put on the case because I knew enough about crystals to fake my way into convincing Deluca I could sell it for him. Mays already had Roger working undercover for Deluca so it was a perfect set up when Roger brought me in as his girlfriend. I was able to snow Deluca not only with my knowledge of crystals, but with all the info I'd been supplied on his contacts. If anyone else is involved, I'm in the dark as much as you are."

Stephen must have been mulling her story around in his head because he took a long time to comment. He ran a hand through his hair, accidently brushing on his bandage. "Ouch. Man, I forgot that thing was there." He sighed. "Look, I'm sorry for gripping at you. I guess the frustration got to me there. We might as well stop and gas up in Wheeling and grab a bite to eat, nobody seems to be following us for a change."

They crossed the wide expanse of the Ohio River and took the first exit into Wheeling, West Virginia, where a truck stop café advertized the best trucker's cuisine in the state.

After they filled gas, they parked in front of the wide café windows where they could keep an eye on the car. As they walked toward the café, Stephen carried the atlas under one arm, the other he slung around Dani's shoulders giving her a firm squeeze. "I don't know about you, but I'll be glad when this wild hare's ride is over. I haven't had a full night's sleep since I can't even remember when." He chuckled. "Of course, that started before I even met you."

Dani was glad to see him back to his good-natured self. She slipped her arm around his waist feeling a comfortable familiarity with him. "I'll be glad too. You think we can make it today yet?"

"That's why I brought the atlas in. I do know that the farther east we get, and the closer to D.C., the heavier the traffic will be. I'm gonna see if I can map out a different route to bypass the congested area south of Pittsburg."

In the end, they decided to turn south on 79, and take 68 through Cumberland, Maryland and pick up 70 again at Hancock.

Back on the road, Dani asked again if he thought they could make it to D.C. that day.

Stephen shrugged. "If the miles we've driven today were in the Midwest where we made better time, it wouldn't be a problem, but we'll be running into more traffic the farther east we get. If we did make it to D.C. today, it would be after dark. I've only been there once, and that was in a chauffeured limo and I stayed less than twenty four hours, so I don't know my way around. Can you direct us to this Capital-Lex Hotel at night?"

"I'm not sure. Maybe it is best if we holed up somewhere between here and there and got an early start in the morning. I suppose I should call Reierson and let him know," she added non-too enthusiastically.

"Nah. Let him sweat a while."

Dani snickered. "I like that idea. I'm afraid if I call him, he'll want to drive straight to where we are and pick up the crystal. He'd have no qualms about driving anywhere within a two hundred mile radius of D.C."

Dani laid her head back and closed her eyes. She wasn't tired enough to sleep, but getting away from the wheel and just resting felt good. It gave her time to think. Mostly about Stephen and her feelings toward him. Was she falling in love with a man who'd be gone the minute the crystal was turned over to Bama Kendu? She was sure he'd stick around until then, out of curiosity if nothing else. He'd never talked about love and neither had she. Were they being cautious or realistic?

They had a nice fling. In spite of being pursued, they'd had some wonderful, memorable nights together. She was suddenly glad they were stopping short of D.C. That would give them one more night. Would it be time to discuss their relationship, or would it be best to accept the inevitable and part ways as friends who'd been a little more than friends? No, a lot more.

About the time Stephen turned south on 79, Dani remembered something Stephen had said earlier.

She sat up and looked at him. "You mentioned you'd been in D.C. only once for twenty-four hours. Why were you there?"

Stephen frowned, shifting in his seat as though he were uncomfortable with the question. "Some of the guys went there when we came stateside after Afghanistan."

When he didn't elaborate, Dani sensed he'd said all he wanted to say on the subject. She thought about it a moment, remembering something his brother Virgil had said the first time she talked to him.

"You received your Purple Heart there didn't you?"

He shrugged indifferently. "Yeah."

"Why don't you want to talk about it?"

"It wasn't a happy time. I'd just found out Nadine had left me and why. My leg was hurting, and I had to hobble up with a cane in to the front of a podium to meet the President. I guess I should have been grateful. I was the only one on my feet. The other two came in wheelchairs. The worst of it was I just didn't feel like I deserved it. I didn't do anything any one of the other guys wouldn't have done. As far I'm concerned, every one of those guys over there are heroes. I wasn't comfortable being singled out to receive a medal."

"If you don't want to talk about it, I understand," Dani said empathetically.

He shook his head. "I do want to tell you so you understand why I'm not a hero."

"Okay, but I reserve the right to make up my own mind."

He chucked her under the chin, smiling. "Just one of the reasons I—like you."

For a second there, she thought he was going to say the L word.

"There were six of us going into this large mountain mansion that was supposed to be deserted. The only way you could get to it was by helicopter. We were working our way through the building in turns, watching each other's backs." Stephen's Adam's apple bobbed for a moment before he went on. "When the shooting started, I was in the middle. The two guys in front of me were killed instantly. I knew I'd been hit because I went down, my leg on fire with pain and blood pumping out of my body like a badly leaking faucet. Brad threw himself on top of me while the other two guys took out the three shooters. Two guys died, two eliminated the enemy, and Brad saved my life. He was the only one among us who'd had medic training. Those five men were the real heroes. I didn't do anything to help anybody"

Dani blinked at the moisture pooling in her eyes. "What about the helicopter missions you flew. How many men did you fly out of harm's way before that day?"

Stephen shrugged as though that was incidental, then reached over and squeezed her knee. One side of his face kicked up in a lopsided grin. "You do know how to make a man feel better, in more ways than one. I don't know if I've told you, but my leg has been pain free since that night in Storm Lake when we made love the first time."

"No. You haven't mentioned that," she murmured. She had to tell him about the crystal before they got to D.C. He'd probably still be angry, but it would be worse if the truth came from another source.

She sat back trying to think of the best way to tell him. Should she just blurt it out, show it to him, or broach the subject slowly. *By the way Stephen, I've been lying to you. You've been risking your life to save a fifty dollar piece-of crap-glass.* Oh yeah, that would go over big.

While she was contemplating her options, something else occurred to her. Stephen giving her flying lessons all but insisting she know what to do if something happened to him. She began to think he'd left out part of his story.

"If you were hurt, who flew the copter out?"

The look he gave her suggested he'd finished with the subject and didn't want to go back to it. But he shrugged and answered, "There are usually at least two guys who can pilot."

"Was one of them killed?"

Stephen frowned at her. "Why are you asking?"

"Just a hunch. Who flew the copter off that mountain, Stephen?"

His fingers worked on the steering wheel flexing and unflexing. With gritted teeth, his mouth tightened and remained closed.

"You did, didn't you?"

He took a long time to answer. "My pain was so intense I barely remember. I was able to lift off, but lost consciousness before we landed."

"But in that time I'd bet you gave someone else instructions on how to do it."

He gave her a weak smile. "I didn't do a very good job. We had a rocky landing and the copter sustained quite a bit of damage, but at least nobody was seriously injured."

Dani through her hands in the air. "I rest my case."

"Maybe you should be the lawyer," Stephen groused. "Or is psychiatry your chosen field." As though looking for something else occupy his mind, she saw him glance in the rear view mirror as he'd been doing since they'd ditched the black sedan, or rather since it ditched them. She assumed all was clear when he turned his eyes back on the road.

Dani reached up and brushed his wayward curl off his forehead then ran her fingertips down the side of his stubbled face. "You've saved my butt more than once, Rando. In my book, you have the makings of a hero whether you want to accept it or not."

He grasped her fingers and placed a kiss in the palm of her hand. A tingle raced from that sensitive part of her, coursing through her body, settling with heated moisture pooling between her legs.

"I seem to remember," he commented, squeezing her hand and releasing it. "That you saved my rear a couple of times too. Maybe we make a good pair."

Dani smiled. "Maybe we do. But..."she said, holding

up her index finger to emphasize an important point. "You did it all for me and the crystal with no agenda of your own." She took a deep breath. Maybe now was the time to tell him. He interrupted her thoughts.

"I have a confession to make," he said. "You jumping in my car, you and your crystal brought me out of a chilling depression. Didn't you wonder why I wasn't scared when you pressed your gun in my back?"

"I thought it was because you knew I wouldn't have the guts to pull the trigger."

He raised an eyebrow at her. "How the hell would I know that? At first I didn't even know you were a woman and you seemed pretty serious to me."

She grinned. "Really?"

Her surprise brought a laugh out of him. "Really. Anyway, what I told you about Nadine was only a half truth. It was a lot more than her leaving me that sent me on a drinking binge. I was more angry than hurt. If she'd asked me for a divorce, I'd have said yes in a heartbeat. I knew I didn't love her, probably never had. It was the way she went about it, getting pregnant and worst of all, taking my car." He stopped talking seeming to be arranging his thoughts.

"Coming home from war, where every day your life is on the line, is tough. I couldn't even walk down a residential street without looking over my shoulder, expecting to be taken out at any given minute. It takes a long time to let it go. I had no job to go back to, but I couldn't have concentrated on work if I'd wanted to. Nadine had given up our apartment, so I had no place to live. Being around my family didn't seem to be an option since I wasn't ready to deal their sympathy and heroic admiration. My brothers, thank god, didn't treat me that way so much, but the women— I love every one of them to the ends of the earth, but they're too...hovering...natural born caretakers every one of them. I'm not knocking that female trait; I just wasn't ready to be hovered over."

"Because you were ill at ease about the hero worship."

"Yeah, that was the biggest part of it. When I met you and you didn't cut me any slack, I started feeling like my old self again." He gave a short laugh. "I had a reason to watch over my shoulder without feeling paranoid."

Stephen's cell phone rang and he nodded at her to go ahead and answer it. The caller ID was unidentified. That was the trouble dealing with a government agency, their phone numbers never showed up.

Dani opened the phone and said hello. It was Tony. "Tony, where are you?"

"Traveling. Sorry I've been out of touch, but I was in a tight situation and I had to leave my cell behind. Was your mission successful?"

Dani smiled proudly. "Sure was, it's been a bitch though. I told Reierson we'd make it this afternoon but traffic was a nightmare. We should be in D.C. tomorrow morning. Tom wants to meet us at the Capital-Lex were Kendu is staying. I thought it might be a good idea if you could be there too."

"I don't know if I can make it. I'm not in D.C. right now. You keep saying 'we', who's with you?"

"I sorta picked up a companion along the way."

"I guess I'd know about that if I hadn't been out on assignment. Just be careful who you trust, Dani."

She glanced at Stephen and grinned. "Don't worry, he's okay."

"Did you frisk him?"

"Classified."

Tony's hearty laughter filled her ear. "Let me know where you're staying. I should be near my phone for the next few hours. If you want, I can send somebody to bring you in."

"Thanks, but I think we have it under control."

"I fully intend to check out this classified guy when you get here."

"I didn't expect otherwise."

His laughter was cut off when he hung up.

* * * *

At six o'clock they crossed the border into West Virginia and took a shortcut to Interstate 68. Forty-five minutes later, they were in Maryland. A green highway sign told them they were two hundred miles from Washington D.C. and forty from Cumberland. Behind them, the sun dipped below the horizon, offering a spectacular red sunset.

"My stomach is growling," Dani said.

"Man, that's a relief. I thought there was something wrong with the car. What say we stop in Cumberland and have Deluca buy us a relaxing supper at a decent restaurant? We'll get the motel first so we can clean up a bit. We can take off early in the morning and be in D.C. by ten o'clock."

"I'm all for that. I just hope we don't have visitors again."

"Yeah, me too."

"I have a thought," Stephen said suddenly. "We have money now. Let's each get a room—preferably adjoining. If one of our fans shows up, we can vacate to the other room. I'm convinced Deluca has a picture of one or both of us and bribed a clerk to get our room number last night. I don't understand how it's possible we can still be followed, but the black sedan indicates someone still knows how to find us."

Dani nodded her agreement but her mind went back to the black sedan. Is it possible it was Tony? He said he was out on assignment. Was he following them? To keep them safe or…giving herself a mental shake, she shuddered. Not Tony, she trusted him. She couldn't handle one more person she cared about betraying her. She refused to even consider it.

* * * *

In Cumberland they stopped at a Motel 8 near the interstate. Stephen went in first and came out with a key card and a map showing his room number 112 on the end.

"Try to be inconspicuous," he said. "Make up one of your monotonous stories about why you need to be in room

111. Hell, tell him you're superstitious or whatever—

Dani's back went ramrod straight in mock annoyance. "What do you mean monotonous?"

"I mean don't use one of your usual obnoxious tales. You'd rather he didn't remember you."

While she was gone, Stephen surveyed the parameter. It was a fairly large three story motel with an expansive well-lit parking lot. No sign of the black sedan or any other vehicle with people waiting in it. There were a couple of pickups with trailers parked on the side away from the building, along with three semi-trailer rigs farther down, and a car towing a small U-haul. Other than that, all the vehicles were parked up against the building, which had at least ten empty spaces. He made a mental note trying to memorize as much of his surroundings as he could.

Dani came out and jumped in the car which he'd park out of view from the office. She looked as pleased as Garfield the cat with bird feathers hanging from his mouth. He groaned. She held up her key card.

"Bingo."

"What did you tell him?" Stephen asked suspiciously starting up the car.

"Well," she said going into her southern drawl. "I didn't even have to tell him what room number I wanted. I just told him my eleven-year-old daughter had a goal every year to sleep in a room with her age in the number. Then I asked if I had to pay extra for her and her six-year-old sister."

"I don't know why I was giving you instructions. You are one clever woman."

Stephen reached over and pulled her toward him giving her a long kiss. Her arm slipped around his neck pulling him even closer.

"I'm really not that hungry for food," she whispered when he drew back.

"Liar. For the last fifty miles, your stomach's been making more noise than farmer Flinn's John Deere tractor. I don't want you passing out on me while I'm having my way with you."

Stephen liked the rosy flush that tinted her cheeks and the way her lips blossomed every time he kissed her. Even earlier, the first couple of times when she'd behaved affronted. Even then he knew she liked it as much he had. In fact, he liked everything about her. But did he love her? He'd already suspected, some time ago, the answer to that question was yes.

Transitional woman or not, he loved her. Probably from the moment she first stepped out of the bathroom pointing her Beretta at him when he'd called the man he thought was her father. After he'd broken down her defenses, she opened up to him like a flower, even telling him about her father. He still didn't know Tony's involvement in her life, but he was sure when the crystal was back in Kendu's hands, she'd be free to tell him everything.

She'd said she wanted to take a vacation. He'd already made up his mind to invite her back to Virgil's cabin after the skull was delivered. Providing his parents weren't there.

"I'm going to call Tony back and let him know where we're staying," she said, interrupting his thoughts.

"What about Reierson".

"Maybe I'll just let him sit at the Capital-Lex and wait."

Stephen chuckled. "Would serve him right. I don't recall ever disliking a man I've never met so intensely."

"I had a similar feeling after I met him. I'm going to walk to the room so we don't appear to be together. We can each enter our separate rooms, then open the door between us. I'll call Tony while I'm walking." She picked up Stephen's cell phone along with her backpack and stepped out of the car.

He watched her go punching in Tony's number as she walked. She put the phone to her ear a moment then started talking. Not being able to hear what she was saying made him wary. He'd have asked her to talk in front of him, but she'd likely think he didn't trust her. It wasn't her he didn't trust, it was Tony. Stephen was curious as to why she wouldn't explain who Tony was, other than her trainer. There was something involving the man she wasn't willing to share. Why the secrecy? Even if Stephen didn't trust Tony, he should trust Dani's instincts. They'd been very good up to this point. If Dani trusted the man, he decided, putting the car into gear when she disappeared inside her room, he should too.

Maybe.

He parked up against the motel but kept a three car distance from his room. Grabbing his duffle bag and the pillowcase Dani had stuck the clean clothes in; he shoved Deluca's Desert Eagle under the driver's seat and headed for his room.

He tossed his stuff on the bed and unlocked the adjoining door. Dani's was already open. She was in the bathroom and he thought about interrupting whatever she was doing, but knew it would only stall going out to eat. And he was hungry enough to eat out of a McDonalds dumpster.

He quickly washed up in his own bathroom, the luxury of having two rooms, took a look as his two-day beard stubble and made the decision to shave later. The bandage at the side of his temple seemed to be holding fine with only a few spots of blood so he decided best to leave it undisturbed. Dani could look at it later with her magic fingers.

That thought brought another smile on his face. It seemed every time he thought of her he was smiling to himself. He then pulled clean jeans, t-shirt and a pair of underwear out of the pillow case and replaced them with the ones he was wearing. Zipping open his duffle bag to find his toothbrush, he was faced with a jumbled mess. He remembered Deluca and Harry emptying it out on the bed searching for the crystal and Dani shoving everything back into it while he sat on the sidelines nursing his throbbing head.

Dani still hadn't appeared from her side so he dumped

it out on the bed. The first thing he noticed was the small arsenal. He set aside the four weapons they'd confiscated from Harry and Marty, two in Utah and two the night before, and took a mental inventory. Counting Deluca's over sized Eagle in the car, Mays' Glock in Dani's knapsack, plus her Beretta, they had a collection of seven pistols—enough to supply a small army. He picked out the best of the four guns from the goons, checked the ammo supply and the safety, and shoved it in the waistband of his jeans.

He wrapped the rest of the weapons in a small towel from the bathroom, emptied the pillowcase, leaving Dani's things on the bed and put his dirty clothes back in the pillow case and started refilling his duffle.

He looked up noticing a movement from the adjoining door and saw Dani wearing a towel and a grin. She didn't say a word, just picked up her clean clothes and vanished back into her room. Chuckling, he speculated, even in Afghanistan where water was often in short supply, he couldn't take a shower as fast as she did. He also knew it wouldn't take her but five more minutes to be ready. Not a typical woman by any means, and that was an understatement if ever there was one. There was nothing typical about Danielle Lovato.

Stephen made haste brushing his teeth and came back to finish stuffing the last of his things in his duffle. He'd just about finished when a small beaded bag caught his eyes.

CHAPTER TWENTY-FIVE

Carrying her backpack with her jacket tucked inside, Dani walked into Stephen's room ready to go. Her gaze fell on the object in his hand and she froze, her backpack dropping to the floor at her feet. Too late and too shocked to formulate any kind of ignorance plan, Stephen looked up and saw her expression.

His narrow gaze never left her face as he spoke.

"Where did this come from?"

"I—" She wanted to say she didn't know, but the words wouldn't come out. With the bed separating them, he waited, holding the Blood Crystal bag, a stark glare fixed on her. A lump rose to her throat, rendering her speechless. She couldn't even begin to think of an answer he'd accept other than the truth.

Dani swallowed, drew a breath from the depths of her soul and found the courage to speak.

"It's the original bag the crystal came in."

"How did it get in my duffle bag?"

"Deluca must have had it and I shoved it in there when I picked everything else up."

He finally took his eyes from her to examine the bag. "Okay," he said drawing the word out as though warning her not to lie to him. "When did your crystal *skull* move from this lovely bag to the cheap velvet one it's in now?"

When she averted her eyes, he came around the bed

like a pouncing tiger. She backed up a step, but he didn't touch her. He stopped within three feet of her.

"Look me in the eye, Dani, and tell me the truth."

She blinked rapidly at the moisture pooling in her eyes as she lifted her head and faced him. "I'm sorry."

"What exactly are you sorry for, Dani?" He voice was calm and brittle, thick with barely controlled fury.

"The skull isn't the real crystal."

His brow rose and, for just a second, it seemed like he couldn't speak.

"I'm going to ask just one time," he said through clenched teeth, "and if I even suspect you're not telling me the truth, I'll be out that door, and you can call your precious Tony to come and get your lying little ass and your fucking crystal, and I never want to see your face again." He stopped long enough to let his words sink in and take a breath. "Where is it?"

Dani resisted the urge to back away from him. "In the car."

He clearly didn't believe her. "Well, why don't we just go out and get it?" He flung the beaded bag on the bed and stepped aside to let her pass, probably expecting her to bolt. She suspected he wouldn't bother coming after her if she did.

She put her chin in the air, walked out the door and stopped. He pointed to where he'd parked the car aimed the remote keypad at it and unlocked the doors.

She walked to the car, telling herself she'd kept the truth from him because it was her job. She knew it was the wrong time to bring that up as she opened the back door, reached between the seats and pulled out the paper bag holding the crystal. She turned around and walked ahead of him back to the room trying to decide if she should warn him about what it could do if he squeezed it.

She didn't get a chance. He slammed the door shut behind him and snatched the bag out of her fingers. He'd dropped the heart shaped crystal in his hand before she could say a word.

Holding it by his fingertips, he turned it over in his hand, scowling." This looks like another piece of shit glass. Where are you hiding the real one?"

That suspicion raised her ire and she couldn't resist. "Squeeze it," she snapped.

His expression was still doubtful as he wrapped his long finger around it and squashed it with pulverizing force.

"Ouch, hot damn, son-of-a-bitch." He dropped the blood red crystal to the floor where it pulsed three times and returned to its original translucent state. He stared at his hand in disbelief while she bent down, picked up the crystal and slipped it back in the paper bag. She laid it on the bed then opened his hand to examine the degree of the burn. It was only slightly worse than the first time she'd squeezed it and that was probably because he'd tried to grind it into dust. Now she knew for sure, it burned hotter each time the same person handled it.

"You better go run some cold water on that," she said.

He ignored her and grabbed her hand. The same one she'd used to rub the wound on his head. It was still a little pinkish as she opened it for him to see.

"That's how you burned your hand."

"Yes. And that's why it's called the Blood Crystal."

"But it doesn't explain why you chose to make a fool out of me. I risked my life to save a worthless hunk of glass."

She thought about telling him she'd paid fifty bucks for it so it wasn't exactly worthless, but suspected he wouldn't appreciate her humor.

By way of explanation she told him the truth. "My mission was to get the Blood Crystal back to Kendu. I bought the skull in Las Vegas thinking that if I showed it to you and you accepted it, you wouldn't know about the real one and I could trust you."

"Obviously that wasn't enough to gain your trust, or you would have told me about it by now. I guess I'll have to ask *Tony* how a man goes about getting that rare commodity from you.

"I'm going to go eat. If you want to come with me, fine, otherwise you can find a place to eat by yourself." He stepped behind her and locked the adjoining doors, then turned and strode out of the room, clearly willing to make good on his word to leave her behind.

Panic gripped her. She the seized the crystal, stuck it in one of the pockets of her clean cargo pants. Securing the button, she grabbed her backpack and hurried after him.

When she got in the car, he stepped back out and she thought he'd changed his mind about letting her come along. She watched as he opened the motel door that had locked behind her, put something up in the far corner of the door and carefully closed it. It was a common trick to find out if someone disturbed your room while you were gone. He came back to the car and all but demanded her key card. She dug it out of her pocket and handed it to him. This time she saw him bend down and pick up a leaf before he walked over and did the same thing to her door. Returning, He tossed her key card in her lap, started the car and backed out.

Neither one of them spoke while he drove, the silence in the car copious. Dani sensed anything she said would only anger him further. She missed the camaraderie they'd shared and feared she'd destroyed it forever. He continued to ignore her, didn't bother asking where she'd like to eat, and made no attempt whatsoever at conversation. She hated his cold shoulder treatment and took comfort only in the fact that he'd asked her to come along, or rather told her she could if she wanted to, making it clear he didn't care one way or another if she did or not.

She could think of only one thing that might bring him around.

He stopped at an Applebee's restaurant about half a mile from their motel. There he got out of the car, didn't bother waiting for her, but stood by the door letting her enter the restaurant ahead of him. She suspected his mother's training forbade him to do otherwise.

They were shown to a booth where Stephen immediately requested a glass of ice water. The waitress showed up with their menus and his requested water. She wasn't surprised when he took a spoon, dipped ice out of the glass and placed it in his hand. He looked up and noticed her watching him, then gave her an accusatory glare that said this was all her fault for telling him to squeeze the crystal.

She was one step away from losing any sympathy for him. The only thing that stopped her was the knowledge that this *was* her fault. He did, however, involve himself when he took money from Mays to *rescue* her.

They placed their orders and ten more minutes of silence went by while he silently tended to his hand. She couldn't stand it any longer and she finally blurted out the words that would get his attention.

"Tony's my brother."

His blue-gray eyes bored into her. "You made a point of telling me you were an only child, or was that just another lie?"

"Half a lie." she said, wanting to smile, but didn't. "He's my half-brother. Dad had a love child with his *other* wife. Peter Lovato is listed as the father on Tony Lovato's birth certificate." Stephen didn't comment so she continued. "When Dad died, what little he had went to his current wife. After she died of a massive heart attack two months later, I went to a lawyer to find out what was happening to the estate, and that's when I found out about Tony. As his mother's only child, he was entitled to inherit everything she had. I packed up and drove to D.C. to have it out with my greedy conniving half-brother."

She stopped talking when the waitress brought their food. When she left, Dani tried to read Stephen's face, but it was a blank mask as he cut into his rare steak. Apparently, her painful disclosure meant nothing to him. She sighed and picked up her fork to start in on her oriental salad.

Dealing with his injured hand, Stephen unwrapped his

baked potato, slathered it with sour cream, and took another bite of steak before he spoke. "So what did your illustrious half-brother do to gain your favor?"

Dani didn't much like his attitude, but at least he was talking. Between bites, she went on with her story. "He started out by asking me if my mother and I were happy with our lives before she died. When I admitted we were, he said they were too. Then he wrote out a check for half of everything he inherited and asked me to be a real sister to him. He explained that he was an innocent bystander just as I was, and since neither of us had any other family, he wanted us to stick together. He had a two bedroom apartment, so I moved in with him and he started training me to be an agent."

She watched him trying to eat with his sore hand and wished she could find a way to alleviate his pain, going so far as to look around the restaurant for anyone with a visible injury. Crazy thinking, she told herself. She wasn't even sure if touching another wound would help his hand, but it was the only thing she could think of to do. Besides, it gave her something to concentrate on since Stephen had gone back to giving her the silent treatment.

"How long are you going to stay mad at me?" she asked finally.

"It's not a matter of how long, Dani. Maybe you and I are two of a kind. You admit being happy with your father until you found out he had a fault you couldn't forgive. That's how it is for me right now. I was good enough to risk my life for you but not good enough to be told why. You betrayed me, and like you with your father, I may never be able to let it go."

Dani choked back tears refusing to cry. Ironically, his words made sense. "Is that how it is with your ex-wife?"

Stephen shook his head. "No, I can forgive Nadine because I never loved her." He picked up the tab and left the table.

* * * *

They rode in oppressive silence back to the room.

Stephen had decided he'd stay with Dani until they reached D.C. and she'd turned her crystal over to Kendu. Then he'd drive the Taurus back to Marion, Indiana, pick up his plane, and head for Minnesota. Maybe take his brother up on the offer to stay at his lake cabin. His parents likely wouldn't be there with the cool weather September tended to bring to the northern states. The last thing he needed right now was a hovering mother.

The first thing Stephen noticed when he pulled into the motel parking lot was all the spots near the building were taken. Business must have picked up in the hour they were gone. He pulled up beside the car with the U-haul.

"Maybe you should stay here while I check the rooms," he said.

Dani shook her head adamantly. "No, this is my mess. You stay here and I'll check."

He made a rude sound and mumbled. "I may have lost something today, but I can assure you it wasn't my brain."

When she grabbed her jacket and got out of the car, he followed, mentally shrugging. This was her mess. Let her go.

Ten feet from his motel door he stopped. The corner of the motel receipt he's stuck in the door was gone. Unless the wind blew it out, there was someone in the room. More important, he could have sworn he saw the curtain move.

Turning quickly, he put a finger to his lips motioning Dani to silence. He pulled out his gun and dipped behind the cars heading for her room. He couldn't believe what he was seeing. The leaf he'd stuck in her door was gone too.

"How the hell did they find us again?"

"The beaded bag," Dani said. "We left in such a hurry, I forgot the beaded bag in the room. There must have been a bug in it."

Stephen didn't have time to think about what she was saying. The door to his room was flung open and Harry stood there. Behind him, Deluca's voice bellowed out, "Marty's behind you and he has a gun on you, Douglas. Lay the crystal on top of the car in front of you, walk away, and nobody gets hurt."

At that moment, the door to Dani's room opened.

"Don't do it," Reierson yelled from the protection of Dani's room. "She's working for me. And I've got five federal officers with guns trained on your door." He motioned to Stephen and Dani to come in.

"Like hell you do," Deluca shouted. "It's probably you and your idiot sidekick trying to get the crystal for yourselves."

Stephen noticed Dani had her Beretta in her hand. They both looked around trying to see if either Deluca or Reierson were telling the truth. Stephen didn't see any movement behind them at all. He looked at Dani and she confirmed by shaking her head. But if they were in the line of fire, they had no cover whatsoever.

"I'm a federal agent," Reierson said.

Deluca laughed. "Up my ass, Reierson. If you have five agents, have one of them show himself."

"I don't have to do that."

"Show him we mean business," Deluca hollered out the door.

A shot blasted from behind Stephen and Dani. The window in Reierson's room shattered.

Reierson swore profusely. "You just fired at a federal marshal, Deluca. And you're under arrest."

"Come and get me, asshole. You and your five officers."

"Maybe we should just sneak out of here and let them shoot it out," Stephen whispered.

"How? Marty's behind us somewhere."

"If he'd have wanted to shoot us, he'd already have done it. I'm sure he has instructions to keep us alive until Deluca gets what he wants."

Dani was breathing heavily, but she shrugged. "Same goes for Reierson—unless he really is here to save us."

"Hah. That's interesting since he's planning to be in D.C. tomorrow to meet you. He had my cell phone number. If he wanted to meet us here, he could have called. I'm going to go first, follow me if I make it."

He was off running before Dani could tell him she should go first because they were less likely to shoot her. Before she even had the thought fully processed in her head, another shot rang out and the window in Deluca's room shattered. This time she was facing the rear and saw approximately where the shooter was. Not the same angle Marty's shot had come.

Another shot split the night and she saw Stephen drop to his knees ten feet short of their car. Dani screamed his name and fired four rapid shots in the spot where she'd seen the flash of the gun. Then she ran. Stephen was crawling toward the car, obviously hit. She had almost reached him when another loud blast sounded, closer this time. A searing pain tore into her side. Gasping for breath and clutching her bleeding side she took five more steps, enough to reach Stephen and fell almost on top of him. He grabbed her, rolling her over to, shield her body with his.

An arsenal of gunfire suddenly exploded around them, seeming to be coming from all directions. Dani gritted her teeth against the burning in her side. Tears flowed freely as she prayed Stephen wasn't being riddled with bullets.

The next minute everything was quiet until a voice boomed through a bull horn.

"THE WHOLE LOT OF YOU ARE UNDER ARREST, COME OUT WITH YOUR HANDS BEHIND YOUR HEADS."

It was Tony's voice coming from the same spot where the flare of gunfire had come from. The shots that had taken her and Stephen down. Tony. Tony had shot them. It was the ultimate betrayal. That was her last thought before she passed out.

Chapter Twenty-Six

Stephen felt Dani go limp in his arms. He called her name, frantically feeling for a heartbeat. With shaking hands and his own heart pounding in his ears, he was unable to detect anything on her. She looked pale as death. He saw the blood seeping from her side and quickly pressed his trembling hand over the wound, trying to stop the life from pouring out of her. Sirens screamed in the distance.

He wasn't sure what was happening, but he saw four men laying face down on the ground being handcuffed. The largest one he recognized as Deluca. A fifth man laying about ten feet away had men attending to him. Stephen was only mildly aware of the pain in his leg when he realized someone was trying to pull Dani out of his arms. He held her tight refusing to give up her body.

"Stephen, let go," a voice demanded. "This man is a medic."

Stephen looked up into the whiskey colored eyes of a dark-haired man trying to pry Stephens's arms away from Dani.

"It's okay," the man said. "I'm her brother, Tony. We'll take care of her. And you too. You took a shot in the leg."

The siren on the ambulance died as it pulled up beside them. Stephen released Dani into their care. He watched, not daring to breathe as they worked on her. The next thing he knew, she was lifted on a stretcher and put in the waiting ambulance. When he tried to get to his feet, pain shot up his lower right leg.

"I'm going with her!" he demanded.

Tony offered his shoulder for Stephen to lean on as he hopped to the ambulance.

Blood seemed to be everywhere, his hands, Dani's clothes, the sheet covering her. He collapsed to a seat, watching with suffocating numbness as the medics worked over her. The sound was like a drum beating in his head when the doors slammed shut. His concentration was fixed on Dani, looking for any sign that she was breathing. Everything was a blur like he was looking from beneath the water. He rubbed his arm across his eyes, tasting salt. That's when he realized the moisture was leaking from his eyes.

"How…how is she?" he managed to choke out. "Is she breathing?"

"She's breathing," one of them, a young fellow barely past peach fuzz, answered.

Stephen sagged back against the metal wall taking comfort in the fact that she was alive at least.

He was only vaguely aware of the kid cutting his pant leg. His injury was on the side of his leg about three inches below the knee and, according to the kid, didn't look too deep. He felt a sharp sting the kid said was to sterilize the wound before he wrapped a snug bandage around it.

"Do you need something for pain?" the kid asked.

"Yeah" he whispered. "I need her to move.

"She should be all right," he said. "Probably nicked a rib but doubtful the bullet hit a lung, since she's breathing fine. Does the injury on your head need attention?"

"No," Stephen murmured, "a miracle worker took care of it."

The kid made a comment Stephen didn't hear over the wail of the siren and went back to work with the other medic on Dani. A few minutes later, they stopped in the emergency entrance of the Cumberland Memorial Hospital. When Stephen tried to follow her gurney inside, they asked if he was her husband. When he said no, they directed him to a cubicle to have his leg stitched up. An RN appeared shortly and asked him who her next of kin was. He had an overwhelming urge to say he'd changed his mind, that he was her husband after all, but feared they might have called the guys in the white coats to test his sanity, which right now, was borderline anyway.

He was refusing to let them work on his leg, explaining he wanted to be with Dani instead when Tony walked in talking on a cell phone. Tony must have seen the frantic look on Stephen's face because he hung up his phone and said, "She went in to surgery, but they assured me she'll be fine. Tony put a hand on Stephen's shoulder, his other hand he held out in greeting.

"Hello, I take it you're the classified man, Stephen Douglas; I'm Tony Lovato, Dani's brother."

In the dimly lit parking lot, Stephen hadn't gotten a good look at Tony. Now he stared at the striking man with dark Native American looks and eyes the exact amber color as Dani's. Peter Lovato must have been one handsome dude to produce such attractive offspring.

Stephen stuck a hand out, but instead of connecting with Tony Lovato's, he stopped and stared at the blood stains on the palm of his hand. Dani's blood. Tony must have understood.

"So," Tony said, "how long have you been in love with my sister?"

That brought Stephen back to reality. He completed the hand shake realizing at the same time that his hand didn't hurt anymore. Just an hour ago he could barely grip his gun with his right hand. "We're...just friends."

"Uh-huh. Well, you best let the doc take a look at your leg. There's nothing you can do for Dani right now. I'll go in and keep vigil while you get fixed up, then you can come in and join me and we'll have a little talk."

"I want to know what happened out there tonight.

Who the hell was shooting at us?"

"I'll tell you as soon as you let them take care of your leg."

Stephen swore then and yelled at a passing nurse wanting to know what was taking so long.

* * * *

Stephen hobbled into the surgery waiting room with a crutch positioned under his right arm. Tony was on his phone again. When Stephen plopped down on a chair, Tony ended his conversation and sat down across from Stephen with a wide magazine-littered coffee table between them.

"How's the leg?" Tony asked.

"Fine, now tell me about—"

"Is it the same one you had injured before?"

"No…how did you know about that?"

"I'm very protective where my sister is concerned."

Stephen rolled his eyes then closed them, inhaled twice, and started counting to ten. He made it to three.

"Fine. I don't give a crap what you know about me. I have nothing to hide. Have you heard anything about Dani?"

"She's only been in there thirty-five minutes."

"I guess that would be a no then. Tell me what you know about what happened in that parking lot tonight."

Tony pulled a notebook and pen out of his pocket. "Let's start with what you know and I'll try to fill in the gaps."

"I suppose that's the only way I'm going to get anything out of you, isn't it."

"Uh-huh."

"Asshole," Stephen muttered.

When Tony wrote something in his notebook, Stephen swore. "What the hell did you write down?"

"Today's date."

Annoyed as Stephen was with this guy, there was something about the man he liked. Then he realized Tony's method of questioning reminded him of sparing with Dani. The next thing that came to mind was they grew up separately with the same father raising them. The only explanation was they both took after their father. That gave Stephen something to admire about Peter Lovato. Plus, many men couldn't keep one wife content. How the hell did Peter Lovato manage to keep two women happy—at the same time?

Tony interrupted his musing. "Why don't you just start with what happened tonight from the time you arrived in Cumberland?"

Stephen had already come to the conclusion that giving his own account was the only way he'd get anything out of Tony. He started with their arriving at the hotel and each renting their own room—figuring that information would set the protective brother back a notch. He mentioned marking both doors, before driving to Applebee's to eat. He told the rest as well as he remembered it, up to the time Tony appeared over him when he was holding Dani, leaving out their argument over the crystal.

"Why the hell didn't you make yourself known before the shooting started?" Stephen asked, irritated.

"I had to drive all the way from Hancock when Dani called to tell me you were stopping in Cumberland. There were shots being fired as we drove up and I had to position my men before I could take charge. Fortunately, Dani gave me the name of your motel and her room number."

"That shows how much she trusts you," Stephen replied sullenly.

"Actually, it's too bad she did because that's how Reierson was tracking you. Mays had your cell phone tapped."

Stephen shot him a disbelieving look. "That's impossible, my phone has a scrambler."

"And you had to turn it over to Mays when you were put in his jail. That's why I didn't dare call you on it."

Apparently Tony knew every step they'd made. "I checked my phone for bugs when he gave it back to me. There weren't any."

"I figured you would have with the Special Forces training you've had, but he had a high tech device that replaced your speaker. It wouldn't have looked any different than the one originally installed in the phone. He couldn't track you but he could listen to your conversations."

Stephen tried to remember the few conversations he'd had, including the one with his brother when he told him he was going to pick up his plane. "Shit. Well that clears up a lot. But it doesn't explain how *Deluca* kept finding us."

"I'm afraid I can't answer that one. I was hoping you knew."

Stephen made a snorting sound, shaking his head. "If I knew, I'd have put a stop to it. We got rid of all Roger's stuff and still he was on our tail nonstop. So who in blazes was following us in the black sedan?"

"Mays. We knew that because we had Reierson's phone tapped. They'd schemed right from the beginning to get the crystal from Deluca. We've suspected Reierson of being crooked for some time now, but were unable to prove it. Even with his phone being tapped, we wouldn't have caught him if Mays hadn't been so loose lipped."

"And you sent Dani right into the thick of it."

"At the time, we didn't know Mays was involved with Reierson. Until you came into the picture, Reierson was just going to let her deliver it to him. Besides, she was the only agent we had with extensive knowledge of crystals. That made her the only one who had a ghost's chance of getting her hands on it."

"She was a rookie. She shouldn't have been out in the field alone."

"We didn't know she'd be alone. She had Roger Farrell and Brick Mays backing her up."

Stephen gave Tony a narrow gaze.

Tony shrugged and said. "That just leaves one more question."

Stephen narrowed his gaze even further, waiting. He had the odd feeling he wasn't going to like Tony's last

questions.
    "Where is the Blood Crystal?"

Chapter Twenty-Seven

A doctor wearing a blood stained smock, loosely hanging mask, and an ID tag naming him as Dr. Richard Hanson came into the waiting room. Both men shot to their feet.

"How is she?" Stephen blurted, not caring that Tony gave him a curious look.

"She came through the surgery just fine. The bullet went straight though, nicked a rib but missed her vital organs," the doctor said, smiling." I do have a question though. Which one of you is the brother?"

"I am," Tony answered.

"Good. Do you recall any injuries she had as a child?"

Tony shook his head. "No we didn't grow up together."

The doctor glanced at Stephen.

Stephen shook his head unable to speak, an icy chill of dread creeping up his spine.

"Well," the doctor said taking a deep breath. "I've found something I've never seen before. There was only minor bleeding inside, most of the blood vessels had cauterized and her shattered rib had granulated tissue forming."

"What the hell does that mean?" Stephen asked.

Dr. Hanson smiled. "Among other things, it's fortunate it wasn't a bone that needed setting because her lesion had already started to heal. That's why I wondered if she'd had any previous injuries with similar results. I guess we could check her medical records, but I can tell you this, the women is a phenomenon. A surgery that should have taken up to three hours was completed in two."

"When can I see her?" Stephen asked.

"About forty-five minutes." The doctor looked from Stephen to Tony. "Procedure is only a relative can go in."

"Screw procedure," Stephen barked, gesturing to Dani's brother. "If he goes in I go."

The doctor looked at Tony. "Okay with you?"

Tony was clearly stiffing a grin. "Sure, even if they are *just friends*."

The doctor left after shaking both their hands.

Stephen dropped back into his seat glaring at Dani's brother. "We spent a lot of time together in the last week," he said, knowing he didn't own Tony an explanation but giving one anyway.

"Uh-huh."

The man certainly had a way with words. "How long has it been since someone called you an asshole?"

Tony looked at his watch and chuckled." Oh, maybe ten minutes." With that, Tony pulled out his phone again, got up, and walked out of the room punching buttons as he went.

Stephen sighed, propped his throbbing leg up on the coffee table, and laid his head back. He closed his eyes, waiting for the minutes to pass until he could see Dani.

His mind drifted to what the doctor had said about Dani being a phenomenon. An amusing thought struck him. Maybe she did have some kind of a magic balm. He remembered the dream he'd had that she was rubbing his injured leg and how much better it had felt in the morning. And then the night in Storm Lake after their fantastic night of lovemaking, the next morning his limp was completely gone. He also suspected her being there, stitching him up, had something to do with the pain disappearing from his head injury.

He started to drift off to sleep thinking about how his hand had quit hurting after he'd tried to stop the blood from pumping out of her limp body.

Stephen didn't know how long he'd slept, but when he opened his eyes, they still hadn't called them to visit Dani and her brother was sitting in front of him with an unfriendly stare directed straight at him.

Stephen pushed himself to a sitting position rubbing his eyes and yawning. "So what's got your tail twisted in a knot?"

Tony lifted one eyebrow as though he might be irritated about something. "Tell me again the last time you saw the crystal.

Stephen swore. That freaking crystal again. "On the bed in my room."

"You're telling me Dani walked off to go eat and left the object of her entire mission, not to mention risked her life protecting, just laying on your bed."

No way was he going to tell Tony about the argument they'd had and how he stomped out ahead of Dani. "I...don't know. Her backpack was in our car. Did you check that?"

"We've gone through both rooms, all your bags, and your car with a fine tooth comb. All we found was this." Tony reached in his jacket pocket and brought out a familiar red velvet bag. He tossed the bag rather carelessly to Stephen.

Stephen had an overwhelming urge to laugh, but stifled it, as he caught the bag. He could feel the shape of the skull still inside. Suddenly something dawned on him. Tony had never seen the real crystal. According to Dani, it went straight from the five murdered curriers to Deluca. Stephen felt an internal chuckle coming on remembering how easily Mays believed the skull was the real crystal.

He made a careful show of opening the string and dropping the skull in his open hand. "What do you call this?" he asked, putting an edge of frustration in his tone.

Tony's expression was unreadable for all of five

seconds which Stephen figured was as long as it took him to realize Stephen was trying to pull one over on him.

"A piece of junk glass," Tony spat out. "What do you take me for, an idiot?"

That comment spurred a gouge in Stephen's ego. *He* was the idiot for believing Dani when she told him that was the crystal.

"No," Stephen said choosing his words carefully, "I never said you were an idiot. I said you were an asshole. Not the same thing. Although, lots of asshole are idiots but I don't think you're one of them."

Tony's eyes narrowed. "If you're trying to piss me off, you're doing a good job of it."

"Thank you."

A corner of Tony's mouth lifted, but only for a second. "Cut the crap, Douglas, where's the crystal?"

Stephen had a sneaking suspicion where it was, but he wasn't ready to give up that information. Not until he talked to Dani.

He pulled his leg off the coffee table and leaned forward making direct eye contact with Dani's brother. "I. Don't. Know." He tossed the skull back to him. "She told me this was it."

Tony made a derisive noise. "And you believed that?"

A surge of heat rose to Stephen's face. He sat back and threw his leg back up on the table, grimacing from the pain his rash movement brought on. Tony's bemused stare irritated him to no end, but he had no way to escape it.

"Holy crap," Tony said finally. "You did believe it."

Stephen gritted his teeth. "Go screw yourself."

Tony reached in his pocket pulled something else out and tossed it across the table. With quick reflexes, Stephen caught it without blinking an eye. Then he realized he was holding the original beaded crystal bag. Shit.

"Where did you find this?"

"On the floor by your bed. One of the guys brought it in a few minutes ago while you were sleeping." Tony let a moment pass then asked, "When did you learn the truth?"

Stephen saw no need to deny it. "Not until tonight, before we went out to eat."

"So... let me guess. You stormed out angry at being duped and Dani ran after you. That at least would explain why she left the crystal laying on the bed. She'd found something in her life more important than her mission."

Stephen shifted in his seat, suddenly feeling uncomfortable. Dani's brother was as sharp as she was. Now he had to decide whether he agreed with Tony's theory or not. And whether or not he wanted to admit Tony was right, at least about the first part. What the hell.

"Yeah," he said. "That's pretty much how it went."

"Is it possible she was so... besotted... over you she forgot her mission?"

Stephen didn't believe that for a minute, but it was something else he wasn't ready to share. Besides, Tony's sarcastic attitude annoyed him.

"Yeah, I guess that's possible."

At that moment an RN walked in. Her tag ID'd her as Cherie Piper. She smiled at the two of them. "You can come in and see Ms. Lovato now, but only for a few minutes. And please avoid anything that might upset her."

Stephen grabbed his crutch and stood up, shoving the beaded bag in his jeans pocket. As they followed the RN out the door, Tony whispered, "Why don't you keep the bag as a little memento?"

Stephen figured it was just Tony's irritating way of acknowledging he knew Stephen had pocketed the bag. Fine, let him think what he wanted. As far as Stephen was concerned, the bag belonged to Dani.

Dani looked deathly pale and she had various tubes including an IV hooked on her, but her eyes were open. She tried to smile, but didn't speak. Stephen moved quickly, edging Tony to the side so he could take Dani's hand.

He reached up and smoothed the hair back from her forehead. "The doc said you're doing good. How are you feeling?"

She murmured something he couldn't hear. Her gaze

settled on Tony then darted back to Stephen. Her look was akin to...fear? Maybe she was worried he wouldn't get along with Tony because of the way he'd reacted to her trusting her brother and not him. He wanted to reassure her.

"Everything's fine, Dani. You're brother and I have spent quite a bit of time together while we waited to see you."

Dani's only response was her gaze flicked to the RN waiting at the edge of the bed. He saw Cherie nod and wondered if Tony caught the exchange as well. He glanced at Tony, but her brother's eyes were fixed on Dani and he'd missed the exchange. Confused, Stephen stepped aside so Tony could talk to his sister. Apparently that's who Dani wanted to see.

Tony's grim smile manifested the concern etched on his face. He leaned over and placed a kiss on her forehead. "You're going to be fine, sis. The doctor said you might be released in a couple of days."

Stephen was a bit chagrined that Tony had that information and hadn't shared it. Tony must have talked to someone while Stephen was sleeping.

"Where's the crystal?" Tony asked. "We can't find it."

Dani's eyes widened. Her gaze moved from Tony to the RN. The question clearly disturbed Dani. She tried to talk, but her voice was barely a hoarse whisper.

"Maybe you should both leave now. We don't want to tax her. You can come back again in a couple of hours or so, but it may be better if you come in one at a time."

Stephen swallowed the knot in his throat. Obviously the news that the crystal had not been found distressed her. As Tony and Stephen turned to leave, the RN made a point of walking around Dani's bed. She caught Stephen's hand and discreetly pressed a piece of paper in it. Stephen turned back to look at Dani and she simply nodded.

"I gotta take a leak," Stephen said, heading for the restroom. Tony acknowledged him with a nod and pulled out his phone heading for the waiting area.

Stephen made his way into a stall and unfolded the

paper the nurse had given him.

Stephen,

I wanted you to know I am able to talk, but chose not to in front of Tony. I need to see you alone. Nurse Cherie knows about it and will try to arrange it. Also, she's going to give you my things. My watch and clothes, etc. Please keep them safe until I'm released. Don't, under any circumstances, let Tony know you have them.

Love, Dani

Stephen reread the note twice. He was certain she was telling him the crystal was in her cargo pants. And she didn't trust Tony to know about it. Why? Why had her loyalties transferred from Tony to him?

Stephen left the restroom and found Tony waiting outside the door.

"You okay?" Tony asked, glancing down at Stephen's leg.

Stephen noted a hint of concern in Tony's question. "Yeah, nothing wrong with my plumbing."

Tony grinned. He slapped Stephen on the shoulder. "You're a good man, Stephen. Thanks for looking after Dani. All shit aside, I appreciate it."

Stephen nodded, not sure what to make of the compliment. Maybe Tony was exactly what Dani believed he was all along. But why the note?

"As long as you're holding down the fort here," Tony was saying, "I think I'll go have a meeting with my team. See if they've come up with anything new. Want me to bring your car back here?"

"Sure," Stephen reached in his pocket for the keys. About the time he realized he didn't have them he saw them dangling from Tony's fingers.

"You left them in the car," Tony said, smiling. "And

by the way, if you get in to see Dani, try to find out where that damn crystal is."

As Tony walked off, Stephen had a sinking feeling. Dani's turnabout in loyalties didn't give Stephen the satisfaction he'd expected. It had taken him a long time to gain her trust, but Tony was the only kin she had. A betrayal from her brother would gouge her deeply.

Stephen waited until Tony left the building then he turned and headed back to Dani's room. Nurse Cherie was working with Dani's IV. When she looked up he saw her gaze go over his shoulder as though checking to see if he was alone. Satisfied, she waved him over to the bed and bent down to talk to Dani.

"He's back, Dani, alone."

Dani's eyes flew open and focused on Stephen. He hurried to her side and took her hand.

"Where's Tony?" she asked in a strained whisper.

"He left and said he'd be back in an hour or so when we were supposed to be able to come back in and see you."

"Okay, good." Her voice was raspy but strong. "Cherie's going to give you my clothes and things I had on me." She nodded to Cherie who stepped away and came back with a plastic hospital bag held shut by a draw string.

Cherie handed the bag to Stephen and said, "I'll leave for a few minutes to give you some privacy." Then she disappeared out the door, pulling it shut behind her.

Dani tried to lift herself to a sitting position but grimaced and laid back down. "Quick," she said, "the crystal is in the lower pocket of my cargo pants."

With an eye on the door, Stephen searched the bag, found the lump that was the crystal and took it out of the pocket still wrapped in the paper bag.

"Hand it to me," she said.

Stephen questioned the request but did as she asked.

She took the crystal, pushed it under her pillow, and breathed a huge sigh of relief. "Thank goodness, that's taken care of. Close the bag back up and put it over there by the closet where it was. I'm sure Tony will get around to asking for it. I'm surprised he hasn't already."

Stephen did as she asked then came back to stand over her. "I don't quite understand," he said. "Why do you suddenly suspect your brother of wrongdoing?"

"When you were hit, I saw the flare of the gun and knew exactly which vehicle the shooter was standing behind. I fired four shots in the dark in the exact spot before I ran toward you. Seconds later, the bullet that hit me came from behind the same car." She stopped talking for a few beats to catch her breath before going on. "Almost immediately, Tony's voice came from the bullhorn beside that same car. I'm sure it was Tony shooting at us, otherwise why did he wait until then to make himself known?"

"Funny, I asked him the same questions. He said they'd arrived after the shooting started and had to get into position first."

Dani closed her eyes and Stephen could see the dampness squeezing from her between lashes." I so wish that was true. But I don't know. The only way I can be sure is if Mays was there and wounded by my Beretta."

"That's going to be tough to find out without going through Tony."

"I know. Did you see if anyone was wounded?"

"Yeah, one person was, but I don't know who. I do know it wasn't Deluca. He's a big guy and I recognized him when they cuffed him. They're all in custody. Maybe I should question Tony when he gets back."

"No. I have a better plan."

CHAPTER TWENTY-EIGHT

"Are you crazy? You can't just walk out of here."

Dani expected resistance but she had to convince him she was well enough to leave.

"I don't see any other way," she said. "If Tony is guilty and he even gets a hint that we'll take off with the crystal, he'll go ballistic. I can't pretend to be unable to talk for much longer. What can I say—I don't remember where I put a priceless relic? There is no way on God's green earth he's going to believe that."

Stephen nodded. "Because he knows your determination. Crystal first, any and every other person, place, or thing second."

"That didn't exactly sound like a compliment."

Stephen bent down and kissed her cheek. "Coming from the guy who accused you of being a greenhorn rookie, it is."

Dani pulled a somber face. "I wouldn't blame you if you hated me."

"Hate is a strong word, honey, reserved for people like Mays and Deluca, not for people who blow your socks off with their dedication to helping a man save his little country. It took me a while to realize that's what was driving you." He paused for a moment, looking down at her. "You have a big heart, Dani Lovato, and that's just one of the many things I love about you."

She was blinking rapidly at the tears building in her eyes. "You better stop or you're going to make me cry." There was a hitch in her voice as her hand squeezed around his fingers. "I love you too, Stephen, and I'm sorry for not trusting you."

Stephen touched her cheek and brushed her tears away with his thumb. "Let's get that crystal delivered then we can talk. You better rest now before that RN stomps on me."

Dani smiled. "Don't worry about Cherie, she's on our side. I've told her I don't want to talk to Tony but I haven't told her why. She'll give him my bag of clothes without telling him you've already seen it"

"Good thinking. You haven't told her you're planning an escape have you?"

Dani shook her head. "Of course not. I've requested a wheelchair so I can get up in the morning. You'll have to bring me some clothes. Do you have the car here?"

"Not yet, but Tony offered to bring it over from the motel." Stephen looked at her, frowning. "Are you sure you're able to do this? Don't you hurt?"

"I actually feel pretty good. Almost no pain at all. Of course, I'm sure I'm on pain medication." She held up her hand with the IV stuck in it. "I'm going to see if I can get her to remove this."

"You know the doctor said you were a healing phenomenon? He asked if you'd had any other injuries that healed so quickly. Later I remembered how quickly your sore hand healed. And it seemed like every time you touched me whatever ailed me felt better."

Stephen smiled at the odd expression on her face. "If you don't believe me, here's proof." He opened his palm toward her. "My burned hand is practically cleared up just from trying to keep you from bleeding to death."

Tony's voice demanding to see his sister drifted in from the hall along with Cherie's admonition that he couldn't go in yet. Dani put a finger to her lips and closed her eyes. Stephen dropped into the chair beside the bed, held her hand and laid his forehead over it.

As they figured, Tony wasn't being put off. He came into the room closely followed by Cherie, but quietly. Stephen stood up and backed away to permit Tony access to his sister.

Clearly Tony's face was etched with concern as he looked at her still figure. "Still sleeping?" he asked rhetorically.

Stephen nodded. "If you have my keys, I think I'll go out and grab a bite to eat. They only want one of us here at a time anyway."

"Sure, I'll sit with her a while." He reached in his pocket, dug out the keys to the Taurus and handed them to Stephen. "It's parked right out front on the left. Maybe you should try to get some rest, you look like hell."

"Yeah, it's been a long day." Stephen grabbed his crutch, started for the door, then stopped. "By the way, was anyone else hurt?"

"Just Mays. He took a couple of bullets, one in the leg and one in the shoulder. They have him in a room upstairs; I've got a man watching his door. By the way, all your bags are in the car. If you're going to get a room, I'd suggest a different motel. Everything at the other place is cordoned off until we find that blasted crystal."

Stephen thanked Tony for bringing his car, took one last look at Dani, and hobbled from the room, but not before he heard Tony asked Cherie where Dani's clothes were.

A healing phenomenon. Stephens's words along with all the other comments he'd made had an unsettling effect on Dani's mind. Stephen had tried to staunch the flow of blood on her wounded side with his sore hand.

Some inner sense warned her that the power of the Blood Crystal would eventually fade if used too many times. Maybe it would be prudent for her to keep it to herself. It was doubtful anyone else would ever figure it out. That she did was a circumstantial fluke. The other side of the coin was maybe it really had no power at all. She'd heard of people who healed faster than others. Maybe she was one of them. Of course, that left a lot of unanswered questions in her mind.

Tony's voice brought her from her musings. "Are you sure no one else has gone through her things?"

"The bag was sitting exactly where I put it when she came up from surgery," Cherie answered, managing to sound a bit testy.

Dani suppressed a smile.

"Is something missing?" Cherie asked.

Dani heard Tony's deep sigh as he picked up her hand and stroked it. "Yeah. And I'm worried about how she'll take it when she wakes up. Why isn't she awake yet? Is she going to be alright?"

"It's after midnight. She should be sleeping. Why don't you go get some rest yourself and come back in the morning? I'm sure whatever is missing can wait until then."

Again Tony sighed. "I guess you're right. Goodnight," he said to Dani, his voice low and husky. She felt his lips brush her forehead. "I love you, honey; you have no idea how much sunshine you brought into my life. You're the only family I have. Please get better and I'll see you in the morning."

His voice moved away as he spoke to the nurse. "It's my fault she's laying there," he said. "I never should have allowed her to go on this mission."

When Dani opened her eyes she looked at Cherie through blurred vision.

"What you're doing is your business," Cherie said quietly. "But I'd say that man really cares about you."

Dani swallowed at the lump in her throat blinking rapidly. "Yes, he certainly appears to."

" I don't know many men who can express themselves like that. Is he married?"

* * * *

I hope to God I'm wrong about him and I pray he'll forgive me if I am.

"Are you sure you're up to doing this," Stephen asked, limping into her room at six a.m.

Dani had already spent two hours lying awake, asking herself the same question. "Yes, I'm ready. Just help me into my clothes."

Within ten minutes, she was dressed and sitting in the wheelchair holding onto the hospital bag with her blood stained cargo pants inside. She'd returned the crystal to one of the pockets.

"Okay, it's now or never," he said, maneuvering her out the door. "This shift doesn't know us, so just act natural and hope to hell we don't run into your brother."

"Where's you crutch?" she asked.

"In the car."

"I didn't even ask if you were able to drive with your right leg being hurt."

"Not a problem."

They made it down to the end of the hall when a nurse showed up, her brows drawn together in a scowl.

Before she could say anything, Dani gave her a friendly wave. "Goodbye," she chirped.

The nurse shook her head. "Sir, you shouldn't be pushing that chair. Wasn't there someone around to assist you? Here, let me do this." She nudged Stephen aside without waiting for an answer. "Are you all checked out?"

"Yes, ma'am," Stephen lied, giving her a dazzling smile. "Our car is right outside."

The nurse wheeled the chair up to the car as Stephen opened the passenger side door. Dani bit back a grimace, got up, and maneuvered herself into the seat. The nurse helped her get her legs inside and said, "You take care now," as she closed the door.

"Thank you so much," Stephen mumbled, two-stepping around the car and getting in behind the wheel. "Jeeeze," he groaned. "That was close. Your nurse Cherie is going to read that woman the riot act."

Dani laid her head back on the seat. "I feel sorry for Cherie having to try to explain to Tony why I'm missing.

She likes him."

"Actually, I do too and I hope you're mistaken about him. You heard what he said. Mays was hit twice."

Dani considered that a minute. "I can't believe it was from my gun. I shot blindly in that general direction while I was running. But why would Mays shoot at us anyway. Reierson would have strangled him if he'd killed us before he had the crystal."

"Whoever it was didn't shoot to kill."

"I agree. Keep in mind, Tony doesn't miss what he's aiming at."

"The whole thing is a little ironic. I don't think either Deluca or Reierson knew they were in rooms next to each other. By the way, Tony told me Mays and Reierson tracked us through my phone. Apparently Mays exchanged my receiver with an undetectable replacement. Tony had no idea how Deluca found us though."

Dani drew a deep breath. "I do."

Stephen stared at her, frowning. "You do what?"

"I know how Deluca tracked us. It was with the beaded bag. I knew the second you held it up and asked me what it was."

"Well shit."

Dani sat up to look at him. "I'm sorry. I should have told you right away."

Stephen bent sideways and dug something out of his pocket. He tossed it toward her. "You mean this?"

Dani took several deep breaths. "Where did you get it?"

Stephen snorted. "Tony gave it to me."

"And now he knows exactly where we are."

"Tony said he didn't know how Deluca was tracking us."

"And you think it's a coincidence that he planted that bag on you?"

Stephen stabbed a frustrated hand though his hair. "Hell, I don't even know how it got in my duffle bag or where it's been for the last three or four days, however the hell long it's been."

Dani sighed. "I hid it in the back seat of the car, between the seats."

Stephen gave her a scathing look. "We've changed cars twice."

Dani turned to look out the window not wanting to face him. "I moved it each time."

"What about in the airplane?"

"It was in the drawer under my seat."

Stephen swore. His hands gripped the steering wheel. "How the hell you managed all that without me knowing tells me what a trusting idiot I am. And then convincing me that ridiculous skull was the crystal." He swore again this time, slamming the heel of his hand on the wheel. "I hate to even ask, but how did it end up in my duffel bag?"

"When we were looking for things that might have a bug, I got rid of it by stashing it in the gas well of a police car."

He gave her another incredulous look. "Where the hell was I when you did that?"

"Sleeping. I—I did it when I went to do laundry."

"Cripes. I don't know why I called you a rookie. You have more slick moves then James Bond. No wonder you insisted on washing clothes. If you put it in the police car how did it get from there to my bag?"

"Deluca must have been close behind us. That's how I know for sure it's bugged. He must have taken it from the patrol car shortly after I put it there. If he'd seen me do it, he'd have followed me to the laundromat. And there's no other way he could have found it unless he had a tracer on it. And now Tony knows where we are. We should stop and plant it somewhere else. Or we could just throw it out the window."

Stephen shook his head. "Do you really think it matters? Tony knows exactly where we're headed. The only thing we have on him is a substantial head start. Plus, leaving this early, we're making excellent time. We've only been on the road an hour and we're already through

Hancock. I'd bet Tony's not even at the hospital yet."

Dani stared out at the expansive blue width of the Potomac River as the bright morning sun did a shimmering dance on the water. She fingered the beaded bag hoping Stephen wasn't underestimating Tony. And she hoped even more that she was wrong about him. Tony's betrayal would be more painful than the wound in her side. Just the thought of it left a bitter taste in her mouth.

Stephen's voice broke into her musings. "Why don't you check the bag and see if you can find the bug. Then you can put the crystal back in it when you turn it over to Kendu."

Dani suspected he knew where her thoughts were going and wanted to distract her. It seemed like a good idea though. She fingered the little beads, feeling for one that might be a different size than the others. They all looked to be the same and too small for a bug.

"Turn it inside out and look," Stephen suggested.

She did as he suggested and immediately found a small lump under the lining. "I think it's here," she said, moving the loose nub, looking for an opening to slip it out. She found it in a corner at the bottom and worked it free.

She held it up in her fingers. "Voilà," she chirped. "Should I throw it out?"

"Yeah, but wait until the next exit. If he is tracking us that might throw him off and buy us some time." He gave her a concerned look. "How are you feeling?"

"I've had better days," she said, shrugging.

"Does your side hurt?"

"A little."

"I know the road from here, at least until we get to D.C. Why don't you put the seat back and get some rest. I'll wake you in about an hour and we can get some fast food to go. You lost a lot of blood—even if you are a healing phenomenon."

Dani frowned at that thought and laid her head back. She'd barely closed her eyes when Stephen's phone laying on the consol between them rang.

Chapter Twenty-Nine

Grimacing, Dani bolted upright, exchanged a look with Stephen, and grabbed for it.

"Don't answer unless the caller is identified," Stephen warned.

She looked at the lighted screen. "It says unknown."

"Besides my family, Tony and Reierson are the only ones who know the number. It sure isn't Reierson. I guess Tony finally made it to the hospital."

Disgusted, Dani flung the phone down. "Is this madness ever going to end?" she grumbled, laying her head back on the seat.

"At least we know Tony won't have a chance of catching us. Do you know how to get to Kendu's hotel?"

"Yes. It's on the north side so we don't have to go through the city."

* * * *

With an alert eye on his surroundings, Stephen approached the parking lot of the eight-story Captial-Lex Hotel. Mammoth twin fountains at least twelve feet wide and eight feet tall kept a melodious rhythm on either side of the extravagant registration drive. Several taxis and limousines waited near the entrance while black clad chauffeurs lulled about talking. Walking paths, entwined within manicured lawns and ornamental shrubs, ultimately leading to the first hole of a lush golf course.

Stephen looked up, noting with interest a helicopter resting on the roof.

He stopped the car facing the entrance and gave a soft whistle. "I was thinking we could get a room here and call Kendu from the there, but this place is a tad out of our budget, even with Deluca's money in our coffer."

"Ya think?"

Stephen laughed. "Well, Ms. Lovato. This is your show. How do you want to handle it?"

Her quick gaze scanned their surroundings. "I don't see Tony's car anywhere. The Limo's and taxi's are normal; a lot of politicians stay here. Why don't you stay here with the crystal while I go in and call his room to make sure he's there and who, if anyone, is with him?"

He shook his head. "I don't like having you out of my sight. What if I follow you in and find a place to wait while you make your call."

"I guess that would work. I'd just as soon have you and the crystal in my sights too."

He raised a brow at her.

"Not because I don't trust you, Stephen. I was the one who suggested you stay here with the crystal, remember?"

"Okay, you're right. We both go in, but seemingly not together. Do you know what room he's in?"

"Top floor, suite 809, unless he's moved." She reached in the back and dug the beaded bag containing the crystal out of her cargo pants. Handing it to him, she said, "Here, you hang on to it. Stick it in your jacket pocket—but be careful not to squeeze it."

"Yes ma'am. Point taken. Once was enough."

She passed him an indiscernible look then tucked one of Harry's guns in the waistband of her jeans and opened her door. Stephen did the same with one of the other guns, hopped out and hurried around the car to assist her.

"How are you doing?" he asked noticing her slow movements.

"Fine. I'm fine. Let's just get this over with."

Stephen stayed by the car, watching her wend her way

across the lot. She was the toughest most determine female he'd ever met. His body reminded him she was also the most desirable. Not because she had big breasts and long curvy legs, her beauty came from a deeper internal place.

When she got to the front entrance, he limped after her. His leg was stiff from driving, but walking would work the kinks out of it. As he walked away, he heard his phone ringing again for the fourth time.

Tony must be getting frantic, Stephen thought as he walked away without bothering to check caller ID.

He watched Dani pick up a couple of brochures and study one, obviously looking for the hotel number as she walked toward a row of pay phones. She was holding her right side but otherwise seemed to be moving normally. He picked up a Wall Street Journal and sat down in a cushy chair where he could keep an eye on her. No one seemed to be paying any attention to either one of them. If Tony was up to no-good, he was obviously in it alone or he could have called ahead to intercept them.

Dani hung up the phone and walked toward a bank of elevators, indicating with a nod of her head that he should follow her. He tucked his paper under his arm and walked toward the elevators. They didn't speak as they waited, when the elevator doors opened, three people got out. Stephen stepped in behind Dani just as a man came hurrying toward them. He held the elevator door from closing and stepped in next to Dani. Stephen slipped his hand into his pocket, cradling his gun. He could see Dani holding her breath as the man pushed the button to number four. The doors closed them in, he turned to smile at Dani, then got out on four. The doors closed behind him and Dani let out a huge burst of air.

"Is anyone upstairs with Kendu?" Stephen asked, breathing his own sigh of relief.

"Yes, two men in suits. One from the Smithsonian and the other a government security agent. They both have credentials and were there yesterday and again today. Plus a guard is stationed outside his door. He was delighted to hear from me."

They stepped out of the elevator on the eighth floor and immediately spotted the room with the guard out front.

He nodded at them. "You can go right in. Mr. Kendu is expecting you."

Stephen saw Dani pull a deep breath as she opened the door and walked in. Stephen followed, noting nothing out of the ordinary.

Bama Kendu, a short rotund man with a pleasant face and kind eyes stood up to greet them, as did the two men with him. One tall, lean, and impeccably dressed, the other shorter, but stocky enough to carry a piano on his back. All three were smiling.

The taller man extended a hand and introduced himself as Richard Pepler from the Institute. He flashed an official looking ID with the same name and his picture. The piano carrier also flicked open a badge. It appeared official and also matched the name he gave them and his picture.

Mr. Kendu clasped Dani hands with both of his. "Ms Lovato, I am most happy to see you. You have Blood Crystal, yes?"

Dani smiled. "Yes sir. I do. It's been an interesting ride and I'm more than anxious to turn it over to you." She turned to Stephen with a questioning look as though asking if he had any concerns. He gave a small shrug, pulled the bag from his pocket and handed to her. This was her moment and he couldn't have been prouder of her.

She handed Kendu the bag. He accepted it with obviously trembling finger. Carefully, he eased it out in to the palm of his hand and held it up for Richard Pepler to see.

Pepler extended a hand, "May I?"

Kendu handed it to him using his fingertips. "Of course, but take care not to squeeze unless you are prepared for consequences."

Pepler chuckled. "All in good time, my friend, I haven't forgotten your warning. We will take excellent care of it. You may come by the Institute tomorrow afternoon and by then we'll have had time to examine it."

Kendu gave him a slight bow. "I thank you and will see you on the morrow."

In spite of the relief she should be feeling, Dani's throat closed as she watched Richard Pepler walk out the door with the Blood Crystal. It was like he carried away a physical part of her. She blinked rapidly at the tears welling in her eyes. Stephen must have noticed her discomfort because he drew Bama Kendu's attention by introducing himself and exchanging some pleasantries. Moments later, he directed Dani to the door with a hand riding on the small of her back.

A sharp knock sounded on the door before they reached it. Dani passed a wide-eyed look at Stephen. Stephen turned to Kendu for directive.

"Would you like me to answer that?" he asked as the knock, more like pounding, came again.

When Kendu nodded and Stephen pushed Dani behind him and motioned Kendu off to the side. Stephen had a gun in his hand as he unlatched the door. It was shoved unceremoniously inward.

Tony strode in the room wielding a 44-magnum. His sharp eyes quickly scanned the room taking in Kendu's shocked look then settled on Dani. "You still have the crystal, right?"

She took bitter satisfaction in shaking her head. "No. It's gone. A man from the Institute picked it up".

Tony swore. "Damn! I tried calling you. What was his name?"

"Richard Pepler."

"How long ago did they leave?"

"Five minutes," Stephen interjected. "You're too late Tony."

"Why did you leave the hospital?"

Dani swallowed the lump ion he throat. "I know it was you who shot me, Tony. I just don't understand why."

Tony gave her an astonished glare. "I don't know what you're talking about Dani, but we have to stop him. You just turned the crystal over to Ambrose Deluca. I'll explain later. Do you know which way he went?"

"No I—"

Tony raced out the door without giving her a chance to finish. He was slamming his fist on the elevator buttons. Stephen hurried into the hall behind him and Dani followed, numbness gnawing at her innards. She pulled the door shut behind her warning Kendu to stay inside.

"If you're lying to us, I'll shoot you myself." she snarled at her brother.

"I'm not lying, dammit. Deluca probably has more ID's and passports than the entire Secret Service. We have to stop him or we're right back to square one."

His words forced her mind to wrap around the memory of the drivers license with the name Samuel Morris on it.

Dani could tell Stephen remembered too and that he believed Tony. "Wait," Stephen said." My brother said Deluca owned a helicopter. There was one on the roof when we drove up. It took Tony all of two seconds to digest the information. He charged for the stairway with Stephen close at his heels. They yelled simultaneously at Dani to stay put even as she yanked her gun out of her waistband.

Tony took the stairs to the roof three at a time; Stephen managed only two with his injured leg. They were both at the top before Dani reached the first landing. When the two men charged through the door to the roof, Dani heard the deafening whirr of the helicopter blades. Breathless, she reached the gaping door to see Tony and Stephen standing behind metal ducts, holding guns aimed at the aircraft and yelling. Then she heard gunfire. She shoved the heavy door open and peered out. Stephen was sending rapid fire into the juncture of the spinning blades as the helicopter started to lift off. Suddenly the noise lessened and the blades began to slow down. The helicopter settled back on the pad. The blades, though still rotating, seemed to have lost their power.

Dani recognized the pilot as the guard who'd stood outside Kendu's door. He was doubled over holding his bleeding shoulder. Dani had no doubts about who fired the shot to incapacitate him.

From the cover of the door, Dani held her gun aimed at Deluca, waiting for him to produce a weapon and give her an excuse to pull the trigger.

Tony gave orders for them all to step out with their hands in the air. The husky guard came first with Deluca following. She saw the beaded bag still clutched in his hand, an evil smile on his face. Then, as though watching in slow motion, she saw him draw his arm back and hurl the bag toward the roof barrier where it vanished over the edge.

Without giving a thought for her safety, Dani dashed screaming for the wall only to watch helplessly as the Blood Crystal plunged downward landing with a trivial splash in one of the fountains. Behind her gunfire erupted and she turned around to see Deluca lying on the tarmac clutching his bleeding chest.

Dani had little doubt the gun laying beside him had been aimed at her. Fortunately, one of the men had had the sense to keep their eyes on the assailants instead of worrying about the fate of the crystal. She really was a rookie.

Holding her side and breathing heavily, Dani ran for the door, down the stairs and to the elevator. She noted that neither Tony nor Stephen followed her. Of course, they both knew exactly where she was headed. The pain in her side had increased. She braced a hand on the wall trying to regain her strength and when the elevator doors opened, she moved inside it with guarded steps.

Back on the first floor she eyed a sofa thinking maybe she should rest a moment, but what if someone else had seen the crystal fall? She couldn't take that chance. Once outside, she spied the fountain about twenty yards to her left and using the outside wall for support slowly made her way toward it.

About half-way there her stomach lurched and her

head started swimming. Her vision blurred and she could barely see. She felt like she was struggling underwater. Then she realized it was tears crowding her eyes. She quickly swiped them away and made a lurch for the fountain. She'd reached it, had her hand in the water when darkness swirled around her.

"Miss, can I help you?"

The voice was husky and flowed over her like smooth warm silk. A hand squeezed her shoulder and she looked up into dark hooded eyes and the most beautiful face she'd ever seen. He looked like Stephen except his eyes were the wrong color. Was she dreaming?

"Stephen?" she asked groggily.

"Oh my God! Are you Dani? Dani Lovato?"

"Who wants to know?" she asked through dry lips, looking up at the handsome stranger who looked all too familiar.

"I'm Virgil Douglas. Stephen's brother. Your brother Tony called me wondering if I knew where the two of you were. I called twice and when I didn't get an answer I decided to fly down. He said you were both wounded and had *escaped* from the hospital. He thought you might be headed for this hotel. I called again when my plane landed, but there was still no answer. What the hell are you doing here? And where is Stephen?"

She pointed a finger to the sky. "He's up there." A look of alarm crossed his features. Thinking he might suspect her of being deranged, she added, "On the roof."

He looked up frowning. "Here let me help you out of here so we can go find Stephen. I hope he can tell me what's going on."

He lifted her to sit on the edge of the gurgling fountain. "Can you walk?"

"No. Not until I find my…bag." She gazed into the swirling pool trying to see it.

"What bag?"

"It fell in the water…please…help me find it."

The look he gave her suggested she might have lost

more than her bag. But he walked around her and leaned close to the water, shading his eyes.

"Man, this thing is at least three feet deep. Maybe they have to switch the fountain off...wait. I think I see something."

Dani, having regained her energy, moved to stand beside him and look. "Yes, I see it," she pointed a finger. "There." It was resting at the bottom near the center, clouded by the churning water.

"I'm going in to get it." Before he could stop her, she stripped her shoes off and put a foot in the chilly pool.

Vigil grabbed her arm. "Be careful, it might be slippery..."

The warning was barely out of his mouth when her feet went out from under her. She gripped his arm with both hands. While he tried to steady her, he lost his balance and, with a mighty splash, fell face first into the water on top of her. She came up gasping and found herself sitting in the cold water up to her chin, the fountain playing a stream down her head. She looked up to see both Stephen and Tony staring down at her.

Behind her, Virgil immerged holding the bag up triumphantly. "I got it."

Stephen's eyes widened. "Virgil? How the hell did you get here?"

"I swam," he muttered, shaking water from his head.

"Have you lost your mind completely?" Tony asked Dani.

"It would appear so," she sputtered, moving away from the overhead stream. "Help me out of here, and be careful about it. I feel like I've been through a wringer."

Tony smirked. "You don't look like you have,"

Between the three of them, they lifted her out of the water and she instantly turned to Virgil. "Give me the bag."

He held it up out of her reach. "First maybe somebody should tell me what's going on."

She held her hand out to Stephen. "Give me your gun."

Stephen handed it to her, grinning.

Virgil quickly brought his hand down. "All right. All right. Here you can have it. It looks to me like the whole lot of you is crazy."

Tony glanced at Stephen "Wise man, your brother is. I hope your gun was empty."

* * * *

An hour later Dani stepped out of the shower of the two bedroom suite Virgil had rented. She wrapped a plush towel around herself, then sat down at the little dressing table and stared at herself in the mirror. She knew Tony and Stephen were in the other room filling Virgil in on everything that had happened.

She'd had questions of her own like who had actually shot Deluca? The answer had surprised her. He died from two gunshot wounds. One inflicted by Tony, the other from Stephen. Neither one of them had taken their eyes off of a dangerous man to watch her run after the crystal. Kendu had been informed that his crystal was safe.

Dani stared at the innocent looking Blood Crystal nesting on top of its wet bag on the vanity in front of her. Tomorrow they would deliver it to the Smithsonian, but for tonight, it was hers. Her hand itched to pick it up and squeeze it, but she didn't have the nerve. Each time she'd done it, it had gotten hotter and she feared if she did it again, it might scorch her to the bone. She'd already made the decision not to tell anyone about the power she believed the crystal had. After all, maybe she'd imagined it. Maybe there really was no magic balm in it at all. Unless she posed the possibility, she doubted anyone would discover the truth.

She sat there so long she heard Stephen moving around in the attached bedroom they would be sharing. She knew his leg was hurting and he was probably as tired as she was.

With the crystal cradled gently in her hand, she walked into the bedroom. Stephen was lying on the bed, fully clothed and sound asleep. It was an endearing sight.

In the hospital they'd talked about love, but they had both been under a lot of stress for the last week. Did she love him? She wasn't sure. They didn't even know each other under normal circumstances, and she wasn't going to make the mistake of getting involved with a man newly divorced. Granted, they'd made fantastic love a few times, but that was hardly enough to base a lasting relationship on. She didn't want him to realize a few months down the road that she was little more than a transitional interlude. And what if she changed her mind? He'd been through enough already with the war and coming home to find his wife with another man. She couldn't do that to him.

They needed some time apart to sort out their feelings for each other. She'd agreed to spend the night with him under the condition that he leave with his brother in the morning. Watching him go would be the hardest thing she'd ever done, especially since she knew he wanted to stay. She choked back silent tears and laid down beside him.

* * * *

Stephen and Virgil were on the road by seven o'clock the next morning. Virgil had volunteered to help Stephen drive the Taurus back to Marion, Indiana to pick up his Cessna.

"You're awfully quiet this morning," Vigil pointed out after an hour of driving in silence.

Stephen breathed deeply and shrugged. "Yeah, I know. It's been a rough couple of months."

"It couldn't have been rougher than fourteen months in Afghanistan."

Stephen glanced over at the older brother he'd always admired and grinned. "You're right about that. I guess I shouldn't complain."

"You wanna talk about it?"

"Which part?"

"Your call, but I really am curious about Dani Lovato. The two of you looked pretty down in the dumps when we left. Are you in over your head?"

Stephen laughed. "I think we both are. We had a wild and fast week, but that's the problem, we've only known each other a week and I'm just out of a bad marriage. I can't see myself jumping right back into it." But he wanted to. In a bad way. One word of encouragement from Dani and he'd have stayed with her.

"So…how does she feel about it?"

"We mutually agreed that we need some time apart." Actually, it was her idea more than his. She said she had a lot of paper work to catch up on. Stephen suspected now that Tony was on her good side again she'd want to spend some time with him. Mays, hoping for leniency, had confessed to firing the shots that struck both Dani and Stephen. He said he wasn't shooting to kill, just to keep them from escaping.

"You've changed since you got back," Virgil said interrupting Stephen's thought.

"Yeah, war will do that to a man."

"Have you decided what you want to do with your life now that you're a free man?"

Stephen shook his head. "I haven't had time to think about it. I'd like to spend some time at your lake place if the offer's still open, and do nothing for a while. Maybe I'll even learn how to fish."

"Maybe she'll follow you after she has some time to think it over."

Stephen gave a derisive laugh. "She's attached by the hip to her brother."

"Ouch, sounds like you don't care much for Tony."

"On the contrary. I like him a lot. Dani just doesn't have any other family so she's bonded with him big time. Did I mention he said if I wanted to come back he could find me a job?"

"In Washington?"

"Uh-huh."

Vigil laughed. "Well that would certainly put Ma into orbit."

"Is she still on your ass to settle down, get married and

have babies?"

"Not so much since Corinne, Hunter, and Quint took care of the grandkid problem."

"How is your love life anyway?"

"Not worth discussing. I'd rather hear about the Blood Crystal and how you got involved with it."

Chapter Thirty

You've been sitting around here moping for almost a week," Tony grumbled. "Why the hell don't you just go to him?"

"I can't," Dani insisted for the umpteenth time.

"It doesn't make any sense. He said he loved you and, if I understand you right, you love him. How complicated can that be."

Dani started jamming dishes into the dishwasher. "It's not that simple. He's barely two months out of a divorce from a marriage he never wanted. How do I know he won't change his mind about how he feels? I refuse to be a transitional woman."

"That sounds to me like a bunch of psychological bullshit. You love each other. People spend a lifetime looking for exactly what you have right under your stubborn nose. He's a good man, Dani."

"We have two different lifestyles. I love my job here—He doesn't even know what he wants to do with his life. Plus, he has a large family and fierce ties to them. He'd never give them up to move to D.C."

"How can you be so sure? Besides, undercover work is dangerous. After everything that transpired with that damn crystal I'm real sorry I got you into it. Even if you did a fantastic job."

"I doubt I'd have made it back without Stephen's

help."

"You made a good team."

Dani turned and stared at her brother who was reassembling his revolver spread out in pieces on the table. She had come to love and depend on him in such a short time. What if she'd never taken the chance to seek him out?

She smiled pensively and released a deep sigh. "Yeah, we did."

Tony's gaze lifted to her face. For a moment silence hung between them while he studied her.

After an uncomfortable couple of moments she made an attempt to change the subject. "What about you? Did you ever call that nurse, Cherie Piper? She liked you, you know."

Tony chuckled. "Yeah, I kinda liked her too. Problem is, you had her thinking I was some kind of a jerk the way you high-tailed it out of that hospital. I still can't believe you did that."

"Yeah well, chalk that up as a stupid mistake. Not the first and probably not the last one I'll make in my life."

"Are you counting sending Stephen off?"

She gave him a nasty scowl. "We were talking about you and the nurse. So did you call her?"

With practiced precision, Tony snapped the barrel on his gun. "She's coming into town day after tomorrow to visit her mother. I had to do some fancy talking but I waggled a dinner date out of her."

"Ooh, I guess I'll have to make myself scarce."

"And I know just how you can do it." Tony pulled an envelope from his breast pocket and tossed it across the table toward her. "Here's a present for you. I was just waiting for the right time to give it to you."

She picked it up, eyeing him warily. Inside she found an airline ticket. It was for a one-way flight from D.C. to Minneapolis, Minnesota. She turned wide eyes up to her grinning brother.

"When did you buy this?"

"Yesterday after you barked at me for the third time."

He shrugged. "I'm not trying to push you into anything—well, maybe just a little nudge—but go, take a month off, have fun and see where things lead. You can always buy your own ticket to come back and be miserable."

She stood there glaring at him.

He laughed. "And you can tell Rando that if he wants to come back with you, I have a job for him he won't turn down."

"What kind of job?"

"Flying the company helicopter. I'd say he's more than qualified."

"You play dirty; you know that, don't you?"

He placed the last pin in his gun and sighted it in on one of her stuffed animals sitting on a miniature rocking chair in the corner. "Yup, that's me."

She stared at the ticket and gave an exasperated sigh. "Minnesota has thousands of lakes. I don't have clue how to find his place."

Tony pulled a folded sheet of paper out of his other pocket. "Here you go. I talked to Virgil this morning. He'd be more than happy to see you come and pull his brother out of his slump."

"You've been scheming with Virgil?"

Tony let loose with a belly laugh. "He paid for the ticket."

* * * *

Dani stood beside the two-story log cabin staring out at Sturgeon Lake. Massive trees of every conceivable fall color hugged the entire shoreline allowing only glimpses of the homes surrounding it. She'd had to cross a quaint little covered bridge to get on the small island. The wood-burning scent of a nearby campfire added to the serene ambience of the lake.

Ten steps below her a dock extended about thirty feet into the water. Stephen sat on the edge of the dock with two chattering kids wielding fishing rods. They actually appeared to be teaching *him* how to the bait his hook.

She walked slowly down the steps enjoying watching

him interact with the animated youngsters, and hesitated before stepping out on the dock, unsure of how she would be received.

The boy, about seven, saw her first. "Hey look, it's a lady!"

His sister, older by a couple of years, smiled and waved.

When Stephen turned to look at her he appeared for a moment to be in shock. Then a smile of recognition erased the frown from his features as he got to his feet and hurried toward her. She met him halfway and fell into his welcoming arms. Tears streaked down her cheeks as his hands captured her face. He sipped away her tears with whisper-soft lips then covered her mouth with a kiss so intense, so all-consuming, she knew she'd never have to doubt his love for her.

She heard the children approaching and knew they'd be staring and more than a little curious.

The boy spoke first, whispering, "Shanna, why is Uncle Rando kissing that lady?"

"Because, Kyle, that's what grownups do. They kiss and get married and have babies."

"Boy, I'm never gonna kiss a girl," Kyle said.

Dani could feel Stephen shaking with laughter and easily read his mind.

"Wanna bet?"

ABOUT THE AUTHOR

Born and raised on a North Dakota farm, Jannifer started writing at the age of twelve, creating novels by memory while walking home from a one-room schoolhouse. After moving to Minnesota, she began serious writing in 1974 while working full-time. She has since retired and spends summers in Minnesota and migrates with the birds to Yuma, Arizona for the winter.

When she's not writing, she's sewing for craft shows, painting rocks, and pursuing her favorite pastime— traveling the world on a cruise ship. And, last but not least, spending valuable time with her children and grandchildren.

Learn more at: www.janniferhoffman.com

What Reviewers Are Saying About Romantic Suspense Author *Jannifer Hoffman*

SECRETS OF THE HEART

"I would definitely recommend this book to anyone looking for a great story that you can sink your teeth into and figure out. This was a good one." —*Rowena, Book Binge Reviews*

"A touching and steamy romance wrapped inside a brain-teaser of a mystery." —*Laura Beck, MFW Book Buddy Reviews*

SECRET SACRIFICES

"A definite page turner! You'll find yourself glued to your seat. With suspense, a mystery, and steamy love scenes, there is plenty to love about this story! It will not disappoint you!" —*Jessica, We Write Romance*

"I would definitely recommend this book to anyone who is in the mood for a steamy romance with great characters and a fast paced storyline." —*Rowena, Book Binge Reviews*

Secret Sacrifices is a keeper. GOOD READING. —*Camellia, The Long and the Short of It*

"All the twists and turns kept the story moving a good pace and kept me wanting to know what next. I look forward to watching this intriguing family and the women they fall in love with." —*Terri, We Write Romance*

ROUGH EDGES

"Ms. Hoffman seems to get better and better with each book she writes. Her characters and plots become more and more complex, with stories that draw the reader in from page one." —*Jessica, We Write Romance*

"Jannifer Hoffman's smooth writing style, revealing descriptions, splendid love scenes, and well-developed characters make *Rough Edges* a novel to be enjoyed more than once—a good one for the library." —*Camellia, The Long and the Short of It*

"The situations in this story keep you on the edge of your seat wondering what new twist or turn will happen next." —*Terri, Night Owl Romance*

Read More from Jannifer Hoffman's *Douglas Family* Series

Secrets of the Heart

Nicole Anderson owns a successful costume design business, has a wealth of small town friends, and sleeps in a lonely bed, haunted by demons from the past. She's convinced herself that her life is exactly the way she wants it, and has shot down every marriageable man within a fifty-mile radius.

When Hunter Douglas is assigned the task of delivering a deceased friend's children to their aunt, he must first convince the belligerent Nicole Anderson that she actually had a sister. Though forced to take his two charges to Minnesota, Hunter fully intends to persuade Ms. Anderson to allow the children to return to New York with him—without sharing his own little secret. The last thing he wants to do is fall in love with a woman who lives in a small Midwest town with neighbors who seem to know every move he makes.

As the heat index between Nicole and Hunter rises, a bizarre puzzle begins to unfold involving false birth certificates, a stolen suitcase, odd pictures, an elusive stalker, and a grandfather's legacy that could turn deadly.

Secret Sacrifices

Driver Jamie LeCorre, competing in the male dominated Stock Car Racing field, needs a tape that will exonerate her from a deadly crash. Weary of dealing with domineering, chauvinistic males, she is suddenly attracted to just such a man. A man who can get her tape.

Quint Douglas has sworn off high profile, overly intelligent women. He discovers the blond bimbo of his dreams trying to change a flat on a pink BMW. Offering help, he uses a bit too much attitude and is shot down. Yet, Quint still tries to win her over in spite of his deep-seated fear of speed.

Together they enter the tight knit Stock Car Racing world to investigate an old murder, a new body, and a highway collision—all tied together with too many suspects. Quint tries to keep Jamie from being the next victim even as she races around the track at 180 miles an hour, pursued by those who would like to see her eliminated, in more ways than one

Also Available from Resplendence Publishing

Rough Edges by Jannifer Hoffman

When Julia Morgan M.D. miscarries twin girls, she divorces her husband, believing he is to blame. He forces her out of her position at the hospital and threatens her credibility as a doctor if she attempts to practice medicine. Without mentioning her medical degree, Julia accepts a position as nanny on a Colorado ranch 900 miles away.

Dirk Travis is in trouble. His wife has gone missing, and his housekeeper is threatening to quit. He is in desperate need of a reliable person to look after his four-year-old twins. Even though Julia appears to be the answer to his prayers, he can't help but think she's a bit too perfect.

Both insist their relationship will be business only. While those plans start to go awry, other things begin to happen. People are getting killed and Dirk is the prime suspect, but that doesn't stop the heat index from rising between Dirk and Julia, even as she appears to be the next target.

Brilliant Disguise by JL Wilson

An undercover FBI agent in a tiny Iowa town finds you can't hide anything from a woman who's determined to find out the truth...

Nick Baxter, an undercover FBI agent, thinks his *brilliant disguise* will fool the hicks in New Providence, Iowa. They won't suspect he's there investigating widow Shannon Delgardie, under suspicion of treason. What Nick doesn't know is that everybody in town is conspiring to protect her and investigate him in return.

Shannon needs help. The men her late husband blackmailed are closing in and the FBI might be involved. When Nick approaches her, can she trust him? With the aid of computer hackers and hair stylists, she uncovers the truth, finding a love she never expected in a tiny Iowa town.

A Perfect Escape by **Maddie James**

A changed identity. A secluded beach. A sniper.

Megan Thomas is running for her life. From Chicago, from the mob, from her husband. She runs to the only place she feels safe—a secluded cottage on an east coast barrier island.

Smyth Parker is running from life. From work, from society, from a jealous ex-wife—his only consolation is the solitude of Newport Island. He doesn't need to anyone to screw up that plan. And he sure as hell doesn't need to complicate it with Megan Thomas.

But when Megan fears she's been found, she runs to the only safe place she knows, and straight into the arms of the one person who might be able to help, Smyth. Her escape might yet still be perfect. Or is it?

Pixels and Pain by **James Goodman**

Explore the dangerous domain of a madman...

Johnny Walker is a FBI agent on a personal crusade to

catch a killer. One year ago, his little sister was brutally murdered and the police still don't have a suspect. Mary Marshall founded a watchdog group to rid the world of online predators after her sister fell victim to a charismatic stranger she met on the popular networking website, HiyaSpace.

As the similarities surrounding their losses draw these two together, they soon embark on a desperate quest for answers—a quest wrought with peril, betrayal, and unimaginable horror. In a virtual world where everyone's a friend, and everyone's a suspect, will Johnny and Mary be able to track down an internet serial killer whose unspeakable deeds threaten to destroy them all?

Or will the hunters become the prey, unable to escape a web of *Pixels and Pain?*

Checkmate by **Kris Norris**

For years he's hidden in the shadows...watching...hunting. His attempts have never been successful, until now. And his game is just beginning.

Kendall Walker and her brother, Trace, share a passion for adventure racing. But when Trace is kidnapped by a psychotic figure from their past, Kendall finds herself immersed in an adventure race beyond anything she's ever known. And if she doesn't reach each checkpoint in time, Trace will die. She'll do anything to get her brother back, even surrendering to a man intent on becoming her lover. Luckily for her, Dawson has other plans.

Special Agent Dawson Cade doesn't know how his life went from complacent to complicated in what feels like a heartbeat. He has absolutely no leads on the bastard terrorizing Kendall, and he can't stop himself from wanting to take her into his bed. He knows he needs to keep distant, but when circumstances force him to succumb to the desires of a man intent on possessing Kendall, Dawson must face the truth. He's going to be Kendall's next lover, even if she doesn't know it yet.

And as the race begins, he can only hope he's able to save Trace, and keep Kendall from sacrificing herself, in a game where even victory has a price.

Find Resplendence titles at the following retailers

Resplendence Publishing
www.ResplendencePublishing.com

Amazon
www.Amazon.com

Barnes and Noble
www.BarnesandNoble.com

Target
www.Target.com

Fictionwise
www.Fictionwise.com

All Romance E-Books
www.AllRomanceEBooks.com

Mobipocket
www.Mobipocket.com

5216755R0

Made in the USA
Charleston, SC
14 May 2010